Dear Reader,

Does art imitate life, or does life imitate art? When I began writing *Things Unseen*, I discovered that both suppositions are true. My first grandchild was born at twenty-nine weeks' gestation, and in this story Sadie helps a young mother with twins in the NICU. As I wrote, I relived those anxious days of worry interlaced with prayer until my granddaughter was able to come home after seven weeks in an NICU.

Also in this book, while Sara and Sadie are out riding, they find an injured bobcat kitten caught in a leghold trap. I was deep in the midst of resolving the care of the fictional wounded infant animal when life imitated art: a cat with a leghold trap still attached to its foreleg was brought into the veterinary clinic where I work. (Spoiler alert! In both cases, the compassion of a Good Samaritan gives the animal a second chance at life.)

Writing about Silver Peak celebrating its pioneer heritage in this story took me back to some wonderful memories in my own life. During my college years, I performed with an international folk dance company. Each autumn, we were invited to Luray, Virginia, to perform Appalachian clogging in a local heritage festival. Many years later, my church's theatre troupe sponsored a production of my hometown's Civil War experience, another source of inspiration from which I drew when writing about the heritage festival.

Regardless of whether art imitates life or life imitates art, I hope you'll enjoy reading *Things Unseen* as much as I enjoyed writing it.

Warmly,
Anne Marie Rodgers
writing as Carole Jefferson

Mysteries of Silver Peak

MYSTERIES
of SILVER PEAK

Things Unseen

CAROLE JEFFERSON

New York

Published by Guideposts Books & Inspirational Media
110 William Street
New York, New York 10038
Guideposts.org

Acknowledgments

Every attempt has been made to credit the sources of copyrighted material used in this book. If any such acknowledgment has been inadvertently omitted or miscredited, receipt of such information would be appreciated.

Scripture quotations are taken from *The Holy Bible, New International Version*. Copyright © 1973, 1978, 1984, 2011 by Biblica, Inc. Used by permission of Zondervan. All rights reserved worldwide. www.zondervan.com

Cover and interior design by Müllerhaus
Cover art by Greg Copeland represented by Deborah Wolfe, Ltd.
Typeset by Aptara, Inc.

Printed and bound in the United States of America
10 9 8 7 6 5 4 3 2

Prologue

WITH SHAKING FINGERS, SHE WRAPPED THE TINY BUNDLE IN paper, smoothing wrinkles from the fine fabric of the christening gown, straightening the lace. Atop it, she laid the picture of the two she had loved, both gone within months of each other. Finally, she added the words she had written. The ink was slightly smeared from the tears she had not been able to hold back, but there was no time to copy it out again. Her husband could never know she had saved these treasures. He couldn't bear to think of them, much less see the gown on another infant.

Setting the packet aside, she turned to the little wardrobe—the armoire that she had planned to use for her coming child until her husband had forbidden it. Quickly now, she pressed the center of the panel that released the false bottom. Putting a fleeting kiss to the little package of priceless treasures, she secreted them away and replaced the bottom of the drawer.

Now she was the wife, soon to be the mother. But the memory of those who had preceded her would live in her heart always.

1

THE ANTIQUE MINE WAS A BEEHIVE OF ACTIVITY ON THE first Thursday in September. Customers buzzed in and out, swarming the shops along Silver Peak's Main Street as they poured into town for the coming weekend's Pioneer Heritage Festival.

Sadie Speers took advantage of a moment's lull to dash into the small back room of her shop and take a quick swig from her water bottle. As she rejoined her friend and employee, Julie Pearson, in the front of the shop, she mimed wiping a hand across her forehead and dashing away imaginary perspiration. "Whew. I think this might be the busiest we've ever been before the festival."

Julie nodded. "I've lost track of how many sales I've made today. It's crazy."

Sadie grinned. "It's a good thing we like crazy."

The bell above the door tinkled merrily once again, and both women turned with a polite smile.

"Hi, Roz." Sadie's smile warmed. The newcomer wasn't a customer but her lifelong best friend, Roz Putnam. Her tall friend was hard to miss today in a bright yellow sundress with a flowing skirt. Roz had added a hot pink belt and a pair of pink sandals to add even more flair to her ensemble.

"Hello, hello." Roz glanced at the customers perusing Sadie's varied items of stock. "The joint's jumping." She hitched a thumb in the general direction of the shop's exterior. "Pretty much all of Main Street looks like this. I bet we break some attendance records at the festival this weekend."

She raised her eyebrows and peered over the top of yellow polka-dotted reading glasses decorated with tiny white daisies along the earpieces. "Are you ready for tonight's dress rehearsal?"

Sadie nodded. "Edwin and I rehearsed our scene again last night and worked out a few little kinks. We're prepared."

Jerry and Jane Remington staged an annual production for the festival called "Silver Peak: Past to Present." The show was a two-hour ensemble of varied acts that showcased the town from its early beginnings to the present. It included song and dance from the major ethnic groups that settled the region, the mining rush, and skits from some of its citizens' lives. It was highly anticipated every year, and this year, Sadie was looking forward to it even more than usual. Both of her grandchildren would be taking part, as would she and her longtime friend and now-suitor, Edwin Marshall.

"I can't wait to see your piece," Julie said. "What's it about?"

"Pioneer days," Roz said. "What else?"

"Actually, it's not." Sadie shook her head. "Jerry has been trying to add more of the town's twentieth-century history as well. This one is about a couple who learns that their son, a member of the Colorado National Guard's Field Hospital Company, has been assigned to then–Colonel Douglas MacArthur's Rainbow Division, which was sent to France in late 1917. It depicts the couple receiving a series of letters from their son until—well, I don't want to spoil the surprise. Let's just say, I encourage you to stick a few tissues in your handbags."

"Oh no. What happens?" Julie demanded.

Sadie mimed zipping her lips. "You'll just have to come and see the show."

"I'm helping with props beginning tonight," Roz said, "so I'll see it tonight." She grinned. "I'll let you know if Sadie has a future treading the boards."

Sadie snorted. "The only boards I plan to tread are the ones right here beneath my feet." She pointed down to the wide wooden planks of the floor in her shop, worn smooth and shiny by the feet of several generations of shopkeepers and their customers through the years.

Roz snickered, but then her face sobered. "Before I forget, I had a reason for stopping in here this afternoon. I just heard that Anna Harrington had her babies this morning."

"What?" Sadie pressed a hand to her heart. Anna was a young member of their church, Campfire Chapel, who was expecting twin girls. The poor thing had been widowed a few months ago when her husband was killed in a construction accident, and the whole congregation had rallied to support her. "Oh no. She's not due yet. How early are they?"

"They're about a month early," Roz said. "One weighed just under five pounds, and the other was five exactly. They are doing well, so they didn't send them to a higher-care NICU. They'll be at the hospital here until they can go home. Jeanne Sweeting is organizing a list of church members so that someone visits every day. You should let her know if you want to get in on that."

"I'll text her right now." Sadie pulled her cell phone from her pocket. She'd found that texting was an easier way to make necessary communications when she was busy at the store and didn't have time to linger on the phone. Quickly leaving the message for Jeanne, Sadie waved as Roz left when a new batch of customers descended.

Before she could do more than say, "Welcome to the Antique Mine," her cell phone *ping*ed. "I'm Sadie, and Julie is over there," she went on, smiling at the newcomers. "Please let us know if you are looking for something in particular, and feel free to browse."

As the shoppers dispersed, appearing satisfied to look through the contents of the shop at their leisure, Sadie pulled out her phone again and checked the message. It was a text from Jeanne asking if she could visit Anna Harrington tomorrow afternoon. After confirming that she could make that work, Sadie replaced her phone in her pocket and went to assist a client who looked as if she might be interested in learning more about a little cherry slant-front secretary Sadie had found at an auction a week before.

The customer proved unexpectedly eager to buy, and within fifteen minutes, Sadie had sold the desk. As she placed the signed credit slip in the drawer and handed the woman the customer copy of the receipt, the bell rang yet again. Glancing up with a smile, Sadie saw a local woman near her own age enter the shop.

"Hello, Rhea. What can I help you with today?"

Rhea Ressler was a small, yet agile sixty-something lady with whom Sadie had served on a few community committees over the years. She didn't know Rhea well, but she found her pleasant. "Hi, Sadie. I'm cleaning out a bunch of family furniture no one wants anymore, and I found an old armoire I'd like to have assessed for sale and possibly restored if anything is needed. Do you do that type of work or know anyone who might?"

"I'd love to take a look at it," Sadie assured Rhea. "I do restoration work on a regular basis, although usually it's on pieces I have purchased for sale in the shop."

"Great. I have it outside in a truck. My grandsons can bring it in, if you'd like."

Sadie was surprised. She had expected to make an appointment to visit and see the piece. "Um, that would be great. Why don't you have them pull into the back lot and bring it into the back of the shop? I should have time in the next few days to look it over and see what it needs. I can call you with an estimate if any repair or restoration is needed."

"Thanks, Sadie. That sounds great." Rhea turned toward the door. "I'll tell the boys to pull around the back."

Sadie had a quick word with Julie and then hurried to open the back door. Two burly young men were muscling a sheet-covered rectangle up the steps. They carefully angled it through the door and set it gently in the middle of the floor. Sadie helped them unstrap the protective coverings and then caught her breath when they tugged the sheets free. "Oh, this is gorgeous."

The armoire was American-made, she was certain, and probably was at least a century old. A glowing deep oak, the piece had beautifully stylized trees carved on the four door panels and an elaborate solid-brass door and drawer handles. It appeared to be in great shape, despite needing some cleaning.

Rhea had entered behind the boys. "It is pretty, isn't it? I hate to sell it, but I'm determined to downsize, and no one else in the family wants it."

"What do you know about it?" Sadie hoped Rhea would have some idea of the provenance of the armoire.

Rhea shrugged. "Not much. We bought it at an auction years ago."

Sadie hurried back to her desk and wrote up a brief description of the piece and its present condition, along with an estimate of a deposit for a simple cleaning. After Rhea had signed it and handed Sadie a check, Sadie gave her a copy of the receipt. "I'll be in touch as soon as I've had time to work up an estimate on any repairs for you if it even needs anything else. It really looks like it's in great condition."

"Thanks, Sadie. I've heard you're one of the best with treasured old pieces. I'll look forward to hearing from you, but there's no rush."

The two women shook hands, and Sadie ushered the Resslers out the back door before closing and locking it again. She needed to get back out front to help Julie, but she couldn't resist opening the doors of the armoire and taking one quick peek.

Inside the large part of the closet, there were two poles in the top for hanging garments. Sawtooth moldings in the corners would support shelving, although it did not appear to come with them. There were two pull-out drawers beneath the large interior space, but as she glanced down, Sadie realized the bottom of the cupboard looked a little odd.

She placed her fingers on the floor of the main storage area. The bottom looked like it was oak, but it didn't really match the rest of the piece. Curious, she ran her fingers around the edges. It appeared to be setting a little crooked, she decided, getting a fingertip wedged along one edge.

Gently, she pulled up—and was surprised when the whole bottom tilted enough for her to get her hands on one end and lift out the whole thing. It was a false bottom.

Sadie's heart beat faster as she realized there was something lying in the previously hidden space. Carefully, she set the false bottom on the sheets still pooled on the floor.

As she turned back to the armoire, she could see that the true bottom was slightly recessed and probably two inches deeper than the false floor had been. A small, flat package wrapped in yellowed tissue paper had been revealed.

Holding her breath, Sadie slid her palms beneath the little package and lifted it out. She set it on the worktable nearby, moving aside several spools of yarn she'd used earlier to repair a crewel pillow. The tissue was so fragile she feared it might crumble as she unwrapped it, so she quickly pulled out her phone and took pictures from several angles before she handled it again.

Pulling on a pair of cotton gloves so she wouldn't transfer oils from her hands to anything old and fragile that might be inside, Sadie began to open the package. As she had expected, the brittle tissue paper didn't fare well when she began to unwrap the contents. But the tissue didn't crumble completely; only the edges broke away a bit. Sadie made a mental note to ask Rhea how long the piece had been in her family and exactly where she'd purchased it. If it had come from the Rocky Mountain region and had never been exposed to a lot of humidity, that might explain the relatively good condition of the paper.

Slowly, giving the paper time to adjust to a new position, she laid back the two overlapping flaps that covered whatever was beneath. Inside lay a brown folio containing a photograph of a woman with an infant atop an envelope. Beneath them was what looked to be an infant's christening gown.

"*Oooooh.*" Sadie breathed a reverent sigh. The gown was carefully folded. Tatted lace edged the neckline and short sleeves, and a tatted lacy heart design had been sewn on to the breast of the gown with tiny, elegant stitches that were the next thing to invisible. It had been a labor of love, Sadie was sure, and she wondered if the tatting had been done by the same person who had sewn the gown.

Hearing voices floating back from the shop, Sadie glanced up. She needed to get back out front. Regretfully, she re-covered her find in the tissue and replaced it in the false bottom. No sense in leaving it exposed when it had fared so well in its hiding place for who knew how many years. The suspense was going to consume her, she acknowledged. Who was the woman in the photo? What was in that envelope? Had the christening dress belonged to the baby? And who had the child grown up to be? So many possibilities existed.

She glanced at her watch as she stepped back into the shop and put Rhea Ressler's deposit check in the till. Twenty minutes until closing. She filed the signed estimate before she moved to relieve Julie, whom she knew needed to leave no later than four forty-five to pick up her sons. My goodness, it had been busy practically all day long.

"Good luck with your rehearsal tonight," Julie said, as she gathered up her handbag.

Sadie clicked her tongue reprovingly. "You're supposed to say, 'Break a leg.' Thespians consider that other phrase bad luck."

Julie chuckled. "Okay. Break a leg. But for goodness' sake, please don't do it literally. After a day like today, I can't imagine what would happen to this shop without you."

"Figuratively only, I promise." Sadie grinned, turning her attention to another customer who had a pleasingly full armload of treasures to be rung up.

After that, things seemed to be winding down. There was a steady exodus of the final browsers still in the shop, and by the time ten more minutes had passed, they had all departed. She checked her watch again. It was five minutes before five, and her rehearsal started at five thirty.

Although she normally waited until after closing to complete the deposit, Sadie went ahead and ran the settlement on the credit card machine and matched up the slips with her printout, then did the same thing with the checks and the cash. There had been an impressive amount of activity in the store that day. She stapled the credit slips to the printout and then laid the deposit bag on the counter. Quickly, she glanced through all the checks to be sure they had been stamped for deposit on the back, listed them all on the deposit slip, and then placed the bundle in the deposit bag. Next she started on the cash, counting it twice and, thankfully, coming up with matching amounts before marking it on the deposit slip and adding it to the bag. Today's haul—cash, checks, and credit—was quite impressive. The Pioneer Heritage Festival was giving her business quite a boost this year.

The tinkle of the bell interrupted her, and her heart sank. Not that she wasn't happy to have more customers, but now it was two minutes till five and she really had intended to turn over the sign promptly so she could get to the rehearsal on time.

Oh well. Summoning a smile, she laid the deposit bag on the counter and greeted the visitors, a couple with two younger children and a teen skulking along behind them. "Welcome to the Antique Mine."

"Thank you. We know you're closing, but we just wanted to take a quick look," the mother said. She had the youngest child's hand in a firm grip, which Sadie appreciated. The teen eyed her from beneath a large black cap, from which untidy blond strands stuck out, and Sadie caught a flash of clear green eyes—quite pretty, really—before the boy turned away.

"Let me know if you have any questions," Sadie told the woman. She walked to the door, turned the dead-bolt lock, and flipped over the Closed sign so no one else got any ideas. She would let them out and relock the dead bolt after the people left.

As she glanced out to the street, she saw Jeanne Sweeting, the pastor's wife with whom she'd exchanged texts earlier that afternoon, driving by. Jeanne caught her eye and they exchanged a wave.

She started back to the counter to put the deposit bag in her handbag, but a knock on the door between her shop and Arbuckle's distracted her, and she veered in that direction.

Luz Vidal stood on her side of the door, a bakery bag and a piece of paper in one hand. "Hi, Sadie. Was your day as crazy as ours was?"

"It was pretty busy," Sadie confirmed. "I may have broken a sales record."

"We were swamped," Luz said. "I'm going to have to bake some extra things for tomorrow." She extended the bag. "Cream puffs. I know you're going to rehearsal tonight, so please take them along and give them out. They won't keep overnight."

Sometimes if Luz had leftovers, she would package them up and sell them for half-price the next day. But she was right—cream puffs were not an item that would keep well enough to put on sale. "Thank you," Sadie said with delight. "I just realized that I neglected to plan dinner anywhere in the next few hours, so one of these may keep me going until I get home."

Luz grinned. "Better have two." She playfully slapped her sides. "One for each hip so they match."

Sadie laughed, shaking a finger at her friend. "Oh, that's great advice. Is that how you sell so much?"

Luz chuckled. "Do you have a moment? I am putting together a new menu, and I'd be grateful if you'd check it over for me."

"Sure." Sadie glanced back over her shoulder at her customers, as Luz stepped to her side. Together they looked over the menu. Sadie found one typo, but she thought the additions, the new font, and the clear category headers worked well.

She glanced up as she finished reading. Through the open door, she could see Hector, Luz's husband, bussing two empty tables. He caught her eye and sketched a wave, and she smiled back.

"This looks great," she said, pointing out the one small change needed.

"Thanks," Luz said. "I appreciate the fresh eye."

The bell over the shop door tinkled, and Sadie turned to see that the straggler family had opened the dead bolt and was exiting. "Excuse me." Quickly, she sprinted over and locked the door behind them again, dropping the bank deposit bag on the counter. "Sorry about that. I didn't want to take a chance on anyone else coming in, or I'll never make it to rehearsal on time," she explained, returning to Luz.

"Hey, doesn't Anna Harrington go to your church?" Luz asked. "I heard her twins were born early."

"Yes." Sadie gave Luz the brief rundown Roz had shared with her. "I feel so bad for her."

"Me too," Luz said. "Losing your husband when you're four months' pregnant would be horrible, and now she has to raise those babies all alone."

"It's just heartbreaking. At least she'll have support from everyone at our church," Sadie said, "but it's certainly not the same as having a spouse to share the everyday moments."

"She's such a sweet soul," Luz said. "She comes into the shop once a week with a couple of other pregnant ladies, and they're so cute. They all drink decaf tea now. I hope the babies are all right."

"I'm going to visit her tomorrow. I'll let you know."

"Oh, could I send along a gift? I can bring it over first thing in the morning."

"Sure thing." Sadie stepped back. "Sorry, but I've got to run if I'm going to get to the bank before our rehearsal. See you tomorrow. Thanks again for the goodies. I promise to share."

Luz chuckled. "You'd better."

As Sadie closed the door to Arbuckle's and locked it again, an odd scuffling sound caught her attention. Had it come from the back room? A shiver ran down her spine, but she briskly walked into the back. Nothing appeared out of place. The door was locked just as she'd left it. The armoire was undisturbed, and when she opened the doors and checked the false bottom, the little discovery she had made earlier was exactly where she had replaced it.

Strange.

But as she turned to walk back into the shop to get her bag and the deposit, her foot caught on something, which skittered across the floor. She bent and picked it up. It was one of the spools of woolen yarn she'd pushed aside earlier. It must have been teetering on the edge, and she hadn't noticed. The noise she'd heard must have come from the spool falling and rolling.

Setting the yarn back on the worktable, Sadie went back into the front of the store. She slipped into the light jacket she'd worn to work that morning, gathered her handbag from the desk drawer, and reached for the deposit she'd left on the counter.

The bank bag was gone.

2

SADIE FLATTENED HER HAND ON THE COUNTER. THE DEPOSIT BAG had been lying right there. Hadn't it?

Her heart sank, but she was sure it had been there just a moment earlier. Had she picked it up and set it down somewhere else when Luz knocked on the door?

Highly possible, she tried to reassure herself. She occasionally did absentminded things like that, and if she wasn't paying attention, they just didn't make it into the ol' memory bank.

Quickly, she retraced her steps. But the bag wasn't lying anywhere obvious in sight. She checked every piece of furniture that was even close to the path she'd taken from the desk to the door to Arbuckle's—

Sadie sniffed. What was that smell? There was a sweet, pleasant odor hanging in the air...was it strawberry? Yes, that was almost what it smelled like.

Great. So a thief drenched in strawberry perfume had stolen her deposit. An invisible thief, no less, because there certainly hadn't been anyone in the shop she'd seen who could have done it.

Forgetting the strawberry scent, she redoubled her search efforts. She felt like an idiot, frantically searching all over the shop. Surely that bag was here somewhere. How hard could it be to find one small light gray bag emblazoned with the local bank's logo? She must have set it down somewhere. Maybe it had slid or fallen off a surface. She got on her hands and knees and crawled across the floor, looking in all directions, checking chair seats and even the edges of the throw rugs that were scattered here and there.

No deposit bag.

Had she carried it to the door and then back again without recalling it? She opened her handbag and double-checked. No.

Stymied, Sadie halted in the middle of the shop. "Retrace your steps," she told herself. "What did you do first?"

She thought back. That family had come in just as she'd finished the deposit and she'd gone to turn over the sign on the door. And she'd turned the lock then, hadn't she? At least, she was pretty sure she had.

She'd left the bag on the counter during that time, she thought. Then Luz had knocked, and Sadie had gone to the side door and they'd chatted over the bakery goodies. Sadie was nearly positive the deposit bag had been on the counter during that exchange.

The family had left while she and Luz were looking over the menu, and she'd gone to lock up behind them. Then she'd heard the noise she'd thought came from the back. And when she'd come back from checking, she'd discovered the deposit bag wasn't on the counter.

Was it possible someone had stolen it?

Who could have done it? Surely not that young family with the three kids. Besides, that literally wasn't possible, since she was pretty sure she'd tossed the bakery bag onto the counter beside the deposit bag after they'd left, as she'd gone back to finish her conversation with Luz. And then she'd heard the noise and gone into the storeroom.

But the front door was already locked, and she was sure she'd locked the door to Arbuckle's before she went into the back. So there was no possible way anyone could have entered and snatched the deposit off the counter. That thought was slightly comforting, but until she had that bag back in her possession, she wasn't going to relax.

With a jolt, she realized she was simply standing still in the middle of the shop. She checked her watch. Rehearsal started in five minutes.

Well, she wasn't going to the bank now, so all she had to do was hurry across the street to the opera house. She gathered her handbag and the bakery bag and couldn't prevent herself from taking one more look around the shop. Perhaps she would come in first thing tomorrow and see the deposit bag sitting right in plain sight.

She went around and double-checked all the doors to be sure everything was locked up, then let herself out the front door and locked it carefully behind her.

Although it had been sunny and in the sixties earlier, the air was rapidly cooling as the start of autumn crept into town. Sadie was glad she'd put on her jacket as she crossed the street and pulled open the heavy glass door.

"There you are." Edwin Marshall was tall and striking in a gray sweater vest over an Oxford-cloth button-down and neat navy slacks. "They're almost ready to start our scene. Busy day?"

"Very." Sadie swallowed the urge to pour out her troubles. She barely had given a thought to her lines, and she really needed to shift gears and try to get through this rehearsal. "Luz said they were slammed all day too."

Edwin smiled, helping her out of her jacket before they walked into the interior of the theater. "Yes, the festival seems to be bringing a lot of folks to town."

Sadie, her mind still on the missing money, didn't respond.

"Sadie? Are you all right?" Edwin was looking at her strangely.

"Not really," she said. "But we don't have time to talk about it." She tried to smile at him. "I'll tell you later. For now, let's just focus on the rehearsal."

"Hi, Sadie." Jerry Remington hurried up, interrupting their conversation. "Glad you're here. Are you guys ready to run through your scene?"

Edwin and Sadie nodded, and Jerry rushed on. "First, we'll get you into costumes, and then Jane is waiting backstage left. That's where you'll enter and exit, and she'll cue you when it's your turn to come on. The act before you is about a man named Hans Bottner, a German immigrant to Silver Peak who wrote a piano solo that was recorded by Emile Berliner's Gramophone Company in 1910." Jerry practically glowed with excitement. "We have a real live, working original gramophone, can you believe it? Anyway, the lights will come down at the conclusion of the Bottner piece, and the stagehands will set up two chairs and a little piecrust table that you two will be using."

"Got it." Edwin took Sadie's elbow, and they hustled toward the steps that led to stage left. A young woman met them at the door and handed each of them a labeled costume off a rack. "Men's, ladies," she said, pointing at separate dressing room doors along the hallway. "I got your measurements, so they should fit all right. Let me know if there's a problem."

Sadie changed quickly. Her costume was a dress of cream cotton lace with a wide, dusky violet silk band at the waist. Lace dripped from the elbows and scalloped the lower-calf-length hem. White not-so-sheer hose and clunky brown shoes that tied over the tops of her feet completed the costume. They had told her not to worry about her hair, though it was far shorter than the original fashions of the day. After all, this was just a vignette in a small local show.

"Hi." Jane Remington, acting as stage manager, pointed at a spot in the wings. "You two wait here for your cue," she whispered. "The stagehands will take the gramophone off of stage right and then bring in your furniture. You'll wait until the guy doing the Bottner piece comes offstage. As soon the lights go down, he'll exit stage right, and then you go."

Onstage, Sadie could hear a man speaking and then the scratchy sounds of an original gramophone recording being played. She had never known that someone from Silver Peak was involved in that early musical effort. Still, she tried to tune out the rehearsal and gather her thoughts. She and Edwin had rehearsed their script several times after each of them had gotten their lines down, but at the moment, Sadie couldn't even remember her opening line.

In just a few moments, Jane gave them a signal. A moment later, the man exited in the opposite direction, and then Jane was pushing them toward the curtain from which they would make their entrance.

It was dark, but she had no trouble seeing the little table and chairs that the stagehands had placed downstage center. In the far wing, she could make out Roz, wearing a headset as she communicated with Jane and Jerry and oversaw the props. Edwin took his mark, standing behind the seat at the left, and she sank into the nearest one. In just a moment, the lights came up.

Edwin, in character as the father of a young Colorado National Guardsman who was sent to France in 1917, spoke his opening line: "We have received a letter from Michael today, my dear."

"From our son? Oh, do read it out loud, Father," Sadie responded.

Edwin did so, mentioning a famous comment from MacArthur: "Colonel MacArthur said that the Forty-second 'stretches like a Rainbow from one end of America to the other,' because we have fellows from so many different states here with us."

Sadie had another line then. But try as she might, nothing came to her. Her mind simply wasn't on her performance. Jerry prompted her, and she was able to pick up the thread of the story and move on. Her character and that of the husband moved forward in time, reading a series of letters from their son as he fought across France with the 42nd Division.

On four separate occasions, Jerry had to prompt Sadie. She began to wish she'd brought along her script. But she and Edwin had practiced just two nights ago and had felt they had their lines down cold, so she'd left it at home this morning.

Desperately, she concentrated on Edwin's delivery; he was speaking slowly and clearly, and she could almost feel him willing her to complete the scene with no further flubs. Finally, they were finished. The young soldier's story had ended, and the lights dimmed. Edwin and Sadie exited and returned to their respective dressing rooms.

As soon as she had changed and hung up her costume, Sadie returned it to the costume mistress. Edwin was waiting there by the rack of clothes for her, a concerned frown on his face.

"Are you all right?" he asked with no preamble.

Sadie sighed. "Physically, yes. But as you saw, my head's all in a whirl. I'm so sorry. I completely ruined that scene. I promise it won't happen on opening night."

"What's on your mind?" Edwin asked.

Before she could answer him, Jerry came toward them, frowning. "Sadie, are you going to have these lines down by Saturday evening?"

She nodded. "Yes. I do know them. I just had an upsetting day, and I let it get the better of me. I promise I'll be flawless on Saturday."

"Do you think you need to go over it again onstage?" Jerry looked concerned.

Sadie shook her head. "No. I'll be ready."

As Sadie and Edwin left the theater, a dance exhibition featuring the Charleston, the tango, and the fox-trot was taking the stage. Such dances had been a common sight at the opera house in the Roaring Twenties, so Jerry had added the suite of dances as a period homage.

"Would you like to get some dinner?" Edwin asked, quietly taking her hand as they walked down the street to where she had parked her car. "And you can tell me what threw you off your stride tonight. I know you have those lines down cold, and the performance will go just fine."

They walked down Main Street to Sophia's in companionable silence. The restaurant was a little busier than usual for a Thursday evening, probably because of the Pioneer Heritage Festival, but there were two open tables in the low-beamed room with its subdued lighting. They were shown to one and greeted promptly by a young server who lit the candle that was seated in the squat wine bottle on the table before she took their orders and brought drinks.

As the server walked away, Sadie unwrapped a straw and inserted it into the soda she'd received. "My deposit bag went missing after closing tonight."

"Went missing?" Edwin repeated. "Was it stolen?"

"I don't know." Sadie shook her head helplessly. "That's the weird part. The doors were locked, and I was standing right there in the store talking to Luz. When I first went to pick it up off the counter and it wasn't there, I assumed I must have set it down in a different spot and just didn't remember. But I've looked everywhere, and I still haven't found it."

Edwin's brow creased. "Tell me how it happened."

Once again, Sadie went through her closing ritual. "It *was* a little abnormal," she concluded, "since that family was still in the shop, but I locked the door right after they came in, and I relocked the dead bolt as soon as they had let themselves out."

"Any chance they could have been the thieves?"

Sadie considered the question. "I know there are people who use children to distract shop owners while they steal things. If the bag was on the counter, it would have been easy pickings for professionals." She shook her head. "But I don't think so. On a few occasions, I've had people in the shop who gave me a funny vibe, as if they might be assessing my inventory with an eye to cleaning me out. But this was just a nice young family with a couple of kids. They didn't let the children run wild through the shop or do anything to try to distract me." She rubbed at her temples, fighting a headache. "I'll have to talk to Luz tomorrow and ask her if she saw anything out of the ordinary, but I think if she had, she would have said something."

Edwin nodded in agreement.

"The worst part is that it was one of the biggest deposits I've ever prepared," Sadie went on. "If the deposit doesn't turn up, I guess I'll have to contact everyone who wrote me a check—at least, those whose addresses I have—and let them know they should stop payment. And then any new check they write will have to be less the amount it costs them to stop payment, since technically this was my error." She sighed. "I really needed that deposit. There's a wonderful auction of a private estate in Leadville next week that has a lot of turn-of-the-century furnishings and goods, and I was hoping to make a couple of purchases."

"Maybe you did just misplace it," Edwin said optimistically. "Perhaps it's lying in some inconspicuous spot waiting to be found tomorrow."

"I really hope so. I just don't think there is any way it could have been stolen." Sadie sighed. "I'm beginning to doubt my memory. I know there are studies that show eyewitnesses' recall of events can be inaccurate."

Edwin nodded. "Yes, prosecuting attorneys have really had to change their approach as more and more research has debunked the validity of eyewitness testimony. Eyewitnesses frequently distort or introduce inaccuracies into their memories of events, even when they think they are being truthful."

"So I might be remembering my afternoon through a distorted memory lens?" Sadie asked with a faint smile. "Great."

"It's possible." Edwin shrugged. "More than three-quarters of wrongful convictions overturned by DNA evidence were originally decided on the basis of eyewitness testimony. No one retells a memory from a completely neutral perspective, no matter how hard they may try."

Sadie leaned forward. "So there may be an unwitting tendency to shade a memory a certain way? I guess when we're distracted, we don't always remember what was right under our noses."

Edwin grimaced. "Exactly."

Sadie cocked her head. "Maybe I'm remembering things a certain way because I don't want to believe someone stole from me."

"Or maybe you mislaid the bag and just don't recall that. In any case, given the size of the deposit, you probably should report it to the sheriff just in case. Have you told Mac yet?" Mac Slattery was the head of their local law enforcement department.

Sadie shook her head. "No time. I realized the deposit bag was missing less than thirty minutes before I had to be at the rehearsal, and I spent most of that time frantically searching the shop. I'll hunt through the shop one last time tomorrow morning, and if I still can't find it, I guess I'll be forced to let the sheriff know. And my insurance company."

Edwin nodded, making a sympathetic face.

Sadie's shoulders sagged. "I'm going to feel like an idiot trying to explain how a deposit bag vanished off the counter when I was standing right there in the same room."

3

SADIE AND SARA WENT FOR AN EARLY-MORNING RIDE THE NEXT day. Although Sadie was anxious to get to the shop and hunt for the deposit bag one more time, she had promised Sara this riding time earlier in the week, and she didn't want to back out now. Besides, if the bag was in the store, it would still be there when she arrived.

"You two are crazy," Alice had said when Sadie picked up Sara. She was already rushing around trying to get out the door to school to get some things done before her students arrived. Theo had left even earlier for a football meeting before the school day started.

After they had mounted and started off at a walk along a familiar trail, Sadie said, "So tell me about your teachers this year. Are you going to like all your classes?"

Sara shrugged. "I'm not sure yet. My English teacher is new this year, and she seems like she's going to be tough. On the first day of school, she passed out a syllabus for this marking quarter that had three projects and three exams on it. And then she launched right into the first novel we're reading. On the *first day*," she reiterated, her tone indignant.

Sadie bit back a smile. "Do the projects interest you?"

"We're already starting the first one." Sara ducked to avoid a branch that threatened to knock into her helmet. "We're supposed to choose a familiar story from childhood and do an author biography, focusing on learning several 'surprising facts'"—she made quotation marks in the air—"that the general public doesn't know about that author."

"That sounds interesting to me," Sadie said, hoping to encourage Sara, who sounded rather dubious.

"Maybe, except we have to work in pairs, and she chose our partners for us. Mine is a girl I don't even really know."

Sadie smiled. "It could be an opportunity to make a new friend. I enjoy meeting new people."

"I do too, but she's supershy. I did most of the talking, and she only answered questions if I asked directly." Sarah sighed. "It was a lot of work carrying the whole conversation."

"I bet she appreciated it though. Maybe she'll be a little more forthcoming once she gets to know you better."

"I hope so," Sara said with great feeling. "We didn't have much in common in terms of books we had read, so we wound up choosing Laura Ingalls Wilder, who wrote the Little House series."

"That should be fun for you. I remember how much you loved those books when you were younger."

Sara nodded. "I think the research will be fun. I'm starting a biography of Laura now. The real Laura," she added. "I've already found out that her real life wasn't nearly as perfect as Laura's life was in the books."

Sadie chuckled. "Life rarely is quite as idyllic as fiction. Authors can manipulate events to give characters a happy ending if they want, but in real life, it's not that simple." Thinking momentarily of her beloved husband who had passed away, she said wistfully, "I wish it was."

They crossed a shallow stream and headed through a meadow filled with short prairie grasses and wildflowers. The early flowers were gone now, and the goldenrod and paintbrush were beginning to go to seed. Milkweed pods hung heavily on their stalks.

"It won't be long before this is covered with snow again," Sadie commented. "I . . ."

"*Sh-sh-sh*. Grandma, listen." Sara held up a hand. "Do you hear that?"

Sadie paused, straining to hear. Her saddle creaked; Scout lipped at the grass. Another sound intruded. A cry, no—a growl?

"What is that?" Sara scanned the meadow. "Sounds like an animal in trouble."

Sadie hoped not. She knew her granddaughter well. If there was a creature in distress, Sara would feel compelled to try to help it, no matter how futile the effort.

"Over there." A movement in the tree line drew Sadie's attention. Sadie began walking Scout in that direction. Sara did the same.

As they drew closer to the source of the movement they had seen, Sara said, "Oh no, Grandma. Look."

Following the direction of Sara's pointing finger, Sadie caught a glimpse of movement. An eerie sound, half-yowl, half-squeal, rent the air, but it faded away almost instantly.

"It's a bobcat kitten." Sadie could hardly believe her eyes.

"And it's caught in a leghold trap," Sara said, her voice thick with disgust and distress. She reined in and dismounted, tying her bay filly's reins to a bush.

"Sara, wait." Sadie scanned the area around them. "The mother could still be close-by."

"I don't think so," Sara said matter-of-factly. "Look at the horses. If there was a full-grown bobcat nearby, they wouldn't be half this calm."

It was probably true, Sadie conceded, also dismounting. The horses' ears were pricked forward, and it was clear they were interested and alert, but their eyes showed no fear.

Together, Sadie and Sara approached the area where the bobcat kitten lay, tethered by one leg to a steel trap that had snapped shut over the fragile bones. Sara was wearing a barn coat. Quickly, she shrugged out of it, leaving her riding gloves on.

"Wait," Sadie said. "What are you going to do, Sara?"

"I'm going to get this baby out of this trap," Sara said. "Then I'm going to take it to the vet and see if it can be saved. Will you help me?"

Sadie smiled. "Of course. But let's talk our plan through first." She looked down at the little creature. The bobcat kitten was probably only a few weeks old, and it was smaller than a toy poodle. It was subdued, eyes glazed with pain and shock, and it barely responded as they approached.

"Okay," Sara said in a quiet, soothing tone, "so here's the plan. If you can open the trap, I'm going to wrap the kitten in my coat. I'm hoping it will stay calm and quiet, and Daisy will allow me to mount her and ride with it. If Daisy objects, you may have to call Milo to come out with a truck to the closest road and I'll walk out to meet him."

"You're going to be late for school," Sadie said, "but I am sure your mother will not mind on this occasion. All right. If you're ready, I'm ready. Just be careful. He might not be as down as he looks, and little as he is, he could still do some serious damage with those teeth and claws."

"I know," Sara said. "I'll be careful."

Sadie studied the trap. She despised these things. Not to mention that they were illegal. This one was small- to midsize, probably set by someone with hopes of catching a mammal with a valuable pelt, such as a fox. Fortunately, it was small enough that she should be able to release the kitten *if* it didn't decide to clobber her while she messed with the trap.

"Ready?" she asked Sara.

Her granddaughter nodded. Kneeling, she laid her coat over the baby bobcat's head and forepaws. One back leg was caught in the trap. Sadie took it as a good sign that the baby didn't move.

Carefully, she stepped forward, placing the soles of her boots atop each of the levers at either side of the trap. Leaning her weight gradually on them, she eased apart the jaws of the trap. Sara immediately pulled the bobcat free. It gave a muffled groan of agony, but it didn't move otherwise. Sadie feared that if the little thing had been out here all night, it might die of shock and exposure before they could even get it to the vet.

While Sara wrapped up the baby, Sadie let the trap snap shut again. She shuddered at the sound, imagining the pain the little animal had suffered. Quickly, she pulled free the pin that fastened the trap to a nearby tree and stowed it in her saddlebag.

"Grandma, I'm turning you into an animal rescuer," Sara said with a grin, cradling the kitten as they started back toward the horses.

"No way am I leaving that out here," said Sadie grimly, "for someone to set again. Milo's going to be furious when he finds out about this." She extended her arms. "Here. Why don't you let me take him while you mount, and then I'll hand him up to you?"

Daisy, good girl that she was, sniffed Sara thoroughly when she approached, but otherwise didn't react as Sara led her to a nearby downed tree and mounted. Sadie came up from the side and handed the little bundle up to Sara.

"He's awfully quiet," she said as she mounted the chestnut.

"I know," Sara said. "That's not a good sign. Let's go." And turning her quarter horse, she headed back to the Henderson barn at a trot, with Sadie right behind her.

As they rode toward the stable a short while later, Sadie saw Milo behind the barn. He was using a pitchfork and a shovel to turn the manure pile, a necessary but less-than-pleasant task. "Milo," she shouted. "Can you cool the horses and put our tack away? We have an emergency."

"Sure thing." Milo stopped his work and came through the barn, emerging just in time to take the reins as both Sadie and Sara dismounted. "You all right?" he asked in concern.

"We found a bobcat kitten in a leghold trap." Sadie pulled the trap out of her saddlebag and handed it to him. "We need to get it to the vet."

Milo's normally gentle countenance darkened. "If I find out who set this, they're going to be mincemeat," he growled.

"I know." Sadie cast him a similarly disgusted glance. "I have to see the sheriff today. I'll mention it to him."

Milo nodded. "I'll hang on to the trap in case he wants to see it." He began to walk Scout and Daisy, knowing they needed to keep moving to avoid their muscles getting tight after their exercise.

"Thank you." Sadie cast him a grateful glance. "We owe you one."

"Great," he said over his shoulder, as he headed toward the barn. "You can help turn Manure Mountain next time you come by."

Both women groaned. Then they laughed.

"We deserve that," Sara said. "I feel guilty leaving him to finish caring for our horses."

"So do I. But until you learn to drive, someone else has to chauffeur you when you're on your animal-saving exploits," Sadie pointed out.

Quickly, they got into Sadie's red Tahoe and headed for the veterinary clinic in town. As Sadie drove, Sara used her phone to call and alert them that they were bringing in the injured bobcat kitten. At Sadie's request, she texted Julie and asked if she could open the shop and stay until Sadie arrived. Thankfully, Julie was available and happy to help out.

Then Sara texted her mother and explained what had happened. "I'm telling her that you're going to write me an excuse, okay, Grandma?"

Sadie grinned. "Okay, Sara."

The minute they entered the clinic, a technician took them back to an exam room. Ben Armstead entered moments later, and the pair carefully unwrapped the bobcat kitten. It didn't even protest, and Ben made a sound of concern.

"He's pretty dehydrated," he said as he examined the baby, "and in shock. His temp and heart rate are low. I'll have to put him under anesthesia to check the leg for breaks and other damage, but I can't do that until he's warmer and more stable. Can I keep him here today?"

Sara nodded. "Do you think he'll live?"

"I hope so." Ben's gaze lingered on the little animal. "Wildlife is often pretty hardy. A better question might be whether or not we'll be able to release him again when he's well. Depends on how much damage was done to that leg."

"Sara's got to get to school," Sadie said. "How about if we check back later today?"

"That should be fine," Ben said. "I do hope he'll respond well, and I'll have something to tell you then."

"Thank you, Dr. Armstead," Sara said gratefully. "I really appreciate your help." Ben had made it clear that he was happy to help Sara with her occasional animal-care efforts.

"No problem." He grinned at the girl. "You know when you finish vet school someday, I'll be offering you a job here. If I help you enough, you'll owe me so big you'll have to say yes."

Sara laughed. "Yes, yes, yes. I'll give you my answer now."

Leaving the clinic, Sadie dropped Sara by her house to change for school, then rushed home and got herself ready before hurrying back, excuse note in hand, to take Sara to school. She could hardly wait to get into the shop and see if the deposit had turned up.

"Hey, you made it," Julie said, as Sadie bustled through the door a few minutes after ten. "I didn't think you'd be here this soon. How's the baby bobcat?"

"Stable. We'll know more later today. Thank you so much for coming in. Did you find the deposit bag?"

Julie looked confused. "The deposit bag? I didn't know I was supposed to look for it."

Sadie felt the hope that had sustained her drain away. "I thought maybe you'd find it when you were opening up this morning. It's missing."

"Missing?" Julie's alarm showed. "You mean, you lost it last night?"

Sadie related the loss—theft?—of the bank bag. "So," she concluded, "the bottom line is that I am not really even sure if it *was* stolen, or if it's hiding here somewhere. I wanted to get here early today and search every corner, but obviously that didn't happen."

"I'll help." Julie immediately walked to the far right side of the shop. "I'll start over here. Let's hope we'll have a little breather before we start getting customers, and maybe we'll find that it was here all this time."

Sadie took the left side of the shop. Between them, she and Julie looked on, in, and under every single item of furniture in the Antique Mine. They opened vintage jewelry boxes and every drawer in every item of furniture, although Sadie knew she never would have placed something in such unlikely spots and not recalled doing so. They looked behind things, under lampshades, and even atop the taller pieces.

Nothing.

The best that could be said was that the shop got the most thorough dusting it had seen in many moons. Sadie then went into the back room. Ignoring the call of the old armoire, she merely checked the false bottom and the other cupboards and drawers to be certain there was no bank bag there. She checked her shelves of supplies that she kept on hand for restoration projects and scoured the room just as she and Julie had the front of the shop.

Still nothing.

Discouraged, she put on her jacket and slung her handbag over her shoulder. "Well, that was a giant dud," she said to Julie. "I guess my next move is to check with Luz to see if she noticed anything amiss, and then I'll go down to the sheriff's office and make a report."

Julie looked as upset as Sadie felt. "I probably don't even want to know how much was in there," she said. "We had a banner day yesterday."

Sadie nodded glumly. "We did." She headed for the door between the two shops. "I'll be back."

She stepped into Arbuckle's and headed back to the kitchen, catching Luz just as she removed two giant trays of chocolate-chunk cookies with walnuts from the oven.

"Good morning, Sadie," her friend called. Working quickly and efficiently, she transferred the cookies to wire racks to cool and dumped the cookie trays into the industrial-size sink.

"Good morning, Luz. Thanks again for the cream puffs. They were a big hit at rehearsal. Some of those folks were there all evening and didn't get dinner."

Luz smiled. "I'm glad I could help stave off starvation. Before I forget, let me give you my gift for Anna Harrington." She hurried to her storeroom and came back with a blue gift bag embossed with baby footprints and smothered in curling ribbon and tissue paper. "Thanks for delivering that. What's up?" she said as she handed the bag to Sadie.

Sadie made a wry face. "After we finished chatting last night, I discovered my bank bag was missing. It had my daily deposit in it. I swear it was on the counter when I came over to open the door for you, but when I returned, it was gone."

Luz's dark brown eyes widened in dismay. "What? How is that possible?"

"I don't know. Did you see anything—anything at all unusual that might help me figure this out?"

Luz thought for a moment, slowly shaking her head. "We were looking over the menu...the family with the children was browsing. But they were not anywhere near the counter when I saw them. And they went to the door, and you went over and locked the door behind them, and it was just you and me." Her brow furrowed. "Oh, Sadie, how could that have happened? Are you sure it's not in your purse, or on the floor behind the counter or something?"

Sadie shook her head. "I looked everywhere. And Julie and I tore the place apart this morning. It's not there, Luz."

"Who could have stolen it?"

"I don't know," Sadie said wearily. "I wish I had an answer. I guess I'm going to go report the loss to Sheriff Slattery, because it is looking more and more like it must be a theft."

Luz clucked sympathetically. "I am so sorry I can't be more helpful. I'll think it through again, and if anything occurs to me, I will let you know."

"Will you check with Hector too?" Sadie requested. "He walked past the door while you and I were proofreading the menu. Maybe he saw something."

Luz nodded. "He just ran to the store for butter." She grimaced. "How can a baker run out of butter? We were so busy yesterday we didn't even realize how low we were."

Sadie nodded, thinking of how much money she'd made yesterday. "Here's to another busy day. Thanks, Luz."

As she retraced her steps through the little restaurant, she pasted on a smile as she greeted several people she knew. But she was conscious of a deep sense of disappointment. She hadn't realized how much she had counted on Luz noticing something that would help her find the missing deposit.

4

EMERGING FROM ARBUCKLE'S, SADIE BLINKED IN THE BRIGHT
sunshine and dug in her bag for her sunglasses. It was a truly
gorgeous autumn day with temps already in the high fifties. Last
night it had dipped into the thirties, and she had no doubt that
before long they would see the first frost—and that meant snow
wasn't far behind. It was hard to imagine that, looking at the clear
blue of the cloudless sky.

Turning right, she started off at a brisk pace along Main
Street. She crossed Washington and Adams before taking a right
on Jefferson and heading into the brick building in which the
sheriff's office was located.

Inside, she went straight to the receptionist's desk. Janet
Parks, who guarded the gates to the sheriff's inner sanctum and
managed the office's many tasks with an efficiency Sadie wished
she possessed, was seated there. "Good morning, Sadie. What can
I do for you?"

"Hi, Janet. I'd like to talk to Mac if he's in."

"He is. Can I tell him what it's about?"

Sadie took a deep breath. "I think I may have to report a
theft."

Janet's penciled-in eyebrows rose behind the large red reading glasses she wore. "A theft? Have you been a little less than watchful with all these tourists who have flooded our town?" She picked up her phone and hit a button, then looked at Sadie expectantly.

Sadie knew Janet was hoping for more details, but she didn't really want to toss information around until she had ascertained that someone really had stolen the money. "I'll discuss it with Mac," was all she said.

Janet listened as Mac picked up his phone. Relaying Sadie's request, she nodded. "He says you can go right on back."

"Thanks." Sadie left the desk and walked along the hallway to the back of the building, where she knew Mac's office was located.

Mac stood when he saw her in the doorway. "Hey, Sadie. Come on in. How can I help you?" He offered her a firm handshake and pointed at one of the two visitors' in front of his desk. "Have a seat and tell me what's going on."

Sadie sat down as Mac took the chair beside her, dragging it around a bit so he could see her more directly. She set down her handbag. "Mac, I think my bank deposit bag was stolen from the shop right before closing yesterday."

"You *think* it was?" He quirked an eyebrow.

Sadie nodded. "Honestly, I was hoping that maybe I just had a memory slip, and I set it down somewhere other than where I thought I had. But I've searched the shop twice. This morning, Julie helped me, and I'm certain the deposit is missing. I can't say for sure that it was stolen, but I am absolutely positive it is not in the Antique Mine."

Mac's brows drew together. He made notes on a pad he had pulled off his desk. "All right. Can you describe it?"

"It's a gray bank bag with burgundy lettering that says *Silver Peak Bank and Trust Company* on it, along with the bank's address and phone number. I always use it for my deposits."

"What was in the bag when it went missing?"

Sadie sighed. "Two hundred and seventy-four dollars and sixty-three cents in cash and fourteen checks, mostly from out-of-towners, totaling two thousand eight hundred and forty-one dollars and seven cents."

"That was from just one day?" When Sadie nodded, Mac said, "I'm in the wrong business, apparently."

Sadie had to smile, and she felt herself relax marginally, which was probably what Mac had intended. "And that doesn't count the credit sales."

Mac whistled. "Definitely in the wrong business."

Sadie shook her head. "It's not as amazing as it sounds. Not when you consider that I pour quite a bit of that back into buying more items, some of which I need to refurbish or repair, and that this is one of the busiest weeks of the year. There are usually a few days in winter when I don't make a single sale."

Mac shifted in the chair, looking down at his notepad. "Do you have a list of people who were in the shop when the bag was—er, went missing?"

Sadie spread her hands. "That's just it. I set the bag on the counter. I hadn't locked the door yet, and a couple came in with three children just to look for a minute. They went to the far end of the shop, away from the counter, and I locked the door behind them so no one else could enter. Then Luz knocked on the door between me and the coffee shop. I answered it and we proofread her new menu. After the people left, I locked the door again. Luz was standing right there the whole time, and when I talked to her this morning, she said she hadn't seen anyone else creeping around in the shop. I noticed the bank bag missing shortly after we finished our conversation."

Mac frowned. "Well, it didn't just grow legs and walk away. Someone gave it a helping hand. Take me through it again."

Sadie repeated her story. This time, she said, "Luz and I were both concentrating on her menu for a little while, and we had our backs to the door. But the door was locked, so I know no one else came in. Oh, and there is one more thing. After Luz left and I closed the door to Arbuckle's, I heard a funny noise. I thought it came from the back storeroom, so I..."

"What kind of noise, exactly?"

"Um, a sort of scuffle, I guess. Not loud, and only for a moment. But it gave me a little shiver since I thought the shop was empty. I walked back and checked the storeroom, but no one was there. One of my spools of thread had fallen to the floor, so I guess that's what it was." But she frowned. "Even though it didn't sound like that sort of noise."

Mac ran a hand through his hair. "Sadie, did it ever occur to you that there might have been someone back there and that you should've called for help instead of charging in to investigate? That's a good way to get knocked over the head. Or worse."

"No, it didn't occur to me," Sadie said with a hint of asperity. "I knew there was no one else in the shop."

"You didn't *think* there was," Mac corrected. "So when did you notice the bag was gone? Before or after you went into the back room?"

"After. But it could have been gone before and I just didn't notice."

"Sounds to me like you had an intruder. You're positive you locked both doors?"

"Fairly sure, yes." But as she searched her memory, she wasn't 100 percent positive. "At least, I think I did." She sighed. "Mac, be honest. Do you think there's any chance of recovering that money?"

The sheriff sighed. "There's always a chance. You know that. But I would have to say, given the number of tourists in town, that the odds of finding your thief aren't great. I'll certainly file a report and look into it, but you should call your insurance company and report the loss, in case it's never recovered. Whoever did it probably took the cash and ditched the checks. Your best hope is to cancel them all and contact the customers who wrote them and ask them to write new ones."

"I don't have all of their contact information," Sadie said glumly. "It was on the checks. I even write the driver's license numbers on them. So all I have is a copy of the deposit ticket with last names and amounts." She grimaced. "Alice has been after me to buy a portable scanner-slash-copier and start scanning all checks along with drivers' licenses for all out-of-town checks. Now I'm wishing I'd listened."

Mac nodded. "Not a bad idea. Or at least record them at the time of sale."

Sadie grimaced. "Sometimes I am just too crazy-busy to add one additional thing to the transaction routine. If people have to wait too long, there's always the chance they'll decide not to buy. I guess a scanner might be the way to go."

Sadie called the shop after she left the sheriff's office. Julie answered, assuring her that things were under control, so Sadie decided to head for the hospital to visit Anna Harrington, the new mother from Campfire Chapel, today. While she was at it, she would grab some lunch and eat on the way. As much as she wished otherwise, there was very little more she could do to find her missing deposit.

Thinking of that, she walked straight to the back of the store, where she'd parked her Tahoe. A few minutes later, she drove toward the hospital, stopping at a sandwich shop on the highway for an eggplant wrap with lemon aoli, spinach, and feta cheese, and a lemonade. Seated at a table outdoors in the sunshine, Sadie reviewed what she hoped to accomplish after the hospital visit.

First on her list was calling the insurance company and reporting the loss. She suspected they were going to be reluctant to consider it a theft until they had a law enforcement opinion on that, but she wanted to get the process started.

Second was taking a closer look at those items she had found in the armoire, and then examining the armoire in detail and making a plan for any repairs it might need. She'd noticed one of the hinges on the upper doors was loose, but there might be other issues.

The third thing was the bobcat kitten. She and Sara needed to go back to Doc Armstead's after school to see how it was doing.

Arriving at the hospital, Sadie parked her SUV in the large lot adjacent to the hospital and headed for the main entrance. Silver Peak was fortunate to have an excellent health-care facility right here in town, unlike many other small towns, where care was being consolidated and merged with larger facilities.

Inside, she waved hello to the receptionist at the information desk. She'd been here many times throughout her life, and her daughter, Alice, had been born here. Of course, the hospital had undergone several face-lifts and major renovations since that time, but it still felt familiar and friendly. She made a stop in the gift shop first and picked up a small vase of blue and white chrysanthemums, asking the cashier to add two blue "It's a Boy" balloons.

Holding the balloons close so they didn't bang into other people, she took the elevator up to the floor that housed the family birthing unit. Labor and Delivery was located there, as well as patient rooms for new mothers, the well-baby nursery, and a small special-care unit for babies who were born early but mostly needed breathing assistance. The hospital was very proud of their Level-II NICU, and there had been a recent article in the paper about it. Sadie felt confident that Anna's twins must be doing relatively well, or they would have been airlifted to a NICU in Breckenridge or Denver that was equipped to care for more seriously compromised preemies.

She signed in at a desk and received Anna's room number before a *click* signaled the unlocking of a set of double doors that permitted her to enter the unit housing the mother-and-baby rooms. Signs overhead indicated that the special-care unit was to the right, and Sadie noted that there was a separate set of locked doors preceding that area. It was a far cry from the casual atmosphere that had been prevalent when Alice had been born. It was a little sad to think about the ways in which the world had changed since she was a young mother. Alice would never think of letting Sara go out without her cell phone, and Sadie even knew people who had tracking applications on their children's phones so they could check on their whereabouts at any time.

Room Twelve was halfway down the corridor on the left. The door was partially ajar, so Sadie knocked gently.

"Come in," called a feminine voice.

Sadie pushed through the heavy door. There were two beds in the room divided by a curtain. The first bed was empty, and the curtain was pulled back so that Sadie could see Anna resting in the second bed near the window.

"Hi, Anna," Sadie said, walking to the bedside and leaning down to hug her young friend. "Congratulations on delivering two healthy little boys." She set the vase with its balloons on the nearby windowsill, which already held two other bouquets.

Anna beamed. "Thank you for coming. The arrangement is beautiful."

"I have a gift for you," Sadie told her, "but if I brought it in, you'd just have to drag it home again, so I decided to wait until you're home. But I did bring one from Luz." She handed over Luz's gift bag. Anna opened it and together they admired the tiny baby-blue sleep sacks with whales printed on them.

"I'll probably be discharged tomorrow," Anna said. "Jenna Henderson has offered to come and get me. My mother-in-law is coming for a few days to help, but she can't get here until next week."

"How was your labor and delivery?" Sadie asked.

Anna smiled, but her lip quivered, and Sadie knew she was thinking of her late husband. "It was really pretty quick and easy." She grimaced. "At least, that's what I've been told."

Sadie patted her shoulder. "I bet it didn't feel that way at the time."

"You can say that again." Anna managed a smile. "The lady who taught the birthing classes offered to be my labor coach. She stayed with me the whole time. I think we're friends for life."

Sadie felt a lump clogging her throat. "That's incredibly sweet. I can't even imagine how hard it was without Guy. But I'm sure he knows how well you did." Guy had been Anna's husband, a good-natured man who always was willing to help with church projects. His passing after an on-the-job accident had been a blow to the whole Campfire Chapel community. "And the boys are doing well? What did you name them?"

Anna's tears welled. "Aaron Guy and Alexander Guy. We had ch-chosen those first names together, and I wanted them each to have their daddy's name too."

Sadie felt her own eyes sting. Losing her husband, T.R., had been devastating, but she was deeply grateful that they'd had so many years to amass wonderful memories together. Guy and Anna had barely had a chance to start making memories before his death.

"Those are lovely names," she said. "I think that's a wonderful idea. You can tell them their daddy will always be with them because they each carry his name."

Anna nodded, grabbing a tissue from the bedside table to blot her eyes and blow her nose. "That was my thinking exactly." She managed a smile. "He was a special man, and I want them to grow up knowing that. They're doing well," she added. "They'll probably have to stay here for a little while. We don't know yet how long. Alex is the smaller one, and he's on a respirator right now. Aaron just has a nasal cannula giving him extra oxygen, so I hope Alex will soon be able to do that. The doctor said they might be able to try that tomorrow."

"That sounds very encouraging," Sadie said.

"It'll be wonderful to have them home," Anna said longingly. "I'm anxious to get started on figuring out how to juggle everything."

"It's a lot to manage," Sadie agreed. "But you won't be alone."

"Most of the time I will though," Anna said. "My mother and I ... well, she's not really in the picture anymore, and Guy's parents live in Pennsylvania."

Sadie was puzzled. She clearly remembered Anna's mother by her side at Guy's funeral. But it felt rude to pry further. "You have a church family that will help you," Sadie assured her. "Jeanne Sweeting has been organizing visitors, and if you tell her what you need and want, she'll organize that too." Sadie smiled. "That lady could make ants march in a straight line, I think."

Anna grinned. "She could. I told Jeanne I'm a little worried about nights, so perhaps she could get a few people to help me just for a week or so."

"Honey," Sadie said, smiling, "you aren't going to have to manage nights alone until you're ready, even if that's months down the road. I'd be happy to come over one night a week, and I know there are a ton of other church members who can't wait to sign up to help you out. We'll help you to get a little more rest when they're wide awake and you're not."

Anna's eyes widened. "That's the ... the kindest thing I have ever heard. You'd really do that? Don't you have to work?"

"Yes, but one night's interrupted sleep won't hurt," Sadie assured her. "It's the 'round-the-clock exhaustion that gets to new mothers. So your Campfire Chapel family is prepared to do what we can to help you cope." She snapped her fingers. "Do you know my shop employee, Julie Pearson?"

Anna shook her head.

"I'll introduce you," Sadie promised. "She has twin sons who are ten now, and I know she would be delighted to be a resource for 'twin questions.'" Sadie told her. "When her sons were born, Julie and her husband had extra help from their church for a long time. That's the beauty of being part of a community. We support one another."

Anna swung her legs over the edge of the bed. "I am so glad we found Campfire Chapel. I don't know how I would have gotten through the past few months without all of you." She stood. "Would you like to visit the babies?"

"Would I?" Sadie's eyes widened. "Am I allowed to go into the NICU?"

"If you go in with me as a guest, yes. Oh, and you'll need your driver's license or some form of photo ID. They sign everyone in and out."

"Just like the bank does with my safe-deposit box," Sadie quipped.

"I guess these babies are the hospital equivalent of the precious items in the bank vaults." Anna said, smiling as she started out of the room. "Come let me show off my boys."

5

Once Sadie was back at the shop after her hospital visit, Julie peppered her with questions about the missing money, her visit to the sheriff, and her visit to the hospital.

"I sort of volunteered you to visit Anna sometime," Sadie told her employee sheepishly. "Or perhaps talk to her on the phone, since you've had the experience of raising twins."

"I'd love to," Julie said. "In a few weeks, those little guys are going to be smiling and nursing well, and she'll feel much more confident." She hesitated. "I know I'm not a member of Campfire Chapel, but do you think I could get on the overnight schedule?"

"That would be wonderful," Sadie said and then grinned. "I don't think your offer of assistance will be turned away just because you're not a card-carrying member of my church. In fact, I'll call Jeanne right now and tell her about Anna's need for overnight helpers and that you and I want to be at the top of that list."

"Great." Julie's voice lilted with anticipation. She giggled. "I can't wait to get my hands on those babies."

Sadie was smiling as she headed for the antique mahogany desk and display case that served as her front counter. But her smile faded as she recalled her to-do list. The next thing after calling Jeanne was to call her insurance agency.

As it turned out, Jeanne didn't answer, so she left a message and moved on to the insurance call. It wasn't exactly a frustrating call, she decided afterward, but it certainly was...inconclusive at best. Her agent dutifully took all the information she had to share about the missing bag and said he'd be in touch with Sheriff Slattery. He couldn't confirm whether or not she could recover any of the proceeds of yesterday's sales through insurance coverage, but the list of exclusions from her policy that he reeled off made her deeply skeptical. Apparently, it would have to be clearly proven to be theft, and it would be highly desirable if they had the thief in custody with a signed confession *and* a statement from the police that none of the money could be recovered.

As she hung up the phone, she rubbed at her temples, trying to stave off the first throbbing pains of a headache.

"Insurance guy give you a splitting headache?" Julie asked sympathetically.

"This whole mess gives me a headache," Sadie replied. "I still can't quite believe my deposit bag practically vanished into thin air."

"There must have been someone in here." Julie smiled and waved as a pair of shoppers exited without making a purchase.

"Yeah, a ghost," Sadie said after waving too. Tired of racking her brain over the problem of the missing money, she headed for the back of the shop. "I'm going to take another look at that armoire that Rhea Ressler dropped off yesterday. If you get a break without customers, come on back, and I'll show you what I found beneath a hidden floor panel."

"A hidden panel?" Julie's eyes sharpened. "You have the best luck. Or maybe I should say the best eye for irregularities?" The bell over the shop tinkled as more shoppers entered, and she visibly deflated. "Oh rats, here comes someone else." Then she mimed smacking herself in the head. "What am I thinking, complaining about customers? We should be this busy every week."

Sadie laughed as she walked into the storeroom. "So true."

The pretty little armoire was just as she had left it. Opening the doors with a sense of anticipation, she lifted out the false bottom and set it aside. To her relief, the items she had discovered and replaced were still there. It wasn't until she saw them that she even realized she had been subconsciously steeling herself for another vanishing act.

Shaking her head at her own silliness, Sadie donned her cotton gloves, before she carefully lifted out the little trio of memorabilia items and laid them on the workbench. Gently, she laid the photograph to one side and picked up the envelope that lay atop the christening gown with the tatted lace.

She opened a drawer in her workbench and pulled out a thin silver letter opener. Barely breathing, she very carefully lifted the envelope's flap a tiny bit. To her relief, the paper didn't crack immediately. It probably hadn't hurt that she had left it in the shop overnight, where the air was slightly humidified to keep the many antiques in good condition. She eased the flap open a bit more and waited patiently, then did it again. Finally, after several more incremental motions in which she eventually had the flap completely upright, she could see that inside the envelope was a folded page that looked like a letter.

Carefully, she laid the envelope down, still keeping the flap open, as she reached into the drawer again for a pair of tweezers with cotton padding on the ends specially designed for handling fragile papers. Holding her breath again, she slowly withdrew the paper from inside the envelope and laid it aside, figuring it might need a moment to adjust.

Putting her attention to the envelope again, she turned it over. There was no writing on the front, so it probably had been meant to be nothing more than a means of containing the paper.

She looked at the photo lying beside it and switched on a light that she kept atop a shelf. In the photo, a woman sat on a chair holding an infant in her lap. The woman stared straight into the camera without a hint of a smile on her face. In fact, she looked exhausted and hopeless, even in repose.

The infant was dressed in the christening gown that had been hidden in the false bottom. If it wasn't the same one, it was an exact replica, she thought, noting the unusual tatted heart design adorning the breast. The woman's hair was fashioned into intricate loops and curls but clearly was quite long with the bulk confined at the back of her head. She wore a high-necked, low-waisted, long dress in a black or very dark fabric with high, gathered sleeve-heads that gave her shoulders a distinct pouf. Below, the sleeves quickly tapered to hug the arms from above the elbows to the wrists. Sadie didn't consider herself an historical fashion expert by any means, but she felt fairly certain the woman's clothing was from the end of the nineteenth century or possibly the beginning of the twentieth.

Both the woman and the baby were very clearly focused, indicating that they had been quite still for the length of time it took for the picture to be made. Although Sadie knew that there were cameras available in the late 1800s that could make photographs in a second, there were still many older models in use that required up to three seconds of stillness or more. Unless an infant was sleeping, it was highly unlikely that the child was going to hold still for very long.

This baby's eyes were wide open and appeared to be staring at something high up near the ceiling—something that a child of only a few months was unlikely to perceive or attend to for any length of time.

Sadie felt a chill run up her spine. She suddenly realized that she was looking at a *memento mori*, a postmortem photograph of the type that was in vogue during the Victorian era. She knew the Latin phrase meant, "Remember that you will die." Many families of the time were not able to afford the cost of a sitting, but when a beloved family member died, especially a child, sometimes families had such photographs made. It was probably the only physical likeness they would have of their departed loved one.

She studied the photograph more closely. The woman was young, and the infant was only a few months old. There were no dates or other information on the front or the back.

Setting down the heartbreaking image, she turned her attention to the letter. Gently, she unfolded it, using the letter opener rather than her hands. Even covered by the cotton gloves, handling such a fragile piece of history was inadvisable.

She went to a file in the corner and pulled out a couple of archival-quality acid-free plastic sleeves. She slipped the photo in its folio into one, the envelope into another, and the letter into a third. Then she picked up the sleeve containing the letter to examine it.

There was writing covering the front of the page, an elegant, flowery cursive script that marched straight across the paper, slanting neither up nor down. She would have thought it was a woman's hand, but she knew that in centuries past, there were many men possessed of equally fine handwriting, so she cautioned herself not to assume anything. But she couldn't help but think that such a lovely, even hand with its luxurious flourishes must have been feminine.

The ink had probably been black when it was written. Although it had faded somewhat, it was still legible.

Slowly, Sadie began to read the flowing script. She grabbed a pad and pen and jotted down the words as she went, because some of the cursive was so complex that she was concentrating too hard on translating it to comprehend its meaning.

When she was finished, Sadie laid down the pen. It appeared that there was a brief message, and then ... a prayer? Most certainly a prayer, she realized, seeing "Amen" near the end of the lines. She read the missive out loud.

> *Oh, faithless wife am I! I cannot bring myself to comply with my beloved husband's wishes in this matter. To destroy the only photo of that precious little face, now beyond our reach forever, requires strength I do not have. To destroy her gown, every tiny stitch made with such loving care by her mother? Unthinkable. Perhaps one day he shall relent. Perhaps one day another shall wear this gown. Until then, I shall hide it away and offer this prayer:*
>
> *Oh, Thou Holy Father,*
> *Behold us prostrate in our grief.*
> *Pour thou comfort on our wounded hearts,*
> *Lord Eternal.*

Most Divine Father, Most Divine Son,
Hold close these two precious souls.
Thou has granted eternal peace to all who believe.

Accept my most humble intercession.
Gather in Your Holy Arms
Those who have gone too soon from ours.
Amen.

~EM, 1899

Sadie put down the pad of paper. So her intuition probably had been right. The author with the fine handwriting had been a female. Someone's wife. But how had she been related to the mother and deceased infant in the photograph? Her words made clear that the child had died, but what had happened to the mother? She looked as if she was alive in the photograph, but the poem clearly implied that both the mother and the infant were resting in heavenly peace now.

She became aware that there were tears running down her face, and she grabbed a tissue and hastily mopped them up. It was the combination of things, she decided, that had lowered her defenses. Not only was she worried about the missing money, but she also had to make sure she didn't mess up tomorrow night's performance with Edwin. Then she'd visited those precious wee ones, who'd lost their father before they could ever know him, and she'd thought of T.R. and the wonderful years she'd had with him. And now she was confronted with another person's grief and apparently the loss of an infant, set down on paper to last long after the writer herself probably had passed away. How could she not be affected?

Just then, Julie popped her head into the storeroom. "The coast is clear. I'm dying of curiosity. Where did you find a hidden panel?" She stopped short. "Why are you crying?"

"Just a maudlin moment," Sadie assured her. "Although I bet this find will get to you too." She proceeded to open the doors of the armoire and show Julie the false floor that lifted up. "And inside here was a little treasure," she went on, gesturing to the items still lying on the worktable.

Julie walked over to examine them as Sadie pointed out the intricate stitchery on the gown and explained why she felt certain the photograph was a *memento mori*. Finally, she held up the letter.

"This was what got to me."

Julie squinted. "I can't read it. I mean, maybe if I studied it for several days..."

Silently, Sadie handed her the pad with the translation.

Equally silently, Julie read it, her lips moving as her gaze traveled down the page. When she was done, there were tears swimming in her eyes too. "You win," she acknowledged. "I defy anyone, especially anyone who is a mother or who has ever loved a baby, to read that without getting emotional." She sniffed loudly as she grabbed a tissue and wiped her eyes. "Where did it come from? Do you think this belonged to the Ressler family?"

"I don't know." Sadie shrugged. "I'm going to ask Rhea about the history of the armoire and tell her what I found. Maybe she has the answer."

"Maybe she's descended from whomever this belonged to. Can you imagine receiving this a hundred years after it was hidden by a member of your family? Why, Rhea might even have someone in her family who would want to use the christening gown."

Sadie traced a gentle finger over the shape of the infant in her mother's arms. "That would be wonderful. I hope Rhea knows who these two are."

Edwin stopped by shortly before closing. "Any luck finding your deposit bag today?" he asked after he'd greeted her.

Sadie shook her head. "Julie and I tore the shop apart today looking for that bag. If it was still there, we'd have found it. I guess it's time to face the fact that someone stole it right out from under my nose. I talked to Mac today, and he seems pretty certain I didn't just lose it."

Edwin winced visibly. "I'm sorry. No wonder you were shaken up last night."

"Do you want to review our lines?" Sadie asked. "I'm confident that I know them. But I think we'll feel better going into the show tomorrow evening if we've had a clean run-through."

"That's probably a good idea, even though I've heard you go through the whole scene without a hitch. It's always good to have a clean run-through fresh in your mind, though, before a performance. I've learned that from rehearsing for trials." Edwin took two chairs from a nearby dining set and placed them in the aisle. "Here we go."

As she'd expected, the scene went flawlessly.

They had just finished when the sound of cheery calliope music reached their ears.

Edwin pointed. "There goes the ice-cream truck."

Sadie turned her head to gaze out the window, where the ice-cream truck was exiting the alley across the street and moving on down Main Street. "I saw it the other day," she said. "But I thought the owners had moved away."

"They did," Edwin told her. "They tried to sell the business for over a year, but no one was interested. Finally, they were approached by a young man who wants to pay his way through school. He offered to lease it from them, and they agreed."

"What an enterprising fellow. Good for him."

"He has to be enterprising," Edwin said soberly. "There's no father in the family and the mother has rheumatoid arthritis. She can barely get around, and she can't work. And there are two younger siblings, I believe."

"What's the family name?" Sadie asked. She didn't claim to know everyone in Silver Peak, but she might know the family. Perhaps there would be a way she could help them.

"I believe it's Avery," Edwin said. "The mother's name is May Belle, but I don't know the children's names."

"May Belle Avery," Sadie repeated. "I don't know her. I'll have to ask Roz if she's heard about them. Maybe there's some scholarship help available for the son if he's serious about school."

She rooted in her handbag and pulled out a pen and notepad. "I'll ask Pastor Sweeting to call on them too. If they don't have a church home, perhaps we could invite them to visit with us."

"Good idea." Edwin smiled at her. "I wish I was as quick to think of ways to help others as you are. It's what makes you special." His blue eyes glowed with warmth, and he reached out and squeezed her hand.

6

———

Sadie picked up Sara after dinner, and they headed for Dr. Armstead's veterinary clinic. Sara had a backpack of things with her; she had decided to stay overnight to help with the care of the bobcat and come back to town tomorrow morning when her grandmother came in to the shop.

"Hello, ladies," Ben said, entering the patient room to which they'd been escorted. "Congratulations. You saved a little life today. I'd like to get my hands on whoever set that trap."

"How's the baby doing?" Sara asked. "I could hardly concentrate on my schoolwork today because I was so worried about him."

Ben smiled. "He got really lucky. Nothing's broken. The skin's torn up where the trap held him, but the fact that there are no breaks means he's going to heal a lot faster." His smile faded. "Unfortunately, the nearest wildlife center is closed until Monday, so you'll have to take him home and take care of him and try to contact them later. We're going to have to be creative about feeding since he's still a nursing baby and he doesn't have mom to feed him."

Sadie's eyes widened. "Are you telling me we're going to have to try to bottle-feed him?" She recalled the snarls and growls that had issued from beneath the blanket in which they had wrapped him.

Ben laughed. "No. He ate a little from a dish for me today. What you're going to need to do is contain him in a large dog kennel and feed him kitten formula mixed equally with ground turkey. He's probably at the age where he's starting to get interested in what his mama eats, so a little meat will be a good thing. Rig up a divider panel to keep him in the back half while you open the door and slide the bowl in. And you'll have to give him a litter pan too."

Sadie was dismayed. "A bobcat in my house? Hank isn't going to go for that."

Ben chuckled. "He's used to living outside. Put him on the porch. With some blankets covering half the kennel and some hay for him to snuggle into, he should be fine for a week or so until he can go elsewhere."

"A *week or so*?" Sadie was aghast. She couldn't imagine keeping such a wild creature for so long.

Sara didn't seem to share her qualms. "That shouldn't be hard," she said matter-of-factly.

Sadie looked at her granddaughter, eyebrows raised. "You and I both know your mother isn't going to let you keep a bobcat at your house. I'm the one who's going to be stuck with it."

"I'll clean the cage," Sara said. "All you have to do is feed it and provide a place for it to stay."

Sadie rolled her eyes, trying to hide her grin. "Oh, is that all?"

Sara returned her grin, unrepentant. "Yes. You're the one who taught me to love wildlife and treasure it. So you can't complain now that I'm following your example."

"So what happens after this 'week or so' ends?" Sadie asked Ben. "Can we release it?"

The vet shook his head. "You should probably call the wildlife center and see if they can take him. I don't think he'll survive on his own with winter coming so soon." He handed her a circular disk about six inches in diameter and maybe three-fourths of an inch thick. It had a cover of fleecy fabric with paw prints on it and a Velcro flap to hold it in place.

The thing was heavier than she'd expected. Sadie almost dropped it. "What's this?"

"It's a heat disk," Ben said. "Stick it in your microwave for five or six minutes. It will hold heat for up to eight hours. Once it's cool, heat it again. You can wrap it in a towel and place it under the hay to help keep the little guy warm."

"Cool," Sara said. "What a good idea."

"Just return it when you're done with it," Ben requested.

"All right." Sadie looked at Sara. "I guess we're as ready as we're ever going to be. Wait." She looked at the vet again. "What about medication? Are we going to have to try to get meds into him?"

The vet shook his head. "I gave him a shot of antibiotics that will last for two weeks. We thoroughly cleaned the wound, so just keep an eye on it to make sure it doesn't start looking infected. And call me if he's licking it too much. We don't want him to make it worse."

Ten minutes later, Sadie and Sara were on their way to Sadie's house with the heat disk and a canister of powdered formula to mix up. The kitten was in a plastic carrying kennel in the back of the car, covered by a towel to help keep him calm. They stopped at the Market for some ground turkey, and when Lou Price found out why they needed it, he wouldn't let them pay for it.

His scowl was ferocious as he wrapped the meat. "Those trappers got no business on Milo's property. Glad you were able to help the little feller out. Here you go. My pleasure. Come back if you need more meat."

Next they made a quick stop at Milo's barn for some hay. Sadie felt a little guilty, stopping with barely a hello for the horses. She hadn't even thought to bring a carrot.

Milo came over to the SUV for a look at the baby, but there wasn't much to see. The distinctive gargling snarl that issued from the carrier when he opened the back door made him grin. "You gals have big hearts, but you're going to have your hands full," he pronounced.

"You're telling me," Sadie said under her breath. "This may rate as one of the more ill-advised things I have ever let Sara talk me into."

"Aw, you'll do fine, Sadie." Milo clapped her on the back and then went to heave the hay bale into the back of the Tahoe. "I called the sheriff to report that trapping activity. Tomorrow I'm going to ride out there and make sure there aren't any more."

"I sincerely hope that if there are, that they're empty," Sadie said. "I can't handle more than one critter like this at a time. Thanks again, Milo." She sent him a wave as she pulled the red SUV back on to the road toward home.

They put the kennel on the front porch, since Hank used the backyard and usually entered through the door into the mudroom off the kitchen. After they got the baby's new habitat set up, they transferred the kitten to his new temporary home with a minimum of fuss and no injuries, which Sadie considered a victory.

"Tomorrow," she said to Sara as they reentered the house, "will you check around to see where we might be able to send him? If someone can just keep him until the spring, surely he'll be big enough then to release."

"Sure thing, Grandma."

Hank, whom Sadie had shut in the mudroom until they were done setting up the kennel, nosed each of them intently, sniffing them all over, apparently fascinated by the strange new scent.

"Hank," Sara said, "you'd better get used to this scent. We're going to be close friends with this bobcat for a little while."

"Speaking of friends," Sadie said, "how's the Laura Ingalls Wilder project going with *your* new friend?"

Sara sat down at the table and began unloading her homework from her backpack. "Okay, I guess. I like Eve a lot, although I think I told you she's really shy. I talked her into helping backstage with the Heritage show to try to get her over it a little."

"That's an excellent idea. Is she enjoying herself?"

"I think so." Sara nodded. "I'm enjoying getting to know her. You know, it's kind of funny that even in a small town like ours, there are still loads of people we don't know."

"Very true. I meet people all the time who have lived here for ages, and I have no idea how our paths didn't cross before. I hope I'll get a chance to meet your new friend and her family."

"I'll introduce you sometime. Eve's so quiet that I believe she just gets overlooked. I mean, she's been in my grade at school for years, but I never really made friends with her before. I've decided

I'm going to try to find other people that I've never noticed and be friendlier."

"That's a lovely idea." Sometimes Sadie was amazed by her grandchildren's wise-beyond-their-years thoughts.

"And Grandma, can you even imagine this? Eve never read the Little House books."

"Unfortunately, I can imagine it. I am often stunned at how many families don't encourage their children to read these days. Do her parents read?"

"I don't know," Sara said. "Her mom's really sick a lot of the time, and I don't think she has a dad."

"Oh? What's wrong with her mother?"

"I don't know," Sara said. "Mrs. Avery moves really slowly, like she hurts, you know? And…"

"Avery?" Sadie recalled her conversation with Edwin over dinner. "Does your friend Eve have an older brother who drives the ice-cream truck?"

"What? Get out! Really?" Sara's eyes lit up. "Eve hardly mentions her brother. Pretty much all she's ever said is that he's going to college this fall and then she is moving into his room. She's really psyched that she won't have to share with her little sister anymore."

"So she does have two siblings," Sadie said, half to herself.

"Yeah. Why?"

"Someone mentioned the family to me recently. I believe Mrs. Avery has rheumatoid arthritis, so that would explain her having trouble getting around. Sara, does Eve go to church anywhere?"

"I don't know. Why?"

"If she doesn't, perhaps we could invite them to come to Campfire Chapel. Mrs. Avery might enjoy having the support of a church family, and the children might like your youth get-togethers."

"That's a great idea, Grandma. I'll mention it to Eve." She cleared her throat. "So you asked me about my project. If you want the truth, I'm a little sad."

"In what way?" Sadie took a seat, noting the glum tone of Sara's voice.

"Remember how I loved all the Little House books? You even got me the cookbook for Christmas one year, and we made some of the recipes just like Laura's."

"I remember." Sadie's eyes twinkled. Sara had been crazy about all things Little House there for a while.

"I've been reading and studying several biographies of Laura Ingalls Wilder, as well as an autobiography that Laura wrote that was only published recently. It turns out the Little House books aren't a true story of her life at all."

"In what way?"

"For one thing," Sara said, her brows drawing together, "Laura's pa sounds like the best daddy in the world in her books, but in real life, he was kind of a—a *criminal*, I think. Turns out one of the reasons the family moved was to skip out on the people they owed money to! That's a crime, right? And Laura had a little brother who died too, which doesn't happen in the books. That's so sad I can hardly imagine it." She sat back in her chair and shook her head. "I'm kind of sorry I chose this author for the project. I think I was happier when I imagined Laura having a more wonderful life."

"But her life wasn't perfect," Sadie reminded Sara. "Her sister Mary loses her sight in the books, right? Did that really happen?"

"Yes," Sara admitted. "So maybe 'wonderful' isn't the right word. But I definitely like the rosy, optimistic worldview in the Little House books better than Laura's real life."

Sadie had to stifle a chuckle. "Who wouldn't?"

While Sara worked on her homework, Sadie went to the tall bookcases on either side of the huge stone fireplace in her living room. Much of her reference collection centered around the history of the state and the local area, but she did have an eclectic collection of other books, and she was pretty sure she had one on Victorian-era antiques and memorabilia. Ah, there it was. She tugged the heavy volume from the shelf, mentally thanking her housekeeper, Claribel, for doing such a good job keeping the shelves clean, then carried it back to the table. Seating herself across from Sara, she started her own homework.

To her delight, there was a sizable section on the evolution of the Victorian *memento mori*. At the end of the nineteenth century, infant mortality was still very high, often over 30 percent. Disease routinely took the lives of young children, and epidemics could wipe out entire families. Sadie knew from rambles through old cemeteries that a stunningly high proportion of infants died. She had often wondered how families could bear such losses.

The custom of the *memento mori,* photographing of the dead, arose as photography became more widespread and people wanted to have something tangible by which to remember their loved ones. Photographers were called on to photograph the dying and the newly deceased, and some even made a specialty out of the gruesome practice.

Sadie wondered if there had been local photographers who took such pictures—if indeed the picture was even local. She jotted herself a note to call Rhea Ressler tomorrow and ask. Today had just gotten away from her.

She thought of the brown folio in which the photograph was inserted. She hadn't examined it closely. Perhaps it bore the name of the studio at which the picture had been made.

She examined a link to a collection of *memento mori* images in the chapter. They were just completely heartbreaking. There were several of mothers holding deceased infants similar to the one she had found, and a few of both parents and other siblings gathered around. One particularly sad image was of two little girls, an infant and a toddler, laid out together. In another, a family gathered at a deceased mother's bedside.

In some of the photos, the photographer had so very cleverly disguised the deceased that it was difficult to tell that they no longer lived. But in most of them, there were telltale details, little giveaways.

Sadie read on, fascinated despite the nature of the research. Some photographers even had frames that they used to prop the deceased upright in sitting or standing positions, placing the frame inside the clothing to hide it.

Fortunately, the advent of more modern medical techniques and medicines dramatically reduced infant mortality by the twenty-first century—

Outside, a piercing shriek rent the peace of the kitchen, startling both Sadie and Sara. Hank began to bark frantically, pacing from one side of the kitchen to the other, then rushing to the door and looking at Sadie expectantly.

"What was that? Is there someone outside?" Sara's hands flew to her heart.

Sadie chuckled, although she had startled, and her own heart rate had doubled as well. "That, my dear, is a bobcat. A grown-up one. Our little friend on the porch will sound just like that when he grows up. I don't hear them often. Hank," she said, "come lie down. I am not letting you go out there right now."

Sara pushed back her chair. "Maybe we should check on the baby. He might be in danger."

Sadie shook her head. "He's safe in that kennel. A bobcat couldn't tear that apart."

"Maybe I should just check through the window…"

Again, Sadie shook her head. "The blinds are closed in the front room. If you try to open them, you're going to disturb our little guest. He's a wild creature, and I don't think we should stress him any more than he already has been. He's had a pretty traumatic day."

As Sara headed up the stairs, she said, "You're right. I'm just anxious. I hope he does all right by himself overnight."

At one in the morning, Hank barked sharply, awakening her. Sadie listened for a moment, in case there was something wrong outside, but she heard nothing. And as she observed the dog, she saw that he didn't look really upset or agitated as he would if there was someone creeping around outside.

The third time Hank alerted again, Sadie simply mumbled, "Please stop, for heaven's sake," and pulled a pillow over her head.

How ridiculous to get worked up over a kitten that couldn't even weigh five pounds.

7

After dropping off Sara at her house on Saturday morning, Sadie headed for the Antique Mine. Since it was a weekend, and one during a special tourist weekend at that, she parked behind the shop and entered through the storeroom. The sight of the old armoire instantly reminded her that she wanted to call Rhea Ressler today and ask her about the furniture and the cherished items she had found within it.

But first, she had her daily chores to get through. Moving as quickly as possible, she unlocked her desk drawer and prepared the cash drawer for the day. Next, she placed a few pieces of outgoing mail in the basket on the counter where the postman knew he could pick up and drop off even if she was busy. She checked the shop's e-mail in case there was anything important there from a potential buyer.

Next she turned to the physical upkeep of the shop. It wasn't cold enough yet to heat up the stove in the mornings. She chuckled to herself, thinking that if she did that, she'd roast everyone out of the shop and probably out of Arbuckle's too. Grabbing a clean rag and her window spray, she cleaned fingerprints from the inside of the glass door and then unlocked the door and walked outside to clean the plate-glass window as well as the door. On her way back in, she flipped the Closed sign over to Open and left the door unlocked since it was nearing ten o'clock.

Back inside, she walked through the shop, eradicating fingerprints on any items of furniture that boasted glass. As she did, she noticed a silver tea service also bore the mark of inquisitive fingers, so she got out the silver polish and touched that up. Next, she grabbed a broom and thoroughly swept up the dust and debris that had entered on the soles of dozens of pairs of shoes on a busy day. Then she gave the floor a light mopping. Nothing like a little moisture to combat the dust, she thought, turning to the trash cans. She'd just emptied them yesterday, and none of them were full again yet. Finally she cleaned and stocked the tiny bathroom and took several boxes to be recycled out to her SUV.

By the time she was done, it was almost ten and the first shoppers of the day could already be seen on the streets outside. Alice entered a few minutes later. Sadie enjoyed having Alice's help in the shop most weekends; it gave them a chance to catch up if their lives had been too busy to get together for a meal during the week.

"Good morning, Mom." Alice smiled. "Thanks for taking on my daughter's latest project. She knew better than to even ask me to let her keep a bobcat in that makeshift area she's got in the backyard. Can you imagine the neighbors' reaction?"

Sadie chuckled. "It's still a baby. I doubt they'd ever know. But I think it's better to keep it out near the mountain where it was found anyway."

"Are you and Edwin ready for tonight? The kids are excited about their parts."

"I can't wait to see them," Sadie said. "I think Edwin and I are prepared. I kind of flubbed the dress rehearsal the other night, but I...Oh, wait. I didn't tell you what happened yet." She went on to outline the puzzling loss of her deposit bag on Thursday evening.

Alice looked stunned. "How could that happen? Are you sure there wasn't someone else in the shop besides you and Luz?"

Sadie shook her head. "I wish I knew. Mac Slattery is looking into it, but frankly, I doubt he's going to have much luck." She felt sick just thinking about it.

"I'm so sorry," Alice said. "Maybe the sheriff will work a miracle."

Then she held up a small net bag stuffed with tissue paper. It was tied with ribbon and had a tag affixed to the top. "I found this on the door of the shop when I came in."

Sadie took the bag and read the tag out loud. "Anna Harrington."

"*Hmm.*" Someone must be in touch with local gossip; they knew she had been to visit Anna and the babies yesterday. Presumably, they wanted her to take this gift to her. Sadie thought through her schedule for the day. She had not planned on visiting the hospital today, since Jeanne probably had someone else from church lined up for a visit...but there was no law saying that Sadie couldn't stop by again if she so desired. She would make it fit into her afternoon. She looked at the small tag again. There was no indication of whom it might be from, but there was obviously something inside the tissue, so she hoped there would be a card inside as well.

The first customers of the day entered the shop, and Alice moved forward to greet them.

"I have a phone call to make," Sadie told her. "And then I'll be available if it gets really busy. We've had a ton of traffic the past few days." Leaving Alice to oversee the people coming through the door, Sadie went over to the counter. She placed the little gift bag in her capacious handbag and pulled out Rhea Ressler's restoration contract.

Calling the number on the sheet, she waited for Rhea to answer.

"Hello?"

"Hello, Rhea. This is Sadie Speers down at the Antique Mine."

"Hi, Sadie. Don't tell me you're done with that dresser already." The little woman chuckled.

"Are you kidding?" Sadie laughed. "We've had so many people shopping here lately, thanks to the Pioneer Heritage Festival, that I've barely had time to look at it. Next week, I hope, will be much better. But I did find something unusual when I took a quick look at it, Rhea, and I have a few questions for you."

"Sure thing. What did you find?"

Sadie told her about the false bottom, the christening gown, the *memento mori*, and the accompanying letter. "It was signed with the initials *E.M.* Is there anyone in your family history who had those initials?"

"I'm afraid I won't be of much help," Rhea said immediately. "It's not a family heirloom."

"Oh." Sadie was immensely disappointed. She simply *had* to know who E.M. was and who the mother and child were in the photograph. "How and when did you acquire it?"

"I bought it at a sale when my daughter was an infant. That would have been in the seventies, I guess. It was such a pretty little piece. We used it for years, but now she's grown and doesn't have a place for it in her own home, and nobody else in the family wants it."

The items were roughly a century old, so there was no way Rhea could have put them in the armoire. Sadie grasped at the important part of her client's statement. "Do you happen to remember where the sale was? Was it a private estate sale or a public auction?"

"It was a public auction over in Aspen at the fire hall, where they used to have auctions every Friday."

"Oh, I remember that. I don't suppose you remember who the auction house was?"

"Sure, I do. I used to go over there with my mother for years. She loved auctions. Never saw a woman buy more junk. Anyway, the auctioneer was Buck Lanniter. He used to do all their auctions."

Sadie remembered Buck well. He was known throughout the area for his superb chanting, the quick-yet-clear speech an auctioneer used to sell items. "He retired and sold the business, didn't he?"

"Yeah, 'bout ten years ago," Rhea told her.

"So when you bought the armoire, there wasn't any information about where it had come from?"

"No. Sorry. I just knew it was a fine piece of furniture in excellent condition, and I wanted it." She chuckled.

"So what would you like me to do with the things I found?" Sadie asked her. "I'm sort of interested in trying to track down who E.M. is and who the christening gown originally belonged to."

"Knock yourself out," Rhea said dryly. "I don't want it. If you can find the family it belonged to and somebody wants the old junk, they're welcome to it. Or you can sell it if you'd like."

"Thanks, Rhea." Sadie felt enthusiasm rise again. "I'll let you know if I'm able to track down its history."

As she ended the call, Luz came through the door from the Arbuckle's side of the store. Catching sight of Sadie, she hurried over. "Oh, Sadie, I owe you an apology," she said. "We got busy again yesterday right after you and I talked, and I completely forgot to ask Hector about your robbery until this morning. Have you found the money yet?"

"Sadly, no. Did Hector see anything?"

Luz nodded. "Yes, he did. He says there was a tall man behind you in the shop when he passed the doorway."

"A tall man?" Sadie was surprised and dismayed. "Is he sure? I don't remember seeing a man in the shop when I locked up."

"You want to talk to Hector?"

"Yes, please, just for a moment."

Letting Alice know she was leaving for a moment, Sadie followed Luz over to Arbuckle's, where she found Hector dismantling the back of the washing machine in the small laundry area.

"Hi, Sadie." He brushed his dark hair out of his eyes as he stood. "Sorry to hear about your theft. Luz and I are going to be keeping a close eye on the till until Sheriff Slattery finds out who stole your money."

"Thanks, Hector. I'm not positive it was stolen," Sadie told him, "although it's looking more and more like that. Luz said you saw someone in the shop whom I didn't notice. Can you tell me what you remember about him?"

Hector looked apologetic. "I don't remember much. I was bussing the tables in the front corner, and I came by the door while you two were looking over the menu."

"Right." Now Sadie could remember the moment more clearly. "I glanced up and smiled at you."

He nodded. "You and Luz had your backs to the shop, so I guess that's why you didn't see him."

"Can you describe him?"

"Tall, like me. Six feet and several inches, though I'm not very good at estimating that. I think he had on jeans and a dark shirt, and he wasn't bulky. Looked kind of thin. Dark hair, kind of untidy but fairly short." Hector spread his hands. "Sorry. I didn't get much more than a glance."

"That's okay," Sadie assured him. "It's more than I knew before. Thanks, Hector."

As she returned to the Antique Mine, she tried to reconcile Hector's information with what she already knew, but it was tricky. When had the tall man entered the shop? Had he been in there already when the tourist family entered and she just hadn't noticed him? Or had he entered with that tourist family and perhaps she hadn't seen him? And how had he gotten out? Oh, how she wished she could talk to that family again.

The bell over the door tinkled. Sadie looked up to see Mac Slattery coming into the shop, his broad shoulders silhouetted in the bright sunshine at his back.

"Hi, Mac." She hurried over to him. "Do you have news for me?" She couldn't prevent the note of hope that crept into her voice.

The sheriff shook his head. "I'm afraid I don't have much, Sadie. No one else in town was burgled or had anything stolen. No other business owners along Main Street have reported anything unusual. No one has tried to cash any checks made out to the

Antique Mine at the Silver Peak Bank, and they said they would notify banks in surrounding towns, as well."

Sadie was deeply disappointed, but she tried to hide it. Mac Slattery, she knew, would do everything he could to help. "So there's really no way to track down what might have happened?"

Mac shook his head. "I suspect the thief just burned or tossed the checks and kept the cash. Trying to cash those checks would have been a big risk."

"Hector Vidal saw something I didn't." Sadie told Mac everything Hector had said.

"I'll go talk with Hector."

"So what's our next step after that?" She spread her hands.

"There's not a whole lot else we can do," Mac said. "I'll talk to Hector, and I'll re-canvass the other shops around here and see if anyone remembers seeing anything even remotely suspicious, but unless those checks turn up, all I have to go on are several unidentified people who probably aren't local residents to try to locate." He scratched his head. "Might be easier if fairies had flown off with your deposit bag."

Sadie swallowed. She had been afraid that those checks were gone for good, and it was looking more likely by the day. "Well," she said, dredging up a hopeful tone, "maybe someone saw something and they just need a little time for the memory to surface. I'll ask Luz again..."

"I'll talk to Hector and Luz," the sheriff told her. "If you rehash it too much, you risk planting false memories of things that didn't really happen."

That was essentially the same thing she and Edwin had discussed. "All right," she said. "What can I do?"

"Just be alert and aware so this doesn't happen again," Mac said.

The words stung a bit. Sadie knew he hadn't meant them unkindly, but she knew she was at fault for having left the deposit in plain sight on the counter—locked door or not—and if there really had been someone in the shop at closing, then she surely hadn't been observant enough. How could she have missed something as large as an adult human being when she was closing up? It was almost easier to believe the deposit had indeed been stolen by fairies.

Moments after Mac Slattery left the Antique Mine, Luz popped through the connecting door again. "What did he say?" she asked.

Sadie realized Luz had been able to see Mac walking down the street and had surmised he'd visited. "Not much," she admitted. "He thinks the money was probably stolen by a tourist."

"Did you tell him about the man Hector saw?"

Sadie nodded, still chagrined at her oversight. "I cannot believe there was a man in the shop that I totally missed."

"If you were as busy as we were the whole day, it's no wonder you can't remember one person." Luz was clearly trying to console her.

Sadie sighed. "Mac said he'll be coming by to talk to both of you soon."

Luz's eyes widened. "I wonder if he'll want Hector to work with one of those artists who draws people from descriptions."

Sadie chuckled despite her discouragement. "I don't think the sheriff's department has a criminal sketch artist on staff. That type of thing is usually done by bigger organizations like the FBI, I believe."

Luz looked disappointed. "Oh." Then she brightened. "Maybe we could find a local artist to try it, at least."

"That's a good idea. I can ask around," Sadie said, not wanting to hurt Luz's feelings. She was certain such portraiture took special training to develop. Still, it was sweet of Luz to try to help, and Sadie appreciated the thought. Anything, at this point, was better than nothing.

8

THEY HAD A BREAK AFTER THE FIRST BUSY HOUR OR SO, AND AS luck would have it, Roz stopped in around eleven thirty.

"Hey, you. Ready for tonight?"

"Yes. I'm sure you saw my flubs on Thursday night, but I promise tonight will be fine."

"I hope so. You looked really distracted. Did something go wrong on Thursday?"

Sadie nodded, glad that her friend didn't think her poor performance was simply a lack of being prepared. Quickly, she told Roz the story of the missing money.

Roz looked utterly incredulous. "But…but how could that happen?"

"Mac Slattery thinks it could have been fairies," Sadie said, deadpanning.

Roz stared at her for a moment, then she broke into laughter. "I can't even imagine him saying that, but I'm inclined to agree."

Sadie shrugged. "Well, I suppose it's no stranger than having my deposit bag vanish while Luz and I were standing right here in the same room." She made a face. "I feel like I am just going around in circles thinking about it. Time to change the subject."

She beckoned to both Roz and Alice to accompany her into the back. She felt compelled to take another look at the treasures she'd found in the armoire, and they were good people for brainstorming ideas as to how she might figure out to whom the items originally had belonged.

"Look at what I found on Thursday." Sadie related the story of Rhea Ressler's armoire and the false floor.

"Oh my heavens." Sadie's daughter picked up a magnifying glass and studied the christening gown, focusing on the tiny stitches holding the tatting in place before handing the magnifying glass to Roz. "Someone spent a great deal of time on this. It's gorgeous." Her gaze was troubled as she looked at Sadie. "But you say the baby who wore this died?"

Wordlessly, Sadie handed her the protective sleeve in which she'd placed the folio and folder.

Alice took the magnifying glass again, studying it closely. She shuddered. "Oh, that's awful. I know infant mortality was a given back in that time, but I can't imagine those mothers were any less devastated than you or I would be if it happened to us."

"I know." Sadie's voice was quiet. "I haven't been able to stop thinking about them. I have to find a way to figure out who they were."

"You don't have much to go on," Roz said.

"No," Sadie admitted. "And even less, since the armoire isn't a family heirloom, but something Rhea purchased at an auction."

"Do auction houses keep records?" Roz wondered.

"I have no earthly idea," Alice said.

Sadie shook her head. "Some probably do, so it's reasonable that they might have some information. This particular auctioneer is retired. I'm hoping to speak with him."

"If he sold his business, the new owners may or may not have kept his records, if he even passed them on," Roz pointed out.

"Pessimist," Sadie said fondly.

"What about this photograph?" Alice asked. "There's no name on this folio, but maybe the design was the logo for a certain photographer."

That hadn't occurred to Sadie. She'd been disappointed when she'd realized there was no studio name on the folio. "That's a good angle to check too. Thanks."

The bell over the shop door tinkled, forcing Alice to return to the front of the shop to oversee another spate of customers wandering in.

"So tell me more about the missing money." Roz had on cat glasses today. Not cat's-eye glasses from the fifties, but glasses that literally had tiny cat faces at the corners of the frames. They were immensely charming, but so distracting Sadie couldn't stop sneaking glances at them.

Sadie spread her hands. "There's not much more to tell. I was talking to Luz. The deposit bag was on the counter. When I finished, it was gone." She shook her head. "It sounds crazy, I know."

"I think you must be forgetting or discounting some things," Roz stated briskly. "Tell me again, step by step, what happened."

Sadie went through it in detail, telling Roz about the family that came in late, and how she had locked the door after their entrance, Hector seeing the tall man that neither she nor Luz had noticed, and how she relocked it again when the family left. She mentioned that she had locked the back door when Rhea left too, so there was no way anyone else could have gotten in through there, but that spool of yarn falling was puzzling.

"It must have been the tall guy. All you have to do is find him." Roz made it sound so simple.

"I never even saw him," Sadie said. "And Hector didn't recognize him. How am I supposed to find him?"

"Good point." Roz grimaced. "Are you absolutely certain you locked the front door? Maybe someone came in and grabbed it while you were back putting away that spool of thread. Or maybe you didn't really lock the back door and someone came in and took the money and knocked the thread off the counter on their way out."

"I don't know." Sadie spread her hands. "I'm almost certain both doors were locked. I'm sure Mac thinks one of them wasn't, and I've just forgotten. Maybe I *did* forget."

"Or maybe there's another explanation we haven't thought of yet." Roz patted Sadie on the back. "But you have to admit, at our age, it could be a memory glitch. I forget things all the time. I think we just have too much information in our brains by the time we reach this stage of life. It gets filed in a drawer in a locked room in here"—she tapped her temple—"and then we can't retrieve it when we need it."

Sadie had to laugh. "That makes an odd kind of sense to me."

"Seriously though," Roz said, "I think you have to try to track down that tall fellow Hector saw. Does anyone on Main Street have a surveillance camera that shows the section of sidewalk out front?"

"I have no idea, but that's a good suggestion. I'll start asking around."

Sadie went up front when Roz left. Seeing that Alice had everything under control, she opened her laptop. She went to the *Chatterbox*'s Web site and read the online blog that reported on social events in the community. The Web site was not always known for its accurate reporting, and sometimes the things written were more gossip than fact.

But this week's *Chatterbox* was unexceptional. The only thing that really caught her eye was a report on the status of the ice-cream truck. As she already knew, the Broermans, who owned it, had moved away and been unable to sell the business. Tobias Avery had leased it, and the whole community wished him luck, as he planned to use the revenues to pay his way through college. The column ended with an exhortation to "get out there and buy lots of ice cream, folks!"

Next, she grabbed the phone book beneath the counter and looked up photography studios in Silver Peak. One Harver Brothers had been "established in 1932," according to their ad in the yellow pages. Punching in the numbers, she waited until a message machine clicked on. Giving her name and number, she said, "I'm trying to track down Victorian-era photographers in and around the Silver Peak area, and I was hoping that perhaps you knew of some."

There was a chance that the armoire and items had come from somewhere far away from their local area, but since Rhea had bought the armoire locally, Sadie was hoping that the owner of the gown had once been a local resident as well.

Exactly how old, she wondered, was that gown? Was there any way to date it from the tatting, or possibly the design of the tatting? Probably not without spending a fortune on testing, she thought ruefully. As curious as she was, she didn't have that kind of money.

Still, maybe she could get some general idea. She didn't know much about tatting and had never tried it, either with a shuttle or with a needle. But she knew someone who might know. Next time she went out, she'd make a stop at What's Needling You, the specialty shop that carried many lovely yarns and taught knitting and other classes.

Shopping traffic slacked off after an initial spurt, so Sadie asked Alice to "hold down the fort."

Stepping out of her shop on to Main Street, Sadie squinted in the bright sunlight, savoring the pleasant warmth of the September morning. All too soon, she'd be inhaling frigid air and wishing she'd worn a warmer coat.

She looked at the shops and offices around her. Arbuckle's didn't have a surveillance camera, she knew. But she really hadn't considered that some of the others might. To that end, she doggedly trudged up and down the street to every business that could possibly have a view of the front of her store.

Putnam & Sons and the *Sentinel* were on her side of the street; Los Pollitos, the opera house, the Historical Society, and the bank opposite her shop.

She thought she'd struck gold when she visited the bank, because she was able to see exterior surveillance cameras before she even entered. She pulled open the heavy glass doors and entered the hush of the marble lobby, passing the teller stations to go to the business offices. A secretary took her name and showed her into the office of bank president James Morgan.

"Hello, Sadie." Mr. Morgan shook her hand and ushered her to one of the plush wing chairs positioned before his desk. "How can I help you today?"

"I'm interested in your surveillance cameras," she told him, briefly explaining her missing deposit.

"Oh, I'm sorry to hear that." Mr. Morgan turned a computer monitor on his desk around. "Unfortunately, our cameras don't show the front of your shop." He showed Sadie the split-screen image that gave him a view of four camera angles: the two Sadie had noticed, one at the door leading to the parking lot, and one focused on the lobby. "As you can see, those two out front show only the 'bank side' of Main Street and part of the street itself." He drummed his fingers on the desk. "I might ask the technician to adjust them the next time he comes. It would be helpful to have a view of the entire street, wouldn't it?"

Swallowing her disappointment, Sadie agreed that it would and took her leave. She walked on down the street, realizing she had to accept the fact that there was going to be no video of the tall man Hector had seen in her shop on Thursday.

One block down, she entered the small shop called What's Needling You that had opened several years ago. In addition to specialty yarns and needlework supplies, the shop offered classes in various types of hand needlework.

Gemma Meijor, the owner, was behind the counter finishing a sale as Sadie approached. "Hi, Sadie," she said. "What brings you to my end of Main Street today? You looking for yarn for something special?"

"Not today," Sadie said. "I just have a quick question for you, Gemma. Do you teach tatting or know much about it?"

"I know how to tat with a shuttle or a needle," Gemma said. "Tatting is finally coming back into fashion, so I've been thinking about adding a beginning tatting class. Why?"

Sadie pulled out her phone and opened the picture of the christening gown. "I recently got this item in, and I think the lace is tatted. Can you tell me anything about it?"

Gemma took the phone and studied the picture, enlarging the screen to study the needlework more closely. "This is definitely tatting," she said. "And beautifully done, from the looks of it. I think— Wait." She headed for a shelf of books behind the counter, pulling down a spiral-bound volume and leafing through it. "Here." She pointed to a completed design. "Look."

Sadie studied the picture. "It's the same heart. Or nearly the same."

Gemma compared the two pictures with an experienced eye. "It's absolutely the same one." She patted the book. "This is a reprint of a Butterick book from 1895 called *The Art of Tatting and Netting*. After over a hundred years, it's still one of the finest books on the topic."

"1895? That's old."

"Well, my book isn't, but the techniques for tatting certainly are," Gemma said, chuckling.

"So the lace on this gown must have been tatted after 1895?"

"Not necessarily. I imagine the pattern was around for a while before this author put it down on paper."

Sadie concluded her visit and walked briskly back to the Antique Mine. That had been interesting, but not as helpful as she could have wished. In a perfect world, she'd have been able to pinpoint the date when that tatting had been done.

As she entered the shop, Alice was just hanging up the phone. She waved a piece of paper at Sadie. "You got a call from Harver Brothers, that photographer who does all the senior portraits.

He said, in answer to your question, that the only photography studio he's aware of that's been around longer than his is Silver Photography in Breckenridge, which has changed names but is still owned by the descendant of the guy who started it. Dean Harver said he's around until five today if you have any more questions."

"Thanks. I'm going to run down to his studio for a few minutes."

Sadie went into the back and took a close-up photo of the gold-leaf design embossed on the folio, which appeared to be a thin layer of leather over pressed cardboard. Grabbing her handbag again, she headed several streets over to Harver Brothers Photography.

The building was one of the original Silver Peak businesses, with wide glass-fronted windows shaded by a deep porch. The current photographer had several displays of senior portraits in one window, and another with bridal photographs in the other.

The door had an OPEN sign much like hers on it, so she stepped inside. She stood on a carpet of dusty blues and greens laid over a gleaming wood floor. There was a parlor to her left that looked like a reception office, and a young woman stood at a table to one side of the room, sorting through photos.

"Hi there. How can I help you?" she asked.

"I'd like to speak to Mr. Harver," Sadie said. She explained that he had returned her call for information, and that she had a question.

"He's finishing up a session," the girl said. "He should be down in just a minute."

Sadie wandered along the hallway while she waited, perusing the many framed photos hung there. She recognized a number of people from Silver Peak in the arrangement. There was even a lovely family portrait of her assistant, Julie, with her husband and twin sons.

Footsteps descending the staircase had her turning to face the photographer.

"Hello," he said, extending a hand. "Will Harver. How can I help you?"

Sadie introduced herself, withdrawing her phone from her purse as she did so. "I appreciate the information about Silver Photography," she told him, "and I was hoping you might be able to tell me something about this. I recently found an old photo in a folio, and I'm hoping the photographer who did the work was from around this area."

Will Harver took the phone and examined the folio that contained her *memento mori*. "Oh yes," he said immediately. "This was used by Silver Photography during its first decade or so. After that, I believe they switched to folios with the studio name on the cover." He smiled. "So it appears I steered you in the right direction."

"You certainly did. Can you tell me anything more about Silver Photography?"

"Absolutely." He smiled. "Artur Silbursky used those folios. He operated his studio in and around Breckenridge between 1886 and 1926. After his death, his sons took over the business, but they changed the logo at that time. The family, a great-grandson, I believe, still operates a photography studio in Breckenridge, now called Silver Photography. I suggest you contact him to see if your find is his grandfather's work." He cleared his throat. "You should know, however, that this was a mass-produced folio and may have been used by other studios as well. Just because I am unaware of any other photographers in Silver Peak, Leadville, Breckenridge, or any other nearby communities of that time that used this particular design doesn't mean there weren't others."

"The only way to find out, I guess, is to check with Silver Photography," Sadie said. "Thank you so much for the information."

Smiling, she thanked him for his time and took her leave. She was going to have to pay a visit to Silver Photography and see what they could tell her about a photograph that was over a hundred years old.

9

WHEN SADIE GOT BACK TO THE SHOP AGAIN, SHE DISCOVERED IT was not nearly as busy as it had been earlier in the week. Leaving Alice in charge, she picked up the little gift bag for Anna Harrington to take it over to the hospital.

Going straight up to the maternity wing, as they had called it back in her day, she thought wryly, she signed in and headed for Anna's room.

"Hi, Sadie." Anna's smile lit up her face. "Thanks for coming again."

"You're welcome." Sadie grinned. "Is it boring in here?"

Anna chuckled. "A little, but I've had a few visitors from church, and I keep reminding myself that when I'm home with both boys, I'll wish I had time to rest again."

"I imagine that's true." Sadie grinned. "How are the twins doing today?"

"I got to try to nurse Aaron this morning," Anna said. "I can't say it was a rousing success for either of us, but the nurse seemed pleased. I'm going to try again later this afternoon."

"Wonderful. And how's Alex?"

"He's off the respirator and breathing well on his own with a cannula," Anna reported, smiling. "The doctor seemed pleased today. I may get to try to nurse him tomorrow."

"It won't be long until you're out of here and home with them," Sadie said hopefully.

"Mrs. Sweeting called. She mentioned that she would be setting up a schedule of helpers at home whenever I was ready. I told her the day the boys come home I'll be ready."

"My friend Julie Pearson has volunteered to come and help too," Sadie told her. "She's the one I mentioned who has twins."

Anna clasped her hands together. "That's wonderful. I can't believe how thoughtful and generous Silver Peak people are."

"I think there are people like that everywhere if you reach out for help," Sadie said thoughtfully. She indicated the little bag she'd brought along. "Someone left this on my shop door this morning. The tag has your name on it."

Anna's eyes widened. "Who is it from?"

"I don't know," Sadie said, "but I'm dying of curiosity. Go ahead and open it."

Anna took the little package and carefully untied the ribbon. She examined the tag, turning it over and frowning. "It doesn't say who it's from."

"It's probably inside," Sadie pointed out.

Anna pulled out the object wrapped in wads of tissue and carefully folded the paper back to reveal not one, but two knitted blankets in a soft ivory. One had a green bow sewn on to it; the other sported a blue one. "Oh my goodness," she said. "These look like they are handmade. What a lovely gift! Do you suppose they were knitted just for the boys?" She picked up the bag and looked inside. Then she turned it upside down and shook it. "But there's no card. I don't know who these are from."

Sadie took the bag and checked. No card. She carefully shook out each piece of tissue paper, and a little card fell out.

Anna pounced on it. "Hand-crafted especially for you," she read. She flipped it over, and her face fell. "But there's nothing to tell me who made it. How am I going to know who to thank?"

"I'm sure it was just an oversight."

"I wonder if it was someone from church."

"How about if I ask Pastor Sweeting to mention the gift at church tomorrow? He can say that the giver neglected to include a name and ask the person to let you know."

"Oh, that would be helpful." Anna indicated a pile of notecards on the rolling tray beside her bed. "I've already started on thank-you notes because I know I'll have a lot less time at home than I do now. And I really must thank whoever made those. They're beautiful."

Sadie noticed a scrapbook lying on the tray beside the stack of notecards. "Do not tell me," she said, "that you have already started scrapbooks for the boys. That would put you in the 'compulsively organized' category, and I can pretty much assure you that if anyone at church learns about it, you'll wind up in charge of at least three committees."

Anna laughed. "Unfortunately for me, I'm not nearly that organized. No, that's a scrapbook I made during my pregnancy." The humor faded from her face, and sorrow replaced it. "Now I'm especially glad I did it."

"I'm sure." Sadie reached over and hugged her young friend. "May I see it?"

Anna's expression lightened once more. "Of course." She reached over and tugged the book into her lap.

The first page had a photo of Anna's husband, Guy, grinning widely as he pointed to the two blue lines on a pregnancy test stick. Anna tapped the page fondly. "He was so excited when we found out we were pregnant. And then, when we learned it was twins, he was just so thrilled." She turned another page that held an ultrasound picture of two tiny little blobs that Sadie knew were first-term fetuses. A second photo of their shocked faces taken by the ultrasound tech made Sadie chuckle out loud.

The scrapbook was delightful. Anna had written down their wonderful memories of all the early days of planning. It all came to a screeching halt at week sixteen when Guy had died so unexpectedly, but Sadie was impressed to see that in her grief, Anna had chosen to include those memories.

Wiping her eyes, Sadie said, "Your boys are going to appreciate this so much when they are older. Seeing how much their daddy loved them and how you have honored his life is a beautiful thing."

Anna wiped tears, as well, but she smiled. "For their sakes, I don't want to dwell on sad things. In an odd way, this scrapbook showed me how important it is to keep putting one foot in front of the other and move forward when your world crashes and burns like mine did. I chose to stay busy and to talk about Guy with other people who knew and loved him, and it really helped me."

Sadie was up to week twenty-four when she saw a photo of Anna and her mother, sitting side by side on a couch, looking unsmiling into the camera. Beside it was another obituary notice. Reading it, Sadie realized it was for Anna's grandmother. "Oh my," she said. "Your grandmother passed away only two months after Guy?"

Anna nodded. "Also unexpected. Heart disease. She had a heart attack and was gone before they got her to the hospital." She rolled her eyes. "She never was one for going to the doctor, and we're pretty sure she covered up some symptoms that might have helped diagnose and prevent it."

"I'm so sorry," Sadie exclaimed. "What a double whammy."

"Triple, sort of," Anna said, her lip trembling. "My mother and I had a falling-out shortly after the funeral, and we haven't spoken since."

Sadie was aghast. Of all the times when a young woman needed her mother to be close, the birth of her children was one of the most important. "Does she know you had the babies?"

Anna shrugged. "I don't know. My labor coach called her, but she had to leave a message because no one picked up."

"I'm sorry." From her manner, Anna clearly assumed her mother had chosen not to respond to the message. But what if she hadn't gotten it? "Would you like me to contact her again to make sure she got the message?"

Anna shook her head. "I don't think so. She knew when the twins were due and that they'd probably come early. I imagine she probably just doesn't want to talk to me. But thank you for the offer." She squared her shoulders and pinned on a smile. "And thanks for asking Pastor Sweeting about those lovely little blankets. I really want to thank whoever it was who sent such a thoughtful gift." She swung her legs to the floor. "Ready for some baby snuggles?"

On her way back to the Antique Mine, Sadie was still basking in baby snuggles. There was probably nothing in the world that compared to cuddling an infant. How sad that Anna's mother was missing such precious moments.

Remembering her promise of asking Pastor Sweeting to find out who had given her the knitted blankets, Sadie decided to swing by the Sweetings' bungalow and tell Don Sweeting about the problem with the gift Anna had received. It was likely, she thought, that the gift giver had been a church member who had heard she'd visited Anna, since the gift had been left with her.

She could also mention the Avery family. She'd intended to do that tomorrow, but there were often so many people waiting to speak to the pastor after church that she thought it might be easier to touch base now.

Parking in the short driveway, Sadie hopped out of her red Tahoe and walked up the flagstone pathway to the Sweetings' door. Jeanne Sweeting had a great eye for color, and Sadie noted that it extended to the exterior. Blooming chrysanthemums were replacing the remains of the summer flowers that had lined the walk earlier in the season.

Unfortunately, there was no answer when she rang the doorbell. She waited a moment and tried again, but still no one came to the door.

As she returned to her car, it occurred to her that she could be more proactive and save the pastor a visit. She would just ask Sara where the Averys lived and invite them to Campfire Chapel herself.

That might actually be less intimidating than having a strange clergyman call, especially since she was Sara's grandmother and one of the daughters was Sara's friend.

The Antique Mine still wasn't as madly busy when Sadie returned as it had been earlier in the week, so Sadie took the opportunity to try to learn more about the armoire. She looked for "Lanniter Auctions" in the business section of the phone book because she knew that had been the business name of Buck Lanniter, the auctioneer Rhea had mentioned. It had closed nearly twenty years ago and, as she'd feared, there was no new listing for such a company.

The only Lanniter in the white pages was James A. Lanniter. The address, she saw, was on a street that she recognized as part of a local independent living retirement community. She pulled her phone from her pocket and dialed the number listed. After the third ring, a male voice said, "Buck Lanniter."

"Hi, Mr. Lanniter. My name is Sadie Speers." Her hunch had been right. "Do you have a moment to talk?"

"Depends on what you want to talk about," he said. "I don't buy anything over the phone. I don't give money over the phone. And I don't make promises to give money over the phone."

Sadie laughed. "Good policies. Actually, I own the Antique Mine in town, and I have a question about an auction item you once sold."

Now it was his turn to laugh. "You know how many things I sold in my lifetime? This should be interesting."

"It is," she assured him. "A client brought in an armoire for me to repair recently, and I found a false bottom in it with some personal items that I thought the family might like to have. But when I talked to her about it, she said she'd purchased it at a Lanniter auction years ago. I'm sure you won't remember the item in question, but if you kept records, I thought there might be a way to track down the original owners. Or at least the people who owned it before she did."

Lanniter was silent for a moment. "That's a pretty tall order," he finally said. "I did keep logs of all the items I sold. Seller, price paid for it, buyer, price sold, my commission, all that sort of thing. Haven't looked at any of it in years, so no telling what shape it's in."

"Could I look through them?"

"I guess so. Everything's in a storage locker now. My nephew deals with all of that. Let me call him about getting the keys, and I'll call you back."

Sadie gave him her name again and her number. "Thank you, Mr. Lanniter. I really appreciate this. I'll look forward to hearing from you."

The rest of her workday passed quickly. At the close of the day, she rushed home to walk and feed Hank and care for the little bobcat.

The bowl in the bobcat's kennel was empty and the litter was disturbed and scattered, so she knew the young one hadn't spent the entire day in hiding. She inserted the partition, set down the fresh food, and cleaned the cage. While she worked, she checked out the injury to his foot, of which she had a good view. It didn't look unusually red or irritated, she noted with relief. Ideally, between the rest and the antibiotics, it would heal without the need for further veterinary intervention.

As she picked up her supplies and turned to head toward the door, she thought she caught a flash of movement on the hillside above her sweeping driveway. Sadie stopped. She scanned the hillside, but it was covered with brushy growth that led right up to the trees perched at the beginning of the mountain, and there was nothing moving.

She shrugged. A bird, maybe?

10

———

AN HOUR BEFORE SHOW TIME ON SATURDAY EVENING, SHE PARKED behind the opera house and hurried inside. Edwin was already there, just getting his costume off the rack.

"Hello," Sadie said. "How was your day?" She had spent some time over a cold supper reviewing her lines just to be sure everything would go well tonight.

"Fine. Hard to believe I'm already starting to discuss Christmas traditions and celebrations with the town council, but I guess the holidays aren't that far away."

Sadie smiled. "It'll go fast, and you'll be making last-minute decisions on December first," she predicted. Finding her own costume by the masking-tape label with her name on it, she headed for the women's dressing room.

The room was a commotion of women in every stage of dress and undress: ladies putting curlers in their hair; dancing girls with large, plumed headdresses attaching false eyelashes; square-dancers in colorful ensembles swishing to and fro; pioneers in far more sober dresses lacing up uncomfortable ankle boots; and more.

Sadie quickly slipped into her costume, realizing as she did so that with its pouf-shouldered blouse, tight lower sleeves, and long skirt it was eerily similar to the dress of the unknown mother in the *memento mori*. She fitted a wig over her own short hair and went to the lady who was helping those less used to stage makeup. The woman applied suitable foundation, a touch of blush, mascara, and lipstick. Looking at some of the dancing girls who would perform a routine from the opera house's glory days, Sadie was thankful she didn't need to plaster on a lot more makeup.

Slipping out of the dressing room, she received an "okay" from the wardrobe mistress overseeing the women's costumes. Edwin was waiting for her just a short way down the hallway, and Sadie chuckled when she saw that he was wearing a light foundation with a touch of blusher and lip color.

He waved his cell phone at her. "I think we need a picture to commemorate this occasion. I have never worn makeup before in my life." He pulled Sadie in close to his side and extended the camera at arm's length. "Smile."

As they laughed together over the picture displayed on his phone's screen, Sara came by. "Hi, Grandma. How was our little patient this evening?"

Sara was dressed in a traditional German costume, a full-skirted dress with a white apron, a white scarf over the shoulders, and flowers at her breast and in her hair for the dance she would be performing as a part of a suite of dances at the end of the first act. Edwin and Sadie's vignette was the second scene that would occur in Act II.

"Oh, honey, you look lovely," Sadie said. "Your baby is doing just fine. Were you able to find a wildlife place that will take him?"

Sara frowned. "I put in two calls today, but both places said they would have to call me back. I'll try again Monday if I don't hear back before that."

Sara's brother, Theo, dressed in leather buckskin frontiersman gear, joined them as she finished the sentence. "Hi, Grandma." He held up a comb covered with tissue paper. "Are you going to watch my instrumental debut?" He laughed, and they all laughed with him.

Theo, Sadie knew, was playing the comb instrument for some of the early dances, along with several other people playing similarly homemade instruments. "We're going to sit out front for the first act, so we'll clap loudly."

"And we'll be in the audience for the second act, so we'll return the favor," Sara assured her.

The last few rows of the opera house had been cordoned off so that the Act II performers could watch Act I and vice versa. At intermission, the two groups would switch.

"Break a leg," Sadie said to her grandchildren. "I guess we're going to head out front now." She and Edwin followed a group of other Act II performers along a passageway that led from backstage to the back of the theater. Much of the crowd had been seated already, and they slipped quietly into their last-row seats without most of the audience even seeing them, as lively fiddle music was piped into the auditorium.

The lights went down, and the music faded. A spotlight came up center stage on Jerry Remington, dressed in a mid-nineteenth-century black frock coat and pants with a vest, swinging watch chain, and tall stovepipe hat. "Good evening, ladies and gentlemen," the emcee intoned. "Welcome to the Pioneer Heritage Festival's annual production of 'Silver Peak: Past to Present'. This year, we have added a few new scenes to better illustrate the history of our wonderful little town. We hope you will…*ENJOY…THE…SHOW!*" Jerry swept off his hat and bowed as the spotlight went off, and the first scene began.

The Ute Indians were Colorado's only indigenous Native American tribe. As members of the tribe were shown engaged in several different crafts that were common to their heritage, a narrator began to talk about the tribe's history. When he finished, a troupe of local descendants of the Utes performed their bear dance.

Theo and his fellow musicians, including a fiddle and a banjo player, were midway through the first act, playing tunes for a set of contra dances, which resembled square dances except that they were danced in lines with every other couple facing up or down the line. That was followed by a set of "play party games" that the early pioneers had enjoyed. Play party games evolved during the nineteenth century, the narrator explained, as a way around strict religious objections to dancing and the playing of instruments in many churches. Participants did choreographed movements to each phrase in a song to the accompaniment of singing and clapping. They included such tunes as "Buffalo Gal," "Skip to My Lou," and "Old Dan Tucker." Sadie was swept back in time, as she remembered her father singing all of those songs. As promised, she and Edwin clapped loud and long.

Sadie enjoyed each act in the show. Sara's group of Bavarian dancers, one of the final in the first act, was hugely popular, with the girls spinning in an outer circle around their partners, who wore lederhosen, short leather breeches with suspenders, and did a unique dance during which they clapped their hands and slapped their knees. It was followed by an Irish step dance as well as Ukrainian, Italian, and Scandinavian dances to illustrate the varied ethnic backgrounds of nineteenth-century settlers.

As the curtain closed on the first act, Sadie and Edwin scurried from their seats back through the hallway to the backstage area. It was chaos. The performers from the first act were urged to get drinks and move out to the side hallway, where they would wait until most of the audience was back in their seats before taking the rows at the back to observe the second act.

A woman with a clipboard was organizing all the scenes in the second act by the order in which they would go onstage. Sadie and Edwin were the third group, after a vignette about the railroad coming to Silver Peak and a woman who read a poem written by a then-twelve-year-old girl whose parents, British immigrants traveling third-class, perished aboard the *Titanic*. Behind them was another group of dancers to illustrate the decadence of the Roaring Twenties.

All too soon, it was their turn to take their places. The stage lights went down, and the crew positioned their table and chairs downstage center.

Before the lights came up on their tableaux, Sadie swished her long skirt into place and took a deep breath. She held perfectly still until the center spot illuminated her. Then she looked to her left at Edwin, standing behind his chair.

"My dear," he said, beaming as he held up a letter, "we have received a letter from our son."

Sadie, in her role as his wife, put a hand to her heart. "After so long! Oh, how thankful I am. Do read it, please."

Edwin read the letter, which told of the son's experiences during First World War battles in France. It was made all the more poignant by the fact that the lines were taken directly from a letter the sergeant's family in Silver Peak had actually received in August 1918.

The young man recounted his division's role in a number of notable battles of the Great War, including the Second Battle of the Marne in July of 1918. "There is a rumor that several of our engineers devised a plan to put false information in German hands. It appears that this may have given us the opportunity to press our advantage in places they did not expect," Phillip wrote. "The Germans fell back under the relentless advance of our new Renault tanks, and we have been advancing ever since. I cannot help but believe that victory shall be ours."

"Oh, Father," Sadie exclaimed. "I scarcely dare to let myself hope that our boy will return to us soon." She had barely finished the words when a clattering knock sounded offstage, and a messenger dashed onstage to deliver a telegram.

Edwin's face crumpled as he received the telegram, and he fell to his knees. "No reply," he choked out, and the messenger backed slowly from the room.

Sadie rose slowly, going to his side. Kneeling, she took the telegram from him and opened it. Taking a deep, broken breath, she read it out loud. "Regret to inform you Sgt. P. M. Anders killed in action France, September 26, 1918."

The lights went down as Sadie bent over Edwin's crumpled form, and a spotlight came up on the narrator at the side of the stage. Holding her pose, Sadie found it all too easy to summon hot tears for the Silver Peak son who had died in a French forest.

"Sergeant Phillip M. Anders of Silver Peak was killed during the initial offensive in the Battle of the Argonne Forest. The Great

War ended six weeks later, on November eleventh." As he spoke, the strains of "In Flanders Fields," a poem written by Canadian physician John McCrae and later set to music, began softly. As the narration ended, the music swelled. Hurrying off stage left as the next act entered under cover of darkness from stage right, Sadie blotted her tears and felt relief that she had successfully completed the scene without blanking out as she had during dress rehearsal.

Roz, dressed in black and directing two stagehands who were moving furniture out of the way, patted her shoulder and whispered, "Great job. You made me cry."

"Then I did it right," Sadie whispered back. As she started to walk past the line of actors waiting to perform, a strong scent of something sweet assailed her.

Strawberry? She stopped in her tracks, immediately caught in a memory she had forgotten. The night her deposit had disappeared, she had smelled that same scent.

Edwin plowed into her from behind, grabbing her around the waist to keep them both from crashing to the ground. "Whoa. What's wrong?" he asked, peering around in the semi-darkness.

"Do you smell that scent?" Sadie demanded.

Edwin sniffed, his nostrils flaring. "Something sweet?"

"Strawberry. I smelled that smell in my shop right after the deposit went missing." She turned and began sniffing the various groups of actors, who regarded her with various looks of amusement, puzzlement, and even a little annoyance.

"Um, Sadie," Edwin said. "This probably isn't the time for a sniff test."

"But someone here is wearing strawberry perfume," she insisted. "And maybe that someone knows something about my missing money."

Edwin nudged her forward, and she realized she was holding up several people. "Can we discuss it after we change out of our costumes?"

She sighed. The scent was gone. Whoever it had been wasn't in the line of people she'd sniffed. She swallowed a giggle, thinking she owed them all an apology. *Pardon me for sniffing you.*

As she walked into the women's dressing room to get her nose powdered so she wouldn't shine during the curtain call, Sadie replayed the events of Thursday evening again.

If only she had seen the tall man! She racked her brain, trying to figure out if there was any way she could find him. She was so disappointed that the surveillance camera angle hadn't paid off. But if he was her thief, did the strawberry scent even play into the theft? Or was it just coincidental? Maybe the lady tourist or the little girl had been wearing something similar?

So when, exactly, had she smelled the strawberry scent? That was after she'd missed the deposit. She clearly remembered thinking she was looking for a strawberry-scented thief, so it must have been after the bag had gone missing.

But wait. She'd gone into the back again, because she'd heard the noise. She'd assumed the noise was that spool of thread falling to the floor, but in retrospect, she had to wonder if it was someone going out the back door. And she hadn't realized the bag was missing until she came back up front...and *that* was when she noticed the strawberry scent. Now she could picture it in her head.

She and Edwin headed up the hallway toward the back of the theater so that they could watch the rest of the show. Before the show ended, they rushed backstage again to line up for the curtain call. The audience gave them an enthusiastic standing ovation, after which she headed back to the women's dressing room. She changed out of her costume and placed it on the rack, and the wardrobe mistress checked her off her list.

Gathering her jacket and handbag, Sadie left the dressing room, responding to a flurry of good-byes as she went. As before, Edwin had finished faster than she had and was waiting for her.

"I wish you didn't have your own vehicle," he said. "I like escorting you home in the evening, especially when it's dark." The September days were getting shorter as they faced the beginning of winter and the shorter amount of sunlight.

Sadie smiled. "What a sweet thing to say."

He grinned. "It reminds me of when we were in high school, and I spent the whole evening hoping I'd get a chance to steal a smooch at the door."

Sadie stretched up and kissed him on the cheek. "There. Since you aren't driving me home tonight. Oh, look." She pointed. "Speaking of sweet, there's the ice-cream truck." Recalling the young man who was earning money for college, she said, "I hope they do a brisk business."

"It looks like he's swamped," Edwin observed, as people pouring out of the theater lined up to purchase cold treats.

"I wonder if he has another vehicle," Sadie said. "Can you imagine having to drive that all around town even when you weren't working?"

The boy at the window counter of the truck looked up and smiled as they passed. He had beautiful green eyes.

"I think picking up a girl in the ice-cream truck might put a crimp on his dating life," Edwin said.

Sadie chuckled and promptly forgot what she'd been thinking about. "Not if she liked ice cream."

Those green eyes lingered in her mind's eye. Hadn't she seen those eyes somewhere before? Of course. The one child in the tourist family who'd come into her shop two evenings ago had pretty eyes like that.

Oh, what she wouldn't give to talk to those people again. Surely they'd seen the mysterious "tall guy" whom Hector had noticed in the shop.

———

Despite being tired after a busy day and the performance, Sadie didn't sleep well Saturday night. Hank barked several times again, and she had to drag herself out of bed when her alarm went off.

She fed Hank, the bobcat kitten, and herself. Her morning devotional was a story about all things happening for a reason, and she had to chuckle out loud. "Okay, God," she said, "I'm listening. What's the reason my dog is waking me up every night? One tiny bobcat kitten can't possibly be disturbing him that much."

Recalling that she wanted Pastor Sweeting to make an announcement about the mystery gift Anna Harrington had been given, she pulled herself together and donned a pretty soft yellow knit sweater with short sleeves and a black wrap skirt with yellow flowers splashed across it. Sliding her feet into practical ballet flats, she headed downstairs.

Hank was barking *again,* and she shushed him more sharply than she usually did. He subsided, going to his bed in the corner of the kitchen, but in moments he was up and pacing again. She hadn't let him into the front room since the bobcat had come to stay, but it was hard to imagine he was still so disturbed by its presence.

Leaving him in the kitchen, she walked to the front window and quietly peered out, just in case there was something wrong.

And she blinked in surprise. There on her porch was a full-grown bobcat. Its coat was a gray-brown color, and it had distinctive black-tufted ears and a whiskered face, along with the stubby tail from which the species derived its name.

Sadie shook her head, hardly able to believe her eyes. But when she focused again, it was still there. It was clearly the mother to the baby in her kennel, because it was lying on its side, oddly pressed up against the kennel bars, so that the baby could nurse despite the barrier between them. The little bobcat's eyes were closed, and his front paws were outstretched as he kneaded his mother's belly through the bars. Sadie suspected he was purring, if only she could hear him.

She backed slowly away from the window and returned to the kitchen to pick up her cell phone. "I'm sorry, Hank," she said sincerely. "You were just doing your job, weren't you, boy?"

Returning to the front room, she carefully approached the window, staying well back from the curtain that shielded her from view. She had to get a picture of this for Sara, or her granddaughter would never believe it.

Moments later, she saved the picture. Then she headed for the garage and jumped into the Tahoe. As the garage door went up and she backed out, she caught a glimpse of motion on the hillside in her rearview mirror. It was the mother bobcat, hardly visible in the brush. The SUV must have spooked her, but now that she knew what had been disturbing Hank, Sadie suspected that the mother would be back before very long. Recalling the bobcat cry she and Sara had heard on Saturday night, odds were good that she'd been coming there all along, and Sadie simply hadn't seen her until that morning.

She shook her head again. Now what was she supposed to do about that baby?

11

As she drove toward Campfire Chapel, located in a restored white clapboard church high on a hill overlooking the historic town, she felt the peace of Christ replace the hectic rush of the past week. She always looked forward to Sunday; church was her reviver, her balance to her often too-busy weeks.

Entering the building, Sadie saw Pastor Sweeting in conversation with Roz's husband, Roscoe Putnam. Both of them were big men, like her husband, T.R., had been, and she had a momentary pang of grief. How many times had she seen Roscoe and T.R. standing together just like that?

"Hey, Sadie, how are you doing?" Don Sweeting reached out to enfold her in a hug. "I heard you had a tough week with a burglary at your shop."

"Not a burglary, exactly," Sadie said. "At least, it could have been, but I'm really not certain yet." She gave them both a brief account of the missing deposit bag, although she was sure Roscoe had already heard the whole story from Roz. Then, tired of thinking about it, she moved on. "But Don, I have something else to discuss with you."

"And what might that be?" His teeth flashed in a smile. "I always get nervous when you ladies tell me you have 'something to discuss with me.' It either means you want me to do something, or that I've done something you wish I'd done differently."

Sadie laughed. "Am I that bad?"

"No, I'm just teasing you," he said. "How can I help?"

"I visited Anna Harrington at the hospital on Friday," she began.

"Aren't those babies sweet?" Don said. "I was in yesterday myself."

"I was too," Sadie said. "I actually hadn't intended to return yesterday, since Jeanne is orchestrating the visitor list, but someone left a gift for Anna on my shop door yesterday morning. So I ran it over to her in the afternoon. It was two darling little handmade knitted blankets. The problem is, there was no card or note saying who it was from, and Anna got herself about half worked up worrying about who to thank. So I thought maybe you could mention it from the pulpit today. It seems as if it almost has to be a church member, because I don't know who else would have known I had visited her. Someone must have assumed I'd be going back."

"*Hmph.* That is a puzzle," Don said.

"Maybe somebody in the Needlework Guild made them," Roscoe suggested. The Needlework Guild was a group of craft-minded congregants who made a variety of gifts for organizations or individuals in need, everything from prayer shawls to socks and mittens.

"Oh, that's a good possibility," Sadie said. "I can check with them." She turned to Pastor Sweeting. "But will you mention it anyway?"

"I'll be happy to. And I'll have the secretary send out an e-mail tomorrow. Shall I tell them to come talk to you or to let you know who it was?"

Sadie shrugged. "Sure. Or just contact Anna directly. Thanks, Don."

Moving toward the rear doors that led into the sanctuary, Sadie saw Sara, Alice, and Theo preparing to enter. She pulled her phone from her handbag as she neared them. "Wait until you guys see who's been visiting my house."

Alice and the kids exclaimed over Sadie's photo of the two bobcats.

"I just can't believe it," Sara said several times.

"Believe it," Sadie finally said. "It never occurred to me that the mother would find her baby. I'm glad I live so close to the mountain, or she wouldn't have been able to find us."

"We can't take her baby away from her now, Grandma," Sara said, frowning.

"I agree," Sadie said. "Tomorrow you can call Dr. Armstead and see if he thinks it would okay to release the baby to its mother instead of sending it to a wildlife center. I think with that extended antibiotic injection that he will do as well with his mother as he would with us."

"All right," Sara said, her frown turning into a brilliant smile that flashed her braces. "And I'll call the wildlife center back and explain that we don't need their help."

After church, Sadie impulsively decided to stop by the shop for a few minutes. She wanted to examine that christening gown more closely. She should have done it right away, but what with the bobcat, the Harrington twins, and the show last night, she had felt like a hamster on a wheel all week.

Letting herself in through the back, Sadie turned on the lights in the storage room and opened the armoire, where she'd laid the items for safekeeping.

She removed the christening gown and laid it on tissue paper on the worktable. Carefully, she began to examine the gown section by section, looking for any information about its owner or maker, or even where the fabric had come from.

Although there were no tags, the detailed stitching suggested that it had been made with love. An elaborately tatted medallion resembling a heart had been stitched on to the breast, and equally careful stitching secured tatted lace at the neck and sleeves as well as several rows of tatted scallops at the hem. It was, plain and simple, exquisite. There was just no other word for it.

Sadie felt her throat tighten as she thought of how much love had gone into the making of the little garment. The infant's mother must have worked on this before the birth. Had she gotten to dress the child in it for a christening before the funeral photo? Sadie wondered why the infant hadn't been buried in the gown. Perhaps the mother had dreamed of having another child who might wear it.

Then she thought of the letter that went with the find. It had certainly hinted that both mother and child were deceased, but clearly they hadn't died at the same time. The letter had mentioned "two precious souls," though, so before the time of the writing in 1899, the mother also must have passed on.

Placing the gown back in the protective bag and laying it in the wardrobe where sun couldn't hit it and damage it, Sadie went to the front of the shop. There was one other thing she wanted to try to do today while it was quiet.

She settled on her stool and pulled a pen and a pad of paper toward her. Time for a little reconstruction: a list of everyone she could remember being in her shop during the last hour of the day on Thursday. She opened the file drawer where she kept her settlement receipts, and she pulled out the one for Thursday. The actual credit card receipts and the settlement total from the credit card machine were stapled to her computer-generated settlement sheet. The idea was that if every sold item was properly entered in the computer at the time of purchase, the credit card settlement plus the total of the cash and checks brought in during that day should equal the computer's total. The settlement had balanced that day, so she wasn't particularly worried about doing it again. What she was after was anything that had happened after four thirty or so last Thursday.

Thinking back, she recalled that she had been in the back of the shop until four forty-five, when Julie had to leave. After that, she'd handled one final transaction. Okay, so that would be her starting point.

She reviewed the final transaction and consulted the invoice on the computer. The woman had used a Visa card to purchase a collection of old postcards; a light oak trifold room screen with beautifully preserved hand-painted flowers on each of the three panels; a rare 1850s four-set of Minton luncheon, dessert, and bread-and-butter plates; and a vintage French 1930s picnic basket made of woven willow with a food compartment on one side and two bottles for wine and water on the other. Sadie remembered her clearly; it had been a nice sale. It had also been the final one of the day. After that, no one else had come into the shop before Luz knocked on the door between them. And then that last family of five had come and gone. She'd finished talking to Luz—and discovered her missing deposit bag. No, that wasn't right. First, she'd heard that weird noise and gone into the back. She'd picked up the spool of thread that had fallen and gone back out front— and that was when she found the bag missing.

Wasn't it?

So many things had made her doubt her memory in the past few days that she was no longer certain of exactly what had happened. Had she gone into the back first or hadn't she? Had she locked the doors or hadn't she? Had the bag still been there when she'd talked to Luz or hadn't it? She thought she knew the answers, but if a judge had asked her to swear to them, she wouldn't have been able to do so.

She hesitated, and then added one last line: *the tall man.* She felt positively negligent that she hadn't even seen the man in her shop. He must have been there when she'd locked up, and she'd overlooked him. Some business owner she was! True, she'd been preoccupied by the upcoming show that evening, and then Luz had distracted her right away, but still... In the future, she would check every corner of the shop before she closed up.

She tossed down the pen in disgust. That had been productive, she thought with a snort as she put away the paperwork and tidied her counter. For the rest of the day, she intended to forget about the theft. She had other things to do.

Closing up the shop, she left and headed across town rather than choosing the route that took her home. In five minutes, she had pulled the SUV to a stop in front of a small white-sided house with deep burgundy trim and a green roof. On a corner, the house was surrounded by a waist-high wooden picket fence on both corners, with a taller fence surrounding the back of the lot.

Sadie stepped out of the Tahoe and approached the door. There was a small patch of flowers still blooming in a carefully tended flower bed along the front porch. She climbed the single step and rang the doorbell.

Running footsteps could be heard approaching the inner door.

Sadie smiled as the door opened and a young girl, maybe nine years old, regarded her through the screen. "Hi. We don't need anything."

"I'm not selling anything," Sadie assured her. "I'd just like to speak with your mother, if your mom is Mrs. Avery."

"Mom? There's a lady here who wants to talk to you." The girl didn't move, and Sadie got the distinct impression she was guarding the door, not about to let Sadie enter.

"About what?" That was an adult female voice, low and melodious.

"About what?" the child demanded.

"Lucinda Rae, remember your manners," the voice rebuked.

"I'd like to introduce myself," Sadie told her. "I'm Sadie Speers. My granddaughter, Sara Macomb, is working on an English project at school with, I believe, your sister."

"Her…"

"I heard her. Invite her in, please." The voice didn't approach the doorway, although Sadie could hear her quite plainly.

"Would you like to come in, Miz Speers?"

"I would, thank you." Sadie was amused at the little girl's sudden display of courtesy.

As Sadie opened the screen door, Lucinda pulled the inner door wide in invitation. Sadie stepped past her into the house, wiping her feet on a pretty rag rug in subdued peaches and browns.

A woman was rising from an easy chair in what looked to be the living area of an open-plan home. The same colors that were in the rug were repeated throughout the room, making it seem warm and cozy. The kitchen occupied the back right corner, and a dining table and chairs were to its left. Back down the hallway to Sadie's right were several doors leading to the bedrooms and bath, she presumed. The house was tiny but relatively neat and clean, with what Sadie considered a normal amount of "kid debris" strewn around.

"Welcome to our home, Sadie," the woman said. The young girl, Lucinda, offered her a cane, and she took a halting step forward, extending her hand as she leaned heavily on the cane. "I'm May Belle Avery, and this is my daughter Lucy."

"I'm eight," said the child. "I'm in third grade. I have a brother and a sister, but they aren't home."

"It's nice to meet you, Lucy-in-third-grade," Sadie said, eliciting a smile from the little girl. She was struck by both the woman's and the child's large, beautiful eyes, a distinct green like those of the brother Sadie had met last night. She wondered if Sara's friend Eve also had inherited the mother's striking eyes. She was a little disappointed that Tobias wasn't home. She had hoped to ask him if he'd seen the tall man enter or leave her shop on Thursday, but no matter, she could find time for that later.

Focusing on the woman before her, Sadie took May Belle's offered hand, but she barely shook it, noting the reddened and swollen joints of fingers and elbow. "It's nice to meet you. Please don't stand on my account."

"Thank you." May Belle carefully lowered herself into the chair again, and Sadie suspected she fought back a wince of pain.

"If today isn't a good day," Sadie offered, taking a seat on the sofa at an angle to May Belle's chair, "I can return another time."

"It's as good as any other right now," May Belle said. "I have rheumatoid arthritis. I had a doctor's appointment late Thursday, and I was also diagnosed with fibromyalgia. Apparently I've been fighting a flare-up, which is why I've been so lethargic and dealing with so much pain."

"I told the doctor I could help her lots," Lucy said.

Sadie smiled. "I bet you're a terrific helper." But inside, she was horrified. May Belle couldn't be more than forty at most. "There's a lady at my church with rheumatoid arthritis," she told May Belle. "She was diagnosed after her son was born. I've heard that it's harder for women to get into remission than men, and that symptoms are often worse."

May Belle nodded. "That's certainly been true in my case. But enough about that. I live it. We don't need to talk about it." She smiled. "It's good of you to come by. Sara has been here twice. She's a charming young lady."

"Thank you. Her mother will be pleased to hear that." Sadie smiled, liking the woman's spirit even though she was obviously drooping with fatigue.

"I haven't had the privilege of meeting your other daughter yet," Sadie said. "Sara said her name is Eve."

"Yes, and I also have a son, Tobias, who's a college freshman this year."

"I believe I heard that he is leasing the ice-cream truck." Sadie grinned. "I saw him last night. He seemed to be doing a booming business."

"He just started college. He's going to attend our local Colorado State branch campus. He's hoping to transfer to the main campus in two years, and I really hope we can manage to make it work but, well, money is tight. He got some good scholarships, and he'd saved some through high school, but he's facing borrowing much too much unless he offsets it with working while he's in school." She grimaced. "It's hard to balance, but he's determined."

"It's nice to hear of a young person who is so enterprising. My grandson, Theo, will graduate this year, so he's beginning his own college search. I think he may be interested in staying relatively near home, as well." Although she imagined Tobias Avery was living at home and going to school locally to save money and to help his mother.

"Eve's friend Sara's mother teaches at my school," Lucy announced. "I never had her but Tobias did."

Sadie grinned. "Mrs. Macomb is my daughter. When I was your mother's age, she was a little girl. Can you imagine that?"

Lucy's eyebrows rose in an adorably adult expression. "No," she said frankly, and both women chuckled.

"I won't keep you long," Sadie said, "but I wanted to invite you all to visit our church, Campfire Chapel, sometime. I'd be happy to pick you up if driving would be difficult for you."

"Why, thank you," May Belle said. "We don't really have a church home. It always just seemed too difficult for me to get the children up and moving by myself on Sunday morning."

"Perhaps some of us at Campfire Chapel could offer helping hands," Sadie said. "We're good at that. In any case, please consider my offer, and call anytime if any of you are interested." She smiled at Lucy as she laid her card on the table, dug for a pen, and wrote her home and cell phone numbers on the back. "I know several boys and girls your age who would be happy to have a new friend. These are my shop, home, and mobile phone numbers if you're ever in a pinch and need assistance. Oh, and also, would it be all right if I gave your name to the friend I mentioned who also has rheumatoid arthritis? Sometimes it helps to have a kindred soul when you're dealing with a debilitating disease like this, and Estelle is a lovely lady. I think you'd enjoy her."

"That would be very nice," May Belle said. "Lucy, run and get a piece of paper and write my name and phone number on it, please?"

The child hopped up from the floor where she'd perched near her mother and ran to the kitchen corner.

Sadie got to her feet. "It was so nice to meet you, May Belle. I hope you won't hesitate to call if there is any way I can help." She approached the chair and took May Belle's outstretched hand, holding it gently between her own rather than shaking it this time before accepting the note of information from Lucy and taking her leave.

As she stepped out the door, she could hear Lucy saying, "Here, Mama. I'll put this blanket over you, and you can take a little nap now. I can make us some lunch too."

It nearly broke her heart. What a heavy burden for a child to carry—for any young person, really, she thought, remembering the two older teens. She felt even more resolved to do what she could to help the family. Oh, she hoped they would consider taking her up on her invitation to visit Campfire Chapel. She just knew her fellow congregants would be so warm and welcoming that the Averys would never want to leave.

12

After church, Sadie had some lunch, changed her clothes, and glanced at the clock. Right on time. Edwin was picking her up soon. They had promised to meet Alice and the kids at the Pioneer Heritage Festival. Theo was participating in a three-mile pioneer handcart race, and Sara was teaching a children's game called "Fox and Geese." Sadie couldn't wait to see them in action. She was so proud that her grandchildren had taken an active role in the historical celebration, both last night and today.

She had barely gotten her soup bowl and spoon rinsed and placed in the dishwasher when she heard Edwin's car approaching the house. Moments later, he appeared at the back door, as she had requested when they made their plans.

Sadie hurried into the mudroom to admit him, holding Hank's collar to keep him from rubbing against Edwin's tailored slacks and leaving them covered in golden fur.

Edwin had a very strange look on his face. "Sadie, I swear I saw an adult bobcat leap off your porch and run up the mountain," he said, his eyes wide.

"Oh, you did," she assured him, unable to smother a grin at his expression.

"You *knew* there was a bobcat out there?" he asked. "That's why you asked me to come to the back?"

Sadie nodded. "It's the mother of the baby we found. She spends a lot of time here nursing and comforting him. I'm hoping Ben Armstead will give me the go-ahead to release the baby tomorrow."

Edwin shook his head. "You amaze me. How many people would take the time to help a bobcat? Lots of people would want someone else to do it, but few would actually consider doing it themselves." He checked his wristwatch. "Are you ready to go?"

She nodded. Turning to the dog, she said, "Sorry, Hank. You won't be confined to the kitchen much longer." She bent and gave him a kiss on the head as his plumed tail waved wildly. Then she and Edwin slipped out the back door, and he led her into his vehicle.

The Pioneer Heritage Festival was held at the county fairgrounds, also the site of other annual events such as the county fair, an AKC-sanctioned dog show, local 4-H events, and a nationally known quilt display and auction.

They followed parking attendants' directions to a vast field, where they parked and walked toward the fair.

She and Edwin had agreed to meet Alice and the kids in front of the Twinkies trailer in the food area at the entrance to the festival. Farther inside, the principal menu items available were authentic "heritage recipes" from bygone days, but Theo's love of deep-fried Twinkies, a staple of any fair or festival in Silver Peak, was an open secret in the family, and they all knew the first place he would go would be the Twinkies booth.

"Deep-fried Twinkies and red-velvet funnel cake?" Edwin asked as they strolled along. "Are they kidding? I bet that's the best food on the planet. Maybe later on, I should make sure."

Sadie laughed. "I wouldn't want you to have to do that alone. Out of the goodness of my heart, I'll assist with your research." They grinned at each other.

True to form, Theo was just turning away from the Twinkies booth with a couple of the deep-fried treats in his hand when Edwin and Sadie spotted him. Alice and Sara were nearby purchasing cider.

"Hi, Edwin. Here. I wasn't sure if you'd tasted these before, so I bought an extra." He gave one of the Twinkies to Edwin.

"Thanks. I was hoping to get my hands on one," Edwin said.

Theo passed another Twinkie to Sadie and one to his mother and Sara, who had decided to share. There was silence for a moment, soon punctuated by ecstatic groans of delight as they all savored the fattening fair food.

"Now I really have to try the red-velvet funnel cake," Edwin said, "to see if it truly is better than this."

"Not possible." Theo shook his head, but Sara nodded.

"That's my favorite," she argued. "Mom, may I get a piece?"

"Maybe later," her mother said hastily. "If you eat it now, you're going to be too full to move when you have to lead all those children during game time."

The festival, unlike the county fair, was completely dedicated to celebrating the pioneer heritage of the area. Local artisans featured pioneer and Indian crafts and cooking, such as tanning hides, needlework, basket making, fletching arrows, cleaning and shooting antique guns, and pot throwing. Sadie winced and hurried past an exhibit on trapping and cleaning pelts. It may have been a livelihood for a significant number of settlers, but her soft heart could hardly bear to think of the animal populations that were practically wiped out to satisfy the thirst for fur. And it hit all too close to home after her recent experience seeing a trap in action.

Much more to her taste was a lively fiddler playing tunes for simple square-dance patterns for beginners, and a large area where pioneer reenactors showed visitors how life was lived out of a Conestoga wagon.

As they stood watching, a woman clad in nineteenth-century pioneer garments and a bonnet coaxes a kettle over a fire to a boil. In it, she placed rations of "antiscorbutics," or thin-sliced dried vegetables, which would rehydrate somewhat in the soup, along with fresh meat, which she explained would have been whatever they had been able to catch for that meal, rabbits or even buffalo if they were lucky, squirrel if they were not. Sadie saw Sara grimace.

"I wonder how many women caught their clothing on fire," Alice murmured, watching the woman whisk her long skirt away from the dancing flames.

Next, the woman took out a bucket and measured out a portion of sourdough starter. Adding wheat flour, salt, water, and lard, she soon had a batch of muffins baking in a Dutch oven nestled amidst the coals.

"Imagine how much time it took just to prepare a meal and clean it up," Alice said.

"Yeah," Sara agreed. "You'd get up, feed your family, bounce and jounce along in a wagon all day, and probably chew on hardtack and beef jerky for lunch, set up camp and cook dinner that night…and get up and do it all over again. Day after day. I'm glad I wasn't a pioneer."

"Hey, isn't your game thingy at three o'clock?" Theo asked her. He held up his phone so she could see the time. "You'd better go get dressed and be ready."

"You're not my boss." Sara tilted her nose in the air.

"No, but he's right," Alice said. "Unless you want to be late. I guess we can watch the rest of the girls if you don't make it on time."

Sara made a face and flounced off, while Sadie, Edwin, and Alice tried not to laugh in front of Theo.

The rest of them continued exploring different exhibitions at a leisurely pace. After ten more minutes or so, Edwin suggested that they make their way to the grassy outdoor arena where Sara would be performing.

As they walked across the fairgrounds, Sadie saw a group of familiar faces. Her heartbeat sped up. It was the couple who had been in her shop last Thursday with the three children. She was sure of it. Maybe she could get their names and find out where they lived so that Mac could question them about the missing money.

"Hello there," she said, catching the woman's eye. "You stopped into my shop, the Antique Mine, last week."

The woman smiled. "Yes. I meant to come back, but we have been so busy trying to do and see all the things this festival offers. It's really amazing for a small town."

"I'm Sadie Speers," Sadie said, offering her hand. "I take it you're not local?"

"Sue Clapsaddle," the woman said, returning the handshake. "This is my husband, Tim." She indicated the man at her side. "We live in Baltimore. I homeschool, so this is part of our children's education. And what a great experience it's been."

Recalling the older boy's aversion to being seen close to his family, Sadie imagined he was off on his own for a while. She was thrilled to have run into the family again. "May I ask you a few questions?" she said. "My deposit bag went missing after closing on Thursday, and I believe it may have been stolen."

"Oh, I'm so sorry," Sue said. "Sure. Anything we can do to help."

"Did you see anyone else in the shop while you were there?" Sadie asked. "I remember when you all came in right before closing, but was there anyone else around?"

"Oh yes," Sue said immediately. "There was a man already in the shop when we got there."

"Can you describe him?" Sadie tried to hide her excitement. Perhaps this was the break she needed.

Sue pursed her lips. "Tall," she said. She indicated her husband, who had moved a few paces off with the children. "Several inches taller than Tim, so probably around six-feet-three. Dark hair, cut fairly short." She grinned. "And kind of cute. I remember he had striking eyes with really long, thick eyelashes, because I thought it was so unfair that men always get those gorgeous lashes while women tend to have to fake them."

"It is totally unfair." Sadie smiled. "Can you picture what he was wearing, or anything else about him?" Sadie had dug a notebook and pen from her purse and was scribbling notes.

"I think he had on jeans," Sue said, "and a shirt with a collar, but it wasn't tucked in. And he had a satchel crossed over his body like people in the city wear. Only it wasn't a man-purse. It was a big brown leather thing with a buckle." She stopped. "I spoke to him briefly. Let me think…" She snapped her fingers. "Oh, I remember. He was looking at pottery, and I said it was pretty. He said he was a history teacher, and he wished he could show his senior advanced placement students some of the things in the shop to bring his lessons alive for them." She paused. "Does that help?"

"Immensely," Sadie said gratefully. "Thank you so much. Do you remember if there was anything on the counter near the cash register?"

Sue hesitated. Then she shook her head. "I'm more of a people person. Tim?" She cocked her head and looked at her husband.

Tim did not have as much memory of the sixth person in the shop, but when she asked about anything on the counter, he immediately nodded. "Yeah. There was a bank deposit bag on the counter. I remember because I almost said you shouldn't leave it lying around like that, but then I realized it was closing time and you were probably heading for the bank the second we left the shop." His smile faded. "But I can't honestly tell you if it was still there when we walked out."

Sadie nodded. "One more question. Sue, do you or your daughter use a strawberry-scented perfume?"

Sue chuckled. "Strawberry? No. I don't usually bother with scent, and Madyson's still a little too young to be into that, thank goodness."

Sadie knew the scent question had been a long shot, since she hadn't noticed it until later, but she was still glad she'd asked. "Would you be willing to give me your contact information so that I can let the sheriff know I spoke to you?" she asked. "He may be in touch if he has any questions also."

"That would be fine," Sue said. "Anything we can do to help you recover your money. That's just terrible." She took the pad Sadie offered her and wrote down the family's name, address, phone number, and e-mail information. "There you go. Good luck."

Rejoining Edwin, Alice, and Theo a few moments after her encounter with the Clapsaddle family, Sadie waved her notepad in the air. "Guess what? That family was in the shop right before closing time on Thursday. They remember seeing someone else there."

"Wonderful news." Alice nudged her along. "We'd better get going if we don't want to miss Sara's performance, but I definitely want to hear more about it later," she said as they approached the seating area around the grassy meadow where Sara's group would be working with the children.

"And now," the announcer said moments later, "we'd like to invite any children in the audience to join us for an introduction to some games that children might have played during pioneer days." One girl taught "Drop the Handkerchief," which, essentially, was the game of "Duck, Duck, Goose" still played in school, while another girl schooled the children in "Blind Man's Bluff." Another teen taught a game called "Chain Tag," in which two people were chosen to be "it." They clasped hands and chased the other children. Those caught joined the chain until all had been caught.

Sara taught a game called "Dare Base." She divided the children into two teams. Each team chose a home base, represented by a flagstick they drove into the ground. Players took turns daring to try to run around the home base of the other team without getting caught. If they were caught, the other team then got to choose a player from the opposing team to come over to their team. The team with all their players still on the original team at the end won the game.

When the games ended, Sara changed out of her pioneer garb and rejoined them. The five of them stayed in their seats for the next events: tomahawk- and knife-throwing competitions, a muzzle-loading demonstration, and another on how the pioneers started fires.

Afterward, they wandered around some more. Theo left them to change into his pioneer garb for his event. They watched a blacksmith at work forging horseshoes and barrel bands, and then went to cheer on Theo, who was participating in a mile-long handcart race. To Sadie's delight, her grandson won the race. He came strolling toward them afterward with a gift certificate to Sophia's, which he promptly presented to his mother.

What a pleasant afternoon it had been. Alice invited Sadie and Edwin for dinner. "It's spaghetti, nothing special," she said.

"Except that Mom's spaghetti sauce is always special," Theo added loyally.

Sara grinned. "And she made two loaves of Italian bread yesterday that I am absolutely dying to taste."

By mutual accord, they moved toward the exit gate. As they approached, Sadie saw that the ice-cream truck had pulled up in the parking lot, its music merrily tempting buyers.

The same young man Sadie had seen last night was at the window. He glanced up, caught sight of Theo, and sketched a quick salute with a grin. Sadie realized that, of course, Theo knew the Avery boy; they would have been only one grade apart. They may even have played sports together.

"Theo, is that Tobias Avery?" she asked, though she already knew the answer.

Theo nodded. "Yeah. Pretty cool that he's the ice-cream truck man now, isn't it?"

"It is. I visited his mother this week. I invited them to come to Campfire Chapel sometime."

"That's a great idea," Sara said. "I can ask Eve too."

Sadie started across the field toward the truck.

"Hey, Grandma, where are you going?" Theo asked.

"I have one quick question for your friend," Sadie told him, never slowing her pace.

At the truck, she waited politely until Tobias was done with two customers. Then she stepped to the window and held out her hand. "Hi, Tobias," she said. "I'm Theo's grandmother, Sadie Speers."

"Oh, you came by my house to visit Mom earlier," Tobias said. "That was nice of you. Thanks."

"You're welcome. I have an ulterior motive for introducing myself though. My deposit bag was stolen out of my shop on Thursday at closing. I saw your truck going down Main Street and then later at the end of the alley behind the Antique Mine, and I just wondered if you saw anyone suspicious entering or leaving my shop."

"Oh, wow. I'm so sorry." Tobias's forehead wrinkled as he considered her question. But finally, he shook his head. "I don't think so," he said. "Nothing stands out. I sure don't recall seeing anyone acting sneaky."

"Did you see a very tall man, or anyone at all, enter or exit?"

Again, the young man shook his head. "Honestly, I don't remember even glancing specifically at your store. I'm usually pretty focused on my driving because kids tend to dart out in front of me unexpectedly. And when I'm not driving, I'm manning the window. Sorry, Mrs. Speers."

"That's okay. I'm just trying to check every angle I can think of. It was nice to meet you, Tobias."

"You too, ma'am. Thanks again for taking time to visit my mom."

What a pleasant young man. As she rejoined her family, Sadie decided it had been quite a productive afternoon, even if Tobias hadn't recalled anything helpful. Running into the Clapsaddle family had been a real bonus.

13

WHEN SADIE AND EDWIN ARRIVED AT ALICE'S HOUSE FOR DINNER, Sadie's daughter was just putting the pasta in the pot to boil. Theo was setting the table and, as he pointed out, that meant he didn't have to clean up.

Dinner was a relaxed affair. All five of them appeared to need some downtime after their big afternoon, as they sat down to spaghetti, Alice's crusty Italian bread, and tasty spinach salads with sliced hard-boiled eggs and a dollop of warm bacon dressing. Alice asked Edwin to offer the blessing, an honor not lost on Sadie, who often did it. Edwin had charmed her family, who were coming to accept him as one of them.

"So who wants to go to church with me this evening?" Sadie asked as they dug in. Tonight Pastor Sweeting was holding a Harvest Service to celebrate the bounty of late summer and fall that benefited the community as winter approached.

"I can't," Alice said. "I've still got a load of papers to grade before tomorrow. Sorry."

"And I have homework," Theo said.

"I'll go with you, Grandma," Sara said, "if you don't mind bringing me home again."

"Since I'm driving, I'll take you both there and home again," Edwin said, and Sara giggled.

"Thank you."

"That was such a stroke of luck this afternoon," Edwin said to Sadie. "Actually being able to find that family who was in the shop the afternoon your deposit went missing."

Alice's head snapped up. "Did they have something to do with your missing money or know anything about it?"

"I don't think they took it," Sadie said, "but they remember another man being in the shop when they came in."

"A man you didn't remember?" Edwin asked.

"That's huge, Grandma," blurted Sara. "Maybe he stole your money."

"I don't want to accuse anyone unless I'm sure," Sadie told her granddaughter, "but I would love to talk to this man." She looked back at Alice. "The lady spoke to him briefly. She said he was a history teacher, that he was tall and dark-haired and had really long eyelashes."

Theo laughed. "She noticed his eyelashes?"

Sara made measuring motions with her fingers about six inches from her eyes. "They were *this* long." Both kids dissolved in laughter.

Alice, however, had an arrested expression on her face. "That sounds like the new high school history teacher," she said. "I remember him from the in-service days before school started, when they introduce all the new people."

"Do you remember his name?" Sadie was thrilled. She'd feared he was another tourist and that she'd never track him down.

Alice shook her head. "Sorry, I don't. I can find out for you though."

"That would be great," Sadie said.

She, Sara, and Edwin left for church after helping with cleanup since Alice and Theo had done the pre-meal work. Others were pulling into the parking lot as they did. Wyatt and Jenna Henderson smiled and waved, and their two-year-old son, Caleb, came running headlong to be scooped up in Sara's arms.

The service was delightful. A farmer in the congregation had helped Pastor Sweeting set up a corn shock at the front of the church. Around it were arranged pumpkins, gooseneck squash, gourds, and basket of apples. Instead of a sermon or homily, a missionary who had spent the last three years teaching sustainable agricultural practices to communities in Tanzania presented a slideshow and talk about her work. Campfire Chapel had pledged a significant gift to help support her mission, so it was gratifying to see what their support had helped to accomplish.

The congregation also had been asked to bring harvested fruits and vegetables from their own gardens, home-canned items, or canned goods. All of them would be donated to the local food pantry, and volunteers from the church had signed up to prepare and freeze or can any perishable items that the food pantry couldn't use immediately.

Martin Deering led the music for worship services, and tonight he had a select choir singing, "All Good Gifts," a beautifully harmonic song from the musical *Godspell* that fit the harvest theme. His wife, Paula, then played the piano for the cherub choir, a group between the ages of five and eight who sang a charming, bouncy tune thanking God for all the good things He had given them.

Before he closed the uplifting service, Pastor Sweeting mentioned Anna's mystery gift again. Then he announced, "There will be light refreshments served in the fellowship hall right after the service. Tina Watson keeps our scrapbooks, and she has brought along a couple from the past few years for you to enjoy. They'll be displayed fa-a-ar away from the food," he added, earning a chuckle from the congregation. "We ask that you not handle the scrapbooks while you are eating."

Sadie was pleased to hear that. Tina did a lovely job with the church scrapbooks, and Sadie couldn't wait to see what new photos she had added.

Edwin and Sadie joined the rest of the crowd moving into the fellowship hall as the service concluded. There was a line forming at the refreshment table already, so Sadie opted to check out the scrapbooks first.

She leafed through photos from the previous years, enjoying the youth group's camping trip, the annual summer picnic, Bible school games and events, a production of *Our Town*, and more. Having participated in many of the events, she and her family were in many of the photos.

Her attention was caught by a photo in the spread showing a group of ladies from the Needlework Guild with a quilt they had made to auction off to support the Tanzania mission project. She remembered what Roscoe had said about Anna's gift-giver possibly being one of them.

Pulling her notepad from her purse, she quickly jotted down the names of the ladies in the picture. Maybe one of them had been the person who gave Anna those dear little knitted blankets.

"What are you doing, Sadie?" Marge Ruxton was one of the ladies in the photo. She was the wife of the church's financial secretary, an often contrary but dependable woman always willing to lend a hand when projects needed extra volunteers.

"Listing these needlework ladies so I can check to see if one of them gave Anna Harrington those blankets the pastor mentioned."

Marge studied the photo. "Why is that your job? Jeanne Sweeting's in charge of getting folks to help with those babies. Seems like she should be the one doing that."

"A gift with no note was left on my shop door for Anna." Sadie wanted to grit her teeth at Marge's critical tone, but she managed to resist. "Anna asked me to find out who the giver was."

"Huh. I still think you should tell Jeanne and let her do it."

"Are you in the Needlework Guild?" Sadie had seen Marge's picture in the group in the photo album, so she knew she was.

Marge nodded. "I'm a founding member." Her chest swelled with pride. "Actually, the group was my idea."

"Does everyone in the guild knit?"

Marge shook her head. "No. I don't. I only crochet and quilt. We have monthly gatherings where everyone brings whatever project they want to work on."

"Can you tell me who in the group does knit?"

Marge pursed her lips. "You should ask them yourself. There's a meeting tomorrow evening at seven here at the church."

"All right. I'll come by and talk to the other ladies. Thank you."

Edwin, who'd been perusing the photos farther along the table, came to Sadie's side then. "The line's getting smaller. Shall we get something to eat?"

Sadie turned to him, glad to escape Marge. "Yes, please. Where's Sara?"

Edwin pointed. "Enjoying toddler time." Sure enough, Sara was seated at a table already with Caleb Henderson in her lap, feeding him bites from her plate.

Sadie said, "Of course. I should have known."

As they walked over to let her know they needed to go, Sadie felt sure she would be able to tell Anna who her "mystery gift giver" was very soon. All she had to do was visit the Needlework Guild and ask them who had made the blankets.

First thing on Monday morning after she had opened the shop, Sadie called Ben Armstead's veterinary office. Identifying herself to the receptionist, she asked if she could speak with Ben regarding the bobcat kitten. A moment later, the vet came on the line.

"Good morning, Sadie. You got a problem with that baby?"

"Not at all," Sadie assured him. "Just an interesting development, and I need your opinion."

"Sure thing. What's up?"

"The mama bobcat has been hanging out on my porch nursing her baby," Sadie said. "She leaves every time we stir, but so far she's come back every time."

"You're kidding." Ben sounded stunned. "They're pretty shy creatures. That's amazing."

"I know, right? My question for you is: Would it be okay to release the baby today since his mother's around to care for him?"

Ben thought for a minute. "How's the foot look?"

"Excellent. The swelling is gone, and there's no unusual redness."

"The antibiotic injection is good for two weeks," he told her, "and the big reason we couldn't just release him immediately was because he's a helpless juvenile. He'd have died on his own. Since Mom's back in the picture, I say, yes, go for it. You can release him today if you want."

"Excellent." Sadie felt jubilant. Hank would be thrilled to have his territory back, and she couldn't say she'd miss the extra work either.

The morning was far less eventful than last week had been. Most of the tourists who had flocked to town for the Pioneer Heritage Festival had departed, and the Antique Mine experienced what she would call "normal" traffic.

The first thing she did after she got the shop cleaned and organized for the day was to call Silver Photography in Breckenridge. A male voice answered the ringing phone. "Silver Photography, this is Gary. How can I help you?"

"Hello, Gary. My name is Sadie Speers." She went on to tell him about finding the folio that she suspected had come from his great-grandfather's studio. "Would it be all right if I brought it by this afternoon for you to see?"

"I'd love to see it," the photographer confirmed. "I'm free until three. Can you make it around two?"

"I'll be there," Sadie promised.

Julie came in at one to relieve Sadie so she could run some errands.

"Has the sheriff made any progress in finding out where your deposit bag went to?" were the first words out of her mouth after they'd greeted each other.

Sadie sighed. "Not really. And I'm starting to believe he must be right. I didn't misplace it. It was stolen."

"We scoured this shop," Julie said. "I can't imagine it's here."

Sadie told Julie about the "tall man" whom the Clapsaddle family and Hector had said was in the shop when they arrived. "Alice is going to try to get his name," Sadie said, "and I guess maybe my next step will be to talk to him."

"Was he still in the shop when the other people left?" Julie asked. "If he was, he's probably your thief, and maybe you should let the sheriff approach him. If he really did take your money, he could be dangerous."

"But if he didn't, I'd feel horrible naming him as a suspect and getting him in trouble with the sheriff," Sadie pointed out.

Julie crossed her arms. "At least promise me that if you do talk to him, you'll do it in a public place so he can't murder you and hide your body before he goes on the lam."

Sadie laughed. "That's a pretty easy promise to make."

Shortly after that, she slipped into her jacket, grabbed her handbag, and headed out to make a trip to Breckenridge.

The Silver Photography Studio was housed in a handsome period Victorian of slate blue with cream and lavender accent trim just one block off the town's sizable historic district. The sign on the door said, "Open," so Sadie turned the solid brass doorknob and entered a foyer with rooms on either side.

"Hi there. Are you Sadie? I'm Gary Silver." A middle-aged man with thinning brown hair and twinkling hazel eyes rose from a desk in one of the rooms and strode toward her, hand extended.

"Not Silbursky?" Sadie asked. "That was your family name, wasn't it?"

"Yes. My great-great-grandfather, father of the first photographer in the family, was a Russian immigrant. He and his son kept the original name, but in the early twentieth century, my grandfather changed it to Silver. I think it was a combination of being sick of the Russian-sounding name and how hard it was for people to spell that did it. And he chose Silver because of our proximity to the silver mining communities here in Colorado."

"How interesting," Sadie said. "Have you ever considered going back to the original name?"

Gary laughed. "Nope. I'm quite content with Silver. No one ever asks me how to spell it, that's for sure." He indicated a set of chairs near a lovely old fireplace. "Have a seat, Sadie. Would you like something to drink?"

"No, thank you. I'm fine. I don't want to take much of your time. I just have a few questions for you."

"I'm dying of curiosity. Did you bring the folio along?"

Sadie nodded. "I did." She set down her handbag and pulled out an envelope in which she'd put the folio, still in its acid-free protective plastic. She related how she found the folio, and her near-certainty that it contained a *memento mori*. "If it is your studio's work, then your great-grandfather may have been the photographer. I'm trying to find out who the subjects in the image are."

"It's entirely possible that he took it," Gary said. "He was rather famous around the area for his 'death portraits,' as they're sometimes called, and I know he often went to people's homes to do them."

Sadie opened the exterior envelope and withdrew the folio, handing it to Gary.

"Oh yes," he said, "this is definitely my great-grandfather's work."

"How can you tell?" Sadie leaned forward.

Gary pointed to a tall window behind the mother's right shoulder. "Because it was taken right here in this studio. Come with me and I'll show you."

Sadie followed him up a flight of steps with a faded carpet runner down the center. The steps rounded back on themselves on a landing and continued to a second floor. Gary led her to the end of the hallway and into a large room that had been set up as a photography studio. He went to one of the windows, turned, and stood facing Sadie. "Here," he said. "She was posed right about here. Sometimes, if there was illness in a household, or for many other reasons, families came here. In this case"—he indicated the folio he still carried—"it would have been easy because the deceased was an infant. Much less difficult to move than, say, an adult."

Sadie shivered. "Ugh. I can't imagine that. It's hard for me to envision anyone wanting a postmortem photograph."

"If it was the only image you would ever have of your loved one, you might feel differently," Gary said simply. "Times were different then."

"Thank goodness we've made so much medical progress," Sadie said fervently. "My heart breaks for those poor parents. Knowing that any time your child got sick it could potentially be fatal would be a horrible thing to live with."

Gary nodded. "You're right. It's hard for us to even grasp how tenuous life was before modern medicine. Now...would you like to see the books?"

Sadie's eyebrows rose. "Books?"

He grinned, rubbing his hands together. "I didn't tell you on the phone, but I have my great-grandfather's appointment books. If you have any idea when this photograph was made—and I may be able to help a little bit with that—we may be able to figure out who the people in your picture are."

Sadie pressed her hands to her mouth. "That's more than I dared to hope for. Let's get started."

Gary laughed, showing her out of the room and down the stairs. Back in his office, he ushered her into a wing chair and took the one across from her. On the coffee table before them were three large leather-bound books that Sadie had not noticed earlier.

"May I look at the photograph?" Gary was still holding the folio in its plastic protector.

Sadie nodded. "I put it in there to keep it safe from the oils on my fingers."

Gary rose. "Lucky for you I handle old photographs more than occasionally." He went to his desk and withdrew a set of cotton gloves very similar to the ones Sadie used when handling delicate materials.

He glanced at Sadie, and she nodded. "Excellent idea." Pulling them on, the photographer withdrew the folio. He examined the front and back, then reverently opened it. "It's hard to describe what a feeling of…is 'rootedness' a word? Anyway, seeing a tangible of the same work I do four generations later gives me a feeling of being very connected."

"I have deep roots in Silver Peak," Sadie told him. "It does give one a feeling of belonging that I think people who are not raised that way can't understand."

Gary gently opened the folio and gazed at the image of the young woman and the baby. Almost immediately, he said, "It's definitely a *memento mori*. The mother is alive, and the child is deceased."

Sadie was startled. "It never occurred to me that the mother wasn't alive."

"Oh, it's possible. I've seen photos where several family members passed away from, say, an influenza, and the surviving family members are posed with the deceased. Sometimes, if the photographer was particularly skilled and had the right apparatus for supporting the corpses, it is difficult to tell which individuals are alive and which are not."

"Heavenly stars." Sadie truly hoped she never ran across one of those photographs.

Gary peered at the image, picking up a magnifying glass lying atop the stack of books to peruse it closely. "If I had to guess, I'd say that this photo dates from my great-grandfather's earlier work. The woman's clothing looks more end-of-the-1800s to me. The Victorian influence was fading then."

Sadie smiled. "There was a rather cryptic letter in with the photo, as well as a christening gown. The letter was dated 1899."

Gary nodded. "That's certainly within a believable time frame." He caught Sadie eyeing the books stacked in front of them. "I guess you want to look at the records."

Sadie clapped her hands together. "I thought you'd never ask."

14

SADIE GRINNED AS GARY SILVER HEFTED THE FIRST OF HIS GREAT-grandfather's record books. "I feel like a kid about to enter a candy shop."

He laughed as he handed it to her. "Here you go. I have some proofs for a wedding I need to finish preparing, so I'll leave you to it." He peeled off the gloves and handed them to her. "Sorry, I only have the one pair."

"No problem." Sadie laid the book in her lap and slipped them on.

"That's probably the one you want," Gary told her. "He opened his studio in late 1886, and I believe that first book contains records up to 1901. So your subject is probably in there. Unfortunately, I can't tell if the infant was a girl or a boy. They all wore those heavily ornamented gowns for the first four months of their lives."

"It's a girl," Sadie said. "Something in the writing I found refers to a female. So that may help some."

"Have at it," Gary said. He rose and retrieved a yellow pad of paper and a pen from his desk and laid them on the table. "Good luck. Let me know if you need to take a break or get a drink."

Sadie chuckled. "Thank you. I'm hoping it won't take that long."

As Gary returned to his desk, Sadie examined the first volume in her lap. Carefully, she opened it and turned the flyleaf page to the first entry. Artur Silbursky had lovely handwriting, neat and clear, that would make her task easier. Each portrait session had a single page. He recorded a number of things: the subject's contact information, the date and time of the scheduled session, the desired reason for the session, the names of all subjects in the photographs, the location, the props used, and the number of images he took. A second entry showed the images purchased by the subject, which images they had purchased, the sizes of the requested reprints. "Can you tell me more about the reprints, Gary? What were the common sizes?"

"Absolutely," Gary assured her, looking up from his desk. "As you probably know, they were called 'plates.' You will see a lot of orders for 'sixth plates,' which were two-and-five-eighths by three-and-a-quarter inches. The next most popular size was 'ninth plates,' and they were two by two-and-a-half inches."

"But the one in the folio is much bigger than those," Sadie said.

Gary's eyes lit up. "So it is. That's a full, or whole plate. Six-and-a-half by eight-and-a-half. That should make your search easier. There were not a lot of those, because there were not a lot of families with the means to purchase the larger, more expensive prints."

"So this family might have been wealthy?"

"Or perhaps they spent their whole life savings on one precious image," he said. "But it's definitely possible. In fact, based on the quality of the woman's clothing and that christening gown, I'd say it's likely that your subjects were at least upper middle class."

Sadie bent to her task again. She discovered that if she first looked at the size of the photos ordered, she could quickly eliminate a lot of the entries. Checking the location also eliminated any that had not been taken here at the studio. If the buyer had ordered a full plate, she looked at the reason for the portrait. Wedding photos could be eliminated, as could family groups. She decided to include all those designated as "christening" just in case. The child could easily have been living when the session was scheduled. She also included "infant" and the most obvious, "postmortem."

If those three categories yielded a potential result, she looked next at the names of the people listed as subjects. Silbursky was meticulous in his record-keeping, for which she would thank him when she entered the Pearly Gates herself someday, she decided. His listings typically included the individual's name and their places in the family, such as "Grandfather," "Mother," or "Female Child, two years."

The work went quite fast, because she was able to eliminate many of them quickly. Those few that appeared to fit more of her criteria always made her heart beat faster, until she got to the listings for the people photographed and saw that the child was a boy.

In the end, it took her little more than forty minutes to peruse the entries and determine that during the period from 1886 to 1901, there were only five entries that had been taken at the studio in which a whole plate had been ordered of a photo of a "Girl infant." One of those had been taken in September of 1900, and since her letter had been written in 1899, that one could be discarded.

That left only four. One was listed as a christening picture and also listed the father as a subject, so that probably wasn't it. She had included it because there was a chance the photographer had made an additional image of only the mother and the child. Another had been one of Silbursky's first commissions in 1886, which she also put in her "unlikely" column; the grief that poured from that beautiful prayer seemed far too fresh to have been written thirteen years after losing a loved one.

That left two possibilities, both of which were postmortem photos of a mother and child. Sadie silently read them. *Cora Howard and Myrtle Howard, Female Infant, twelve months.* That one had been taken in 1890. A definite possibility, although she hadn't thought the baby in "her" photograph was a full year old.

Her heart beat faster as she read the second option, which was recorded in December 1895: *Fanny Maxfield and Magdalena Maxfield, Female Infant, six months.* She thought of the initials *E.M.* from the letter. Of course, the letter-writer might have been a friend or someone whose initials were totally different. But all the other criteria fit like, well, like a glove, she thought as she removed the borrowed cotton ones from her hands.

"Find anything interesting?" Gary stopped pecking at his computer and looked over at her.

Sadie gave him a tremulous smile. "I may have found them." Her voice, more hushed than she had intended, sounded stunned and reverent.

Gary looked astonished. "You're kidding."

"I'm not." Sadie set the book back atop the stack and picked up the notepad. She explained her search process step by step, receiving Gary's approval as he realized how careful she had been to eliminate those who could not have been the ones she was seeking. She showed him the photo his great-grandfather had taken again, and he agreed that the infant looked quite a bit less than a year old.

"I think you may be right. These Maxfields could very well be the family. I can't believe it. I thought you'd get a list a mile long that would really be of no help. It never occurred to me to whittle it down by the size of the picture and the gender of the baby."

"I have to get going," Sadie told him. "But I really appreciate your help. If you're ever in Silver Peak, please stop in at the Antique Mine and say hello."

As Sadie took her leave, Gary waved at her from the door of the studio. "You'd better let me know how this turns out!"

She grinned as she hopped into the Tahoe. "Absolutely. I promise." As she started the car and pulled away from the curb, she waved, her thoughts already returning to the momentous discovery she'd made.

Were the Maxfields the family she sought?

———

On her way back from Breckenridge, Sadie decided to stop at the Silver Peak Hospital and visit Anna Harrington.

As she parked the Tahoe, she was surprised to see Anna also walking toward the hospital. "Anna," she called.

As the young woman turned, Sadie asked, "What are you doing out here?"

"I was discharged yesterday," Anna told her. "Jeanne Sweeting took me home. I just took a break for lunch, but now I'm headed back to spend the afternoon with the babies."

"And the doctors said you're okay to drive?"

Anna shrugged. "I didn't have surgery or any major medical issues, so I'm allowed. Jeanne offered to drive again today, but I felt all right."

"How are the twins doing?"

"Wonderfully. They anticipate Aaron will be ready to come home in another day or so, and I'm hoping Alex will be home by next week." A vertical line furrowed between her eyebrows. "I want them both home, but this might be better for me. I need to get used to dealing with one before I am responsible for two."

"Yes, I'm sure handling both of them is going to be a balancing act. It's a good thing we're getting you some help."

Anna nodded. "And Guy's mom is coming for three days, but they live in Pennsylvania, and she works full-time. She gets two weeks' vacation a year, so we'll see her then, at least."

Anna didn't mention her own mother, but Sadie recalled her definite statement about their falling-out. She hesitated, not wanting to probe.

Into the silence, Anna said, "I think I told you my mother and I are no longer in touch."

Realizing the young mother wanted to talk, Sadie murmured, "That must be difficult."

Tears filled Anna's eyes, and she stopped walking along the sidewalk outside the hospital. "My grandma left me her nursing-school class ring, one she'd always told me I would have. My mother got really upset and told me that ring should have been left to her. She was a nurse too, so I guess that made sense to her." The tears spilled over as she faced Sadie. "I was pregnant with twins and widowed, and she stopped talking to me when I needed her the most."

Sadie took the weeping young woman into her arms, wrapping comforting arms around her. "I'm so sorry."

"It was such a stupid falling-out," Anna said. "Grandma always promised me that ring. Mom knew that. I don't know what happened."

"Grief does odd things to people," Sadie said. "Sometimes people react badly to others around them and then they're sorry later."

"I don't think she's sorry. If she was, she would have apologized by now."

Sadie didn't have an answer for that logic, although she knew it wasn't always the easiest thing to simply apologize when you'd wronged someone so deeply. She turned to her young friend and continued toward the hospital entrance. "Could I go with you back to the NICU and hold whichever boy you can't be with?"

"That would be great," Anna said shakily, regaining her composure. She pulled a tissue from her purse and wiped her eyes. "I hate having to divide my time between them."

Anna took her into the NICU, where Sadie signed in, left her driver's license, and received a special visitor's badge that she wore around her neck. First, Anna took Sadie to Alex's bedside, where a nurse helped her get seated in a rocking chair and got the baby from his bassinette. He was trailing a couple of monitors and he still wore an oxygen cannula. "What do I do if one of the alarms goes off?" Sadie asked, feeling rather anxious. Alex was the tiniest baby she'd ever seen, and he felt like a feather resting against her as the nurse tucked him against her with his little head beneath her chin.

The nurse laughed. "Don't worry. If an alarm goes off, one of us will be here in a minute. You stay put. It probably just means we need to adjust his position so his oxygen-saturation level doesn't drop. No big deal."

No big deal? Sadie felt that was a very big deal, but Anna was already smiling and walking away to visit with Aaron.

After a frozen moment of panic that they were leaving her alone with this needy little human being, she took a deep breath, feeling a wave of tenderness sweep through her. Oh, there was nothing like a baby. She began to hum, and then sing in a quiet voice as the words to one of the nursery songs she had sung to Alice, and later to Theo and Sara, came back to her.

As she rocked and sang to the tiny scrap nestled against her, she thought of poor Anna's reaction to the mention of her family. The young mother was a shy soul, and now a bereft one after losing Guy, who had been her rock. Her story of the falling-out with her mother was so sad. As she'd told Anna, she'd seen people do awful things while they were grief-stricken, things they never would have done at any other time. She couldn't help but wonder if this was such a case, and if there was any way to help mend the rift between the pair.

The baby squirmed and shifted against her, giving a tiny thin cry. Sadie gently rubbed the tiny back, continuing to sing. She didn't want to get into the middle of a family squabble, but perhaps Anna needed an advocate. If ever a girl needed her mother's support, Anna surely did right now.

Her time at the hospital had been an unexpected blessing, she thought as she drove back to the shop. How often did one get to cuddle a baby for an hour? It probably had the same effect on blood pressure as holding a purring cat in a lap—at least, it might if the baby wasn't screaming.

Still thinking about Anna and her mother, Sadie called Julie at the shop.

"The Antique Mine. This is Julie. How can I help you?"

"Hey, how's business?"

Julie snorted. "Deader than a doornail." She paused. "Whatever a doornail is."

"It's a really long nail that was used to..."

"Never mind," Julie said hastily. "What are you up to?"

"I was going to make a stop at the town hall and look at their census documents. They have them on digital files now, but you still have to go there to view them."

"What are you looking for? Or should I say *whom* are you looking for?"

"Fannie and Magdalena Maxfield," Sadie said. "I'm not positive yet, but I think they may be our mystery mother and child in that old photograph from the armoire."

Julie's gasp was loud and clear. "How did you find that out?"

Sadie shared her visit to Gary Silver's photography studio. "He was incredibly helpful," she said. "I must do something to thank him."

"Maybe a gift certificate to the shop," Julie said. "Photographers are always looking for unique props for sittings."

"That's a great idea," Sadie said. "Leave me a note so I don't forget. And if you don't need me, I'm going to stop at the town hall for a few minutes."

"I enjoy your company, but I don't *need* you today," Julie said, laughing.

"Thanks." Sadie was chuckling too, as she disconnected. As she parked, she thought briefly of visiting Edwin. But she felt pressed for time, and his job was a busy one, so she decided she'd just catch up with him later.

Walking back down the hall after checking in at the reception desk, she entered the records room. There were filing cabinets along three walls and down the center of the room, but she went straight to the computers along the remaining wall. Thankfully, nearly all the old records had been entered in digital data banks, and she intended to run both names she had found yesterday to see what came up. She would run Cora and Myrtle Howard too, but since that infant was twice as old as Magdalena Maxfield, Sadie doubted she was the subject of the photograph she had found in the armoire. The baby in that photograph was much younger than a year, she felt almost certain.

First, she entered Cora Howard. The computer gave her immediate results. Cora had been born in 1872, and her daughter, Myrtle, had been born—and died—in 1890. Reading further, Sadie saw that Cora had lived to be sixty-eight years old and had given birth to six more children after Myrtle, five of whom had survived to adulthood. She blinked, realizing that this confirmed her hunch that Cora wasn't the woman in the photo. The prayer accompanying it had clearly said that both mother and child were deceased at the time of the writing in 1890, and Cora had still been healthy and having babies at that time.

Her fingers actually trembled as she entered the next name: *Fannie Maxfield*, and hit ENTER.

Like magic, the empty screen populated with information. Sadie's breath caught in her throat as she read the bare bones of Fannie Maxfield's life story. Born Fannie Elizabeth Hayes, January 1874, Silver Peak, Blake County. Married Carlton Cole

Maxfield, May 1893, First Congregational Church, Silver Peak. Died February 1896, Silver Peak.

Fannie Hayes Maxfield fit the facts. Sadie felt both glad and incredibly saddened as she absorbed the information. Fannie had been so young, just nineteen when she'd married. And only beginning her twenty-second year at her death.

Magdalena Alice Maxfield was listed as her only offspring of record. Born June 1895 and died December 1985. Again, Sadie was struck by how difficult life in the nineteenth century had been. Carlton Maxfield had lost his baby, and then his wife only two months later. How did a person go on from there?

With that melancholy thought in mind, she looked more closely at Carlton's information. Her heart sank even further. The young father and husband was a few years older than Fannie, having been born in 1868. But he had died at what could only have been a premature age in 1904. He would have been thirty-six years old.

A whole family, gone before their time. For the past few days, every time her hectic pace had lessened and she'd had time to think of the things she'd found in the armoire, she'd felt compelled to try to find the descendants of the people in the picture. Surely someone would treasure that beautiful christening gown...and if not, she'd buy it from them and donate it to the Historical Society. It was a stunning piece of local history, even more so if she could uncover the story behind it.

But what if there *were* no descendants? Sadie didn't know why she was so inexpressibly saddened, but she felt acutely aware of how fortunate she had been to be born nearly a century later, a century during which some of the most extraordinary medical advances that would ever be made had occurred. She couldn't help but contrast the empty christening gown with the baby she'd held in the NICU earlier, tiny by any standards but with a very rosy future ahead. Antibiotics, vaccines, sterile surgical protocols, nutritional standards, high-quality infant care, and so much more had enhanced and extended the quality of life in the last century.

Tapping her index finger against her chin, Sadie let her mind wander. When she had first discovered the gown and memorabilia in the false bottom of the armoire, she had suspected that the child's mother might have secreted them there.

But it had become clear as soon as she had absorbed the contents of the lovely little prayer that the mother probably had not written it. Although there was some room in the way the poem was worded for different interpretations, Sadie had assumed that the "two precious souls" were the mother and the infant in the photo. Now that she thought about it, she really hadn't had a good reason for that supposition, but it appeared they were indeed the pictured subjects. The mother, at that time, had been alive, though she'd passed away only two months later.

So who was E.M.? A Maxfield relative, perhaps? The poem had been written four years *after* Fannie had died, and five years *before* Carlton Maxfield died. Was Carlton the "he" mentioned in the paragraph prefacing the poem?

She needed to go back and read that poem again. Sadie couldn't remember all of it. Then she had a thought. Reaching into her handbag, she pulled out her phone and called Julie at the shop.

When her friend answered, Sadie said, "Are you busy?"

"Well, hello, Sadie, how nice of you to call," Julie replied, laughing. "No, I'm not busy. What's up?"

"Could you go into the back room, open up the armoire, and get out that poem I found? I need you to read it to me."

"Hold on a sec." Julie didn't bother muting the cordless phone, so Sadie could hear her walking through the shop and into the back room. "Here it is. '*Oh, faithless wife am I! I cannot bring myself to comply with my beloved husband's wishes in this matter. To destroy the only photo of that precious little face, now beyond my reach forever, is beyond me. To destroy her gown, every tiny stitch made with such loving care by her mother? Unthinkable. Perhaps one day he shall relent. Perhaps one day another shall wear this gown. Until then, I shall hide it away and offer this prayer—*'"

"Stop," said Sadie. "So whoever wrote that is the wife of a man who wanted the gown *and* the photo destroyed?"

"That's the way I read it," Julie agreed.

"Why would anyone want to get rid of such precious memories?" Sadie wondered.

"You just said it," Julie told her. "Memories. The only reason I can imagine someone not ever wanting to see things like these again is grief."

"Oh, smart lady," Sadie said, and Julie laughed. Sadie went on. "I think you're right. Whoever the writer's husband was, he couldn't bear to be reminded of Fannie and Magdalena because he had loved them so much. Maybe the writer is Carlton's mother?" Inspired, she said, "Thanks, Julie. Gotta go."

Sadie turned back to the computer. She typed Carlton Maxfield's name into the computer. She felt immensely excited at the thought that she might have figured out who the writer was.

But as she saw Carlton's parents' names, her elation drained away. The father had been Joshua Cole Maxfield, and the mother

Rebecca Alice Maxfield, formerly Smythe. Not an *E* initial anywhere.

"All right, 'E,'" Sadie muttered. "Who are you?"

Carlton had three sisters, she saw. And, oh, didn't that lighten her heart a tiny bit? Perhaps there was a descendant somewhere who would love to have these mementos of a family member from the past. Painstakingly, she checked each sister's profile. But as it turned out, Carlton had been the youngest child, and all three sisters had married prior to his marriage in the early 1890s. And not one of them had either a first or a married last name beginning with *E*.

Sadie sighed. "Back to Carlton again." She couldn't help but feel that Carlton was the key. He'd been the husband, the father who'd lost both his reasons for living within a few months. She went down to the second page of Carlton's family history—and blinked. She read it again. Somehow, she hadn't been expecting that.

15

————

CARLTON MAXFIELD HAD MARRIED AGAIN. SADIE EAGERLY READ the information listed before her. He had married Bridget Murphy in February of 1898, almost exactly two years after Fannie's death. And they'd had a child, Iris Rose, in 1899.

Eighteen ninety-nine? That couldn't be a coincidence. If it weren't for the fact that the second wife's name had been Bridget and not something like "Elizabeth" or "Edith," she could almost believe that she'd been the writer of the prayer. Plus, there was another little problem with that scenario, Sadie thought ruefully. A second wife who had only been married because a first wife was gone was not going to be "prostrate in grief," as the author had written. Except in very unusual circumstances, she supposed, circumstances such as the second wife having been the first wife's sister or best friend?

Maybe it hadn't been the second wife who wrote the poem, but Sadie thought she had better go back and look at Fannie's family. Had she had sisters?

She entered Fannie's name and perused her family history, even moving out to her first cousins who had been born locally. It was almost incredible that there wasn't an *E* initial among them.

Regina, Phoebe, Martha, Agatha, Wilhelmina, Georgina, and Sarah.

Maybe a friend? Sadie was grasping at straws now. But of course, friends wouldn't be listed in local genealogical information. For that, she'd have to try the library. The local newspaper, the *Silver Peak Sentinel*, had begun publishing sometime in the 1870s, she recalled. Perhaps by the mid-1890s, there would be things like wedding announcements. If Fannie had had a friend close enough to mourn her passing with the beautiful poem Sadie had found, perhaps she had been *in* the wedding.

Sadie returned to the shop later in the afternoon. There were plenty of empty parking spots along the street, so she pulled into one almost right in front of the Antique Mine and got out of the Tahoe.

"Hi, Sadie." A female voice called her name, and Sadie turned her head to see Jeanne Sweeting coming out of Arbuckle's. As she did, a sudden memory assailed her.

On the day her deposit had been stolen, Jeanne had been driving past the store. Sadie had waved at her *as she was locking the door* behind what she had thought then was a family of five. She was thrilled to know her memory wasn't faulty. And it confirmed her suspicion—no one else could have entered the shop after that group, because in addition to the front door being locked, it helped make her certain that her memory of locking the door after Rhea left was probably accurate, as well. So both doors had been locked.

"Hi, Jeanne. I have a question for you," she said as they met on the sidewalk.

"I'll give it my best shot," Jeanne promised.

"Last Thursday, I waved at you as I was locking the shop door. You were driving past. Do you remember that?"

Jeanne nodded. "Sure do."

"Did you notice anything or anyone unusual near my shop?"

Jeanne thought for a moment, but then she shook her head. "Not that I recall. I mostly remember how annoyed I was that I got caught behind the ice-cream truck, and I was already running late for a meeting."

Sadie laughed. "I hope you weren't too late."

"No later than I usually am," Jeanne said cheerfully. "I hear you've been visiting Anna Harrington almost every day. Thank you. That young woman needs friends."

"Yes, her own mother is estranged from her by the mother's choice."

Jeanne sighed. "That's more detail than I knew. Poor Anna. She could really use support right now."

"I've considered approaching the mother to see if she's interested in mending the rift between them. I don't want to be a busybody, but it might be worth attempting a conversation, at least. Maybe the mother is looking for a way to fix it and doesn't have the courage, or isn't sure how."

"I don't think that's being a busybody," Jeanne said. "A busybody snoops and gossips. I'll say a prayer for God to smooth the path to reconciliation between Anna and her mother. By the way, Don said he checked with the church secretary this morning, and no one has come forward to admit to giving Anna that gift you asked about. So I guess that's still a mystery. It's kind of odd, because I know a number of people have been spreading the word about identifying the donor."

"I'm going to stop by the Needlework Guild tonight and ask if any of them could have done it."

"Oh, good idea." Jeanne nodded emphatically. "I bet that's the answer.

When Sadie returned to the shop, Julie greeted her and handed her a note. "We haven't been a bit busy this afternoon either. The only person who stopped in was Sheriff Slattery. He says if you call him, he'll drop back by before five. He wants an update on anything you've learned about the theft of the deposit."

"Anything *I've* learned? He's the sheriff. I should be questioning him."

Julie laughed. "Yes, but we all know you probably have found out as much or more than he has, so why don't you pool your resources?"

Chuckling, Sadie made the call and left a message for Mac Slattery to stop back by the shop. Next, she called Sara's cell phone.

"Hello, Grandma."

Sadie grinned. "Hi, honey. How was your day?"

Sara sighed. "Long. Lots of homework. I'm making cookies because Eve is coming here to work on our English project."

Sadie rather thought Sara should have started on that homework, but saying so was probably not the greatest idea. Besides, Sara's grades were always excellent, so she must manage her time relatively well. "Would you guys like to come to dinner?"

"I'd love to," Sara said, "and I'm pretty sure Mom and Theo can come too. When we talked about our schedules this morning, nobody had anything planned for tonight."

"Great." Sadie was hoping to talk to Alice about the history teacher again. "Any menu requests?"

"Corn on the cob," Sara said immediately. "Soon it'll be winter and the corn will be gone." She sounded mournful, and Sadie laughed.

"You do love corn on the cob, don't you?"

Sara laughed. "It's one of my faves. What time do you want us?"

"Six o'clock, unless that pushes your mom too much. I know sometimes she doesn't get home from work on time."

"I don't think she had any parent conferences or meetings after school. She usually tells us if she's going to be late."

"Okay. Let's shoot for six."

"Why don't you pick me up on your way home?" Sara suggested. "Then I can help you make dinner."

"All right. You'll text your mom and Theo?"

"I will. See you soon."

After she concluded that call, she dialed over to the office of the *Sentinel*, the town's weekly newspaper. When editor Troy Haggerty answered, Sadie said, "Hi, Troy. I have a question for you. Did newspapers publish society weddings in the 1890s?"

Troy laughed. "Hi, Sadie. I'm fine, thanks."

She laughed sheepishly. "Sorry."

"Yes, in answer to your question," he said. "The media of that time was just as invasive as today's more aggressive newshounds, the chief difference being that they didn't have the sophisticated electronic methods of snooping. They had to pay people to gather information, most of the time. There was an essay published in the *Harvard Law Review* in 1890 advocating the right to privacy. Primarily written by Louis Brandeis, the article advocated the 'right to be let alone.' Although there apparently was a specific inciting incident in which journalists intruded on a society wedding, the article was really aimed at the increasingly invasive way in which journalists were publishing intimate details of personal lives of the rich and the famous."

"It doesn't sound like very much has changed in the past hundred and thirty years. Famous people are still being hounded by the press."

Sadie thanked Troy. She suspected that in the information he had shared lay the answer to her question. If Carlton and Fannie Maxfield's wedding had been considered a society event in 1893, chances were good that she might find some mention of it...thanks to reporters who were as nosy as their modern counterparts. Should she try the historical society or the library?

Probably the library first, she thought. All of the old published editions of the *Silver Peak Sentinel* had been put on microfiche some years back. Although they hadn't made it to digital yet, microfiche was still a great resource, and maybe she could find some mention of the Maxfields. That would be a task for tomorrow.

The bell over the door tinkled, and Sadie looked up to see the sheriff entering, his wide shoulders blocking the bright light of the late afternoon. "Hi, Mac," she said. "Thanks for coming back. I'm sorry I missed you earlier."

"No problem," the sheriff rumbled. "I just wanted to touch base on your missing money. I'm sorry to report that nothing has turned up anywhere that would lead us to believe someone tried to cash your checks. The currency, of course, is nearly impossible to track."

Sadie nodded. "I know."

"Have you learned anything else?" Sheriff Slattery shot her a piercing glance.

Sadie hesitated. "Not really. I've remembered that I definitely did lock the doors. One family came in, and I went to the front door and locked it behind them. The back door was already locked. But here's something." She went on to tell him about her recent encounter with the Clapsaddles. "Here's their contact information," she said, offering him a note. "I am starting to believe the tall man may have something to do with my missing money. He could have gone out the back door, I suppose. It's possible to lock it and pull it closed behind you." She thought about Alice's notion that the history teacher from the high school was her mystery man. But she didn't feel right telling Mac that. What if the fellow was perfectly innocent? She certainly wouldn't appreciate someone giving her name to the police if she hadn't done anything wrong.

Mac, unaware of her dilemma, was still considering her theory. "That sounds very plausible," he admitted. "You've got enough furniture in here to obscure someone tall, so he could have been concealed from your view when you locked the doors."

Sadie felt a little defensive, even though she knew it was just an observation. "My business is selling antiques," she said. "I try to keep as much inventory in-house as possible."

Mac wisely chose to ignore that. "And then he unlocked the back door and bolted." He sighed. "I'm sure sorry about this, Sadie. I don't think there's much chance you're going to get any of it back. If he was a tourist, or in town to scam people during the festival, he's long gone. I don't think it was a pro, though, because no one else has reported any thefts."

"I've accepted that the money's gone for good," she said. *Mostly.*

"I've already talked to the neighbors, but I'll re-canvass now that we have a description, see if anyone remembers seeing a tall fella like that anywhere downtown."

"Thanks for your efforts," Sadie said. Again she hesitated. Should she mention the history teacher? No. That wasn't fair. She wanted to talk to Alice about him before she did anything irrevocable.

Sadie closed the shop promptly at five. After swinging by the bank and dropping the day's deposit into the slot, she headed for Alice's house.

She knocked on the door and entered, calling out, "Hello."

Footsteps could be heard overhead, and a moment later, Sara came bounding down the stairs. "Hi, Grandma. Eve and I are almost finished. Can you give us five minutes?"

"Sure." Sadie went into Alice's kitchen and got herself a glass of water.

A few minutes later, she heard voices on the stairs, and then the front door opened and closed. Sara came into the kitchen, dumping a loaded backpack on the table. "I'm ready to go, Grandma."

"Where's your friend?"

"Oh, she left."

"Shouldn't we give her a ride home?" The Averys lived all the way on the other side of town. Granted, it was still close, but Sadie was happy to offer the girl a ride.

"No, she said she walks all the time." Sara grabbed the backpack. "Let's go. I can't wait to see the baby bobcat."

Sadie and Sara locked the house and climbed into the Tahoe. As they drove to the end of the street, Sadie noticed Sara's friend

Eve waiting at the corner for the light to change. "Ask her again if she'd like a ride," Sadie told Sara.

Sara rolled down her window and hollered, "Hey, Eve, are you sure we can't give you a lift home?"

Eve shook her head vigorously, her blonde hair falling about her face. She stood with slumped shoulders and her head down, as if she bore the cares of the world on her shoulders, and Sadie thought she probably did, recalling the girl's mother's health. "No, thank you," she said. "I'm good."

"Okay. See you tomorrow." Sara rolled her window back up as the light changed and they headed out of town. "Don't worry about Eve. I think she's just really shy."

Sadie smiled. "We can't all be social butterflies, dear."

Sara laughed. "What a silly phrase. Where do you suppose that came from?"

Sadie shrugged. "Because butterflies flit from flower to flower, chatting with other butterflies as they go?"

"Huh. That's a stretch. But possibly true." They looked at each other and laughed.

On the way out of town, they stopped at a fruit and vegetable stand and picked up some sweet corn. Then they headed on to Sadie's ranch home, where Sadie let Sara take a peek at the baby bobcat before they took Hank out and played ball with him for a few minutes before coming in to feed him and start dinner. She had been hungry for fish tacos for several days, so she had picked up some flaky white mahimahi. Sara fed Hank, washed her hands, and then helped chop lettuce and tomatoes and grate cheese, while Sadie thinly sliced red onion and set out sour cream, the slim glass jar of hot sauce, and quickly mixed up an avocado-cilantro sauce.

Theo and Alice arrived moments after Sara had set the table. "So where's this famous bobcat?" he asked as he entered the kitchen. "I saw the crate on the porch with the little one, but I want to see the big kahuna."

"She's not here right now," Sadie said. "She won't come in while you're here, probably."

Everyone enjoyed the fish tacos. Theo ate four as he regaled them with tales from football practice. They had a new coach this year who reveled in the art of the prank, and the boys had been taking turns coming up with ways to prank him back.

Alice was struggling with a particularly challenging student who was unable to stay quietly in his seat without disrupting the students around him, and Sara gave them all an update on her Little House project.

"My friend Eve is a really hard worker," she reported. "She hadn't read the books as a child, so she decided to read *the entire series* so she'd have a better handle on what we were doing."

"My goodness," Sadie said. "That's ambitious. That's the blonde girl I saw today, right?" When Sara nodded, Sadie said, "She's the only member of the Avery family I haven't met yet."

"I invited her to come to church with me sometime," Sara said, "but she said she wasn't sure. She was going to talk to her mom about it."

"Mom, what's the latest on your missing money?" Alice asked. "Has Mac found out who stole it yet?"

Sadie shook her head. "No, and I don't think that's going to happen. He thinks it might have been a tourist, and at this point, I'm starting to think he might be right."

"That's pretty bold," Alice remarked. "To linger in your shop, steal the money, and then flee without being seen seems like it would take more planning than an impulsive grab."

"But someone would have noticed if there was someone creeping around casing your shop," Theo protested.

"I know." Sadie didn't say more, but she couldn't stop thinking about the history teacher.

As they carried items to the counter, placed dishes in the dishwasher, and put away the leftovers, Sadie quietly said to Alice, "Have you found out the name of the history teacher yet?"

"Trey Collins," Alice said. "This is the beginning of his second year with the district. He graduated from Colorado State, he's originally from Denver, he's single, and he lives in a townhouse out along the highway."

Sadie chuckled. "Goodness. You certainly were thorough."

Alice looked troubled. "How are you going to handle it? You're not positive he's the tall man you're seeking, right?"

"Not positive at all, although he fits what we know in a very general way. That's why I want to talk to him. I thought perhaps I would stop by and introduce myself tomorrow." She grinned. "Since I used to teach the same subject, it gives me a perfect 'in.'"

16

AFTER HER FAMILY HAD LEFT, SADIE DROVE OVER TO CAMPFIRE Chapel, where the Needlework Guild was meeting. She parked the Tahoe and entered the building, heading for a room in the Sunday school wing from which a flood of light illuminated the hallway.

As she stopped in the doorway, Marge Ruxton caught sight of her. Turning to the rest of the group, she said, "Oh, I forgot to tell you all that Sadie was asking questions about our group."

Helene Daly, a friendly lady from the congregation whom Sadie knew, waved. "Hi, Sadie. You planning to join us tonight?"

Sadie shook her head. "Hello. I'm just stopping by. What are you working on?"

There were seven women in the room, including Marge and Helene. Sadie knew them all from church. Helene held up a square on which she was stitching. "We're making a quilt for the ingathering next month. All the churches in town have been asked to create a quilt to be donated to a new nursing home that's opening in November down at the far end of Main Street in the old hotel."

"What a nice idea," Sadie said. "So everyone in the group can quilt?"

"Not everyone, but everyone sews well enough to contribute to it in some way," Marge said. She appeared to be less confrontational than she often was with Sadie, which was interesting. Perhaps she got along better with these fellow stitchers. "We're a pretty crafty group, but each of us has some types of needlework we most enjoy. So when we don't have a special project like this, everyone does her own thing. I'm normally a crochet enthusiast, so I make little sweaters and afghans for new babies in the congregation."

"But you don't knit." Sadie was certain the twins' blankets from the mystery donor were knitted.

Marge shook her head.

"I'm a knitter through and through," Helene said. "It's the only type of needle art I ever learned, other than basic sewing and enough quilting not to disgrace myself."

"Are there just the seven of you?" Somehow, Sadie had expected the group to be larger.

"There are three people missing tonight. The other two knitters aren't here, and my friend Eleanor, who is our quilter, will be coming when she gets finished with another meeting."

"Helene," Sadie said, "maybe you can help me since you knit. Someone left a gift for Anna Harrington on my shop door on Saturday. It was a set of darling little knitted blankets, but there was no card with them. You didn't leave it, did you?"

Helene shook her head. "Sorry, it wasn't me."

"Anna's a little distressed," Sadie said. "She really wants to thank the giver. So I'd like to figure out who it was."

Helene looked thoughtful. "There are two other knitters who aren't here tonight. Genevieve Olney only knits sweaters now. I can't remember the last time she made anything else. She says other things are boring." She laughed. "The other one, Carey Snader, does make a good many blankets and afghans. Maybe it was Carey."

Thanks," Sadie said. "I know her. I'll check with her, and let's hope that will solve our mystery."

Business was slow again on Tuesday morning, so slow that she closed the shop over her lunch hour and went back to the town hall. She wished she'd thought to look up the descendants of Carlton Maxwell's second child, Iris, the first time she'd been there, but she'd been on information overload and she just hadn't thought of it.

She waved at the receptionist as she went straight into the records room, set down her bag, and pulled up a search engine. Typing in *Iris Maxfield*, she waited for the information to populate. Instead, nothing happened. She tried again and still got no results. She closed the search engine, waited a minute, and put Iris's name in again.

Nothing.

Sighing, she closed it and picked up her handbag, then made her way back to the receptionist's desk.

"Hi, Sadie. Find what you wanted?" Kaitlyn McCarthy was manning her desk, as she had been when Sadie breezed in a few minutes ago.

Sadie made a face. "No. There seems to be something wrong with the computer. I put in the name and nothing came up."

Kaitlyn looked apologetic. "There's probably nothing wrong. I forgot to tell you the data entry is only about seventy-five percent complete. If no results were returned, it just means the data hasn't been entered yet."

"Oh." Sadie felt foolish for thinking she'd just be able to waltz in and print out a list of Iris Maxfield's descendants. She'd anticipated that she might even find one or more of them still living in Silver Peak. In her ideal world, the family would be thrilled with the links to their past.

She should have known it wouldn't be that easy.

Walking much more slowly than she had on her way over to the town hall, she returned to her shop. She felt as if she'd hit a dead end. She wondered if she should call the auctioneer she'd spoken with on Saturday. The only option she had now was to try to work backward, to find out who had owned the armoire before Rhea Ressler.

As soon as she flipped over the "Open" sign again, the phone rang, and she hurried to grab the receiver.

"The Antique Mine, this is Sadie. How can I help you?"

"Sadie, this is Buck Lanniter," said a male voice. "We spoke last week about looking through some auction records from back when I had my business."

"Mr. Lanniter! I was just thinking of you."

"I got those keys I told you about. If you're still interested, I could meet you at five today," said the retired auctioneer. "My stuff is in that climate-controlled storage place out on Sixty-five."

Sadie knew he was referring to Route 65, the highway that ran just east of the town. She'd been by the storage facility, which was just past a strip mall called the Plaza, although she'd never had need of storage and had paid it little mind.

"That would be great. Better make it five fifteen. I drive a red Tahoe."

It's unit forty-one," he said. "Go in the second door in the first row. Unit forty-one's on the left. I'll be looking for you."

"Wonderful. Thank you so much. I'll see you then."

He chuckled. "It'll be an adventure. I have plenty of time on my hands these days."

Sadie called Julie after lunch. "Hey, do you want to work for the last few hours of the day? I've got some things on my plate that I'd like to accomplish."

"Sure. The twins are going straight to swim team practice after school with a friend's mom. I'm doing pickup at five thirty, so I'd be happy to work until five."

"Great. Thanks."

"I'll be in around two."

Alone in the shop, Sadie thought again of her conversation with the Needlework Guild ladies last night. Digging in a drawer, she unearthed the extra copy of the church directory that she kept at the store and looked up the home number for Carey Snader.

Moments after she dialed, Carey's husband answered the phone. "Hello?"

"Hi, John," Sadie said. "This is Sadie Speers. May I speak to Carey, please?"

"She's not here, Sadie. She's been in Florida with our daughter, who just had a new baby, since the twenty-fifth of August. Would you like her cell number?"

Sadie thought quickly. If Carey had been gone that long, there was no way she could have been the one to leave the baby gifts for Anna, unless she had made them early and had had John deliver them. "John, do you know if Carey made any baby afghans for Anna Harrington?"

"Is that the lady who just had the twins?"

"Yes." Sadie held her breath. Maybe John had put the gift bag on her door.

"No," he said. "She was kind of upset that Anna delivered while she was away, because she's been working on two little sweaters, and she hasn't finished them yet."

"Oh." Sadie snapped her fingers, even though John couldn't see her. "Thanks, John. That actually helps me a lot. Tell Carey I said hello and congratulations to you both on the new addition to the family."

"Thanks, Sadie. I'll pass it on."

Julie was as good as her word. With heartfelt thanks, Sadie handed over the role of shopkeeper to Julie and grabbed her handbag. And Roz, Sadie's best friend and confidante, chose that very moment to walk in the door.

"Hey there," Roz said. "I'm so glad the heritage festival show is over. I feel like I've hardly seen you in a week."

"I know," Sadie said. "Festival Week is always hectic, but this year it really ramped up. The shop was swamped every day."

"I came to chat, if you aren't busy today," Roz said. "But it looks like you're headed out somewhere."

"The library, first," Sadie said. "Want to come along?"

"Sure." Roz turned and held the door, her black-and-red-patterned skirt flaring. This skirt had tiny bells attached to the drawstring waist ties that jingled pleasantly if she let them swing free. Sadie noticed she had slipped them into a side pocket when she'd entered the store.

After they exited, Roz fell into step beside Sadie. "Why are we going to the library?"

"Remember the things I found in the secret compartment of that armoire last week?"

When Roz nodded, Sadie caught her up on everything she had learned so far. "Gary Silver was so helpful," she said. "Without him, I never would have learned so much. The rest of what I know, I found out in the records room at the town hall. But when I tried to find out who Iris Maxfield's descendants are, it turns out the records haven't been uploaded to digital format yet. So I'm back to going at it from the other end. I have an appointment to meet Buck Lanniter, who was the auctioneer who sold that armoire to Rhea. He's going to let me look through his old records and see if we can find out who owned it before she did."

"But that could still be someone other than the Maxfield family," Roz pointed out. "You know it started in their hands and ended in Rhea's. But who knows how many owners it had in between? Those first Maxfields might have sold it out of the family at the turn of the last century."

"Very true."

"So why are we going to the library?"

"Because I want to see if Carlton and Fannie Maxfield are mentioned in the *Sentinel*. If they were society families, it's possible that the mysterious E.M. who wrote the poem might be mentioned somewhere."

"Oh, good idea." Roz clapped her hands. "I can help research. I already put a meat loaf in the oven on a timer, so I have a couple of hours to spare."

"It could take a couple of hours," Sadie warned, "although I hope it won't."

At the library, the pair greeted Kimama Temoke, the head librarian. The stunning woman wore her long dark hair in a sophisticated updo today, one that showed off a lovely pair of turquoise and silver chandelier earrings. Her simple black dress was belted at the waist with a large oval Western turquoise and silver buckle. Kimama often played up her Native American heritage with incredible jewelry. Kimama favored turquoise even though the Utes, a more local tribe, had made most of their jewelry of bear claws, antlers, and bone.

Kimama's face broke into a smile at the sight of Sadie and Roz. "Here comes trouble," she said in a teasing tone. "Good to see you, ladies. How can I help?"

Sadie smiled. "Hi, Kimama. We'll just help ourselves to the microfiche room, if that's all right."

"Fine with me. I would ask you not to cause any trouble but I know better." Kimama chuckled.

The friends laughed. Then they proceeded on through the library, waving at Anthony Parker, the assistant librarian, before heading up the steps to the little microfiche room off of the reference room. As usual, it was chilly. The air-conditioning that kept most of the library at a comfortable temperature always made the back room a little too cool. Sadie and Roz had come prepared, and both pulled on sweaters.

"Since you know what you're looking for," Roz said, "why don't I go through the papers and look for the names of interest? You can write them down for me. Then, if I find anything, I can send it to the printer, and you can read the actual articles."

"Sounds good to me," Sadie said. "There are five names to look for. Well, six, if you count the last name *Maxfield*. I want anything with that name in it." Quickly, she jotted down the list of names for Roz:

Maxfield (any family member) but especially:

Carlton Maxfield

Fannie Maxfield

Magdalena Maxfield

Bridget Maxfield

Iris Maxfield

"Got 'em. What year shall we start with?" Roz sat on the stool before the large microfiche reader and turned it on, while Sadie went to the wall files that held the film. They were organized chronologically, and she pulled out 1893. "This was the year Fannie married Carlton. Let's start there."

Roz pulled the film from the box and carefully placed it beneath the rollers before securing the right side. Within moments, she had wound the reel through the machine and was looking at images of the newspaper.

In very short order, she said, "Bingo. Here's a mention of a Maxfield endowing a chair at the Rocky Mountain School of Nursing. Want it?"

"Absolutely. I imagine you'll find a fair number of things like this, but I would like them all if it's not too tedious."

"I didn't even know there was a Rocky Mountain School of Nursing," Roz said as she hit the button to print out a hard copy of the article.

"When the Silver Peak Junior College opened in the early thirties, the nursing school merged with it," Sadie said. "And then later, the whole school became a branch campus of the University of Colorado in, I believe, the fifties."

"Here's another article about a Lurlene Maxfield who was the president of the local Women's Christian Temperance Union."

Sadie chuckled. "In a mining town, she must have had her work cut out for her."

"I wonder if she might be Carlton's mother."

"Or sister. He had four, all older," Sadie told her friend.

Roz's eyebrows rose. "I bet his father was happy when an heir came along. I'm getting the impression that these people were some of Silver Peak's leading citizens." She printed out another article, and then said, "Oh, Sadie, I found the wedding."

"What does it say? Never mind, just print it out," Sadie exclaimed, eager to read it. Perhaps there was a mention of "E.M."

Roz dutifully printed it, and Sadie hovered over the printer until she could snatch up the sheet of copy paper.

"Tell me what it says," Roz begged. "I'm still scanning for more."

"This was a Society wedding with a capital *S*." Sadie scanned the article. "Fannie Hayes was a debutante and the daughter of a Silver Peak banker, and Carlton Maxfield the son of—get this— the wealthiest resident of Silver Peak, according to this article. It must have been a monetary match made in heaven."

"I wonder if they were in love, or if it was arranged because of the influence it would bring to the families."

"I don't know that we'll learn that from the newspapers. But you should read the description of the banquet they threw to celebrate this wedding. Megabucks."

"I'm into 1894 now," Roz said. "Sadie, there are mentions of the Maxfields nearly every week. The younger ones and his parents. Attending a musicale at the opera house, having dinner with the governor, breaking ground for a new church for which they had donated a significant sum…"

"Just print anything that mentions their guests," Sadie said. "We can always come back, but I can't imagine we need all those."

She continued to read while Roz scanned and printed.

"Eighteen ninety-five," her friend announced.

"That's when their daughter was born," Sadie said. "June."

"And here it is." Roz hit the Print button again. "Magdalena's birth." Her hands stilled. "Poor little dear. I can hardly bear to think of losing an infant."

"I know." Sadie stopped reading, and their eyes met. "I've thought of that a lot too, especially since I've visited Anna Harrington and held her baby boys. Those little ones are so lucky to have been born today. They might not have survived in 1895."

After a moment of thoughtful silence, Roz seemed to shake herself. "So what's the next date I'm looking for?"

"Early 1896," Sadie said. "Fannie passed away just a few months after Magdalena."

"A double whammy," Roz murmured as she turned back to the machine. "Poor guy." Moments later, she printed out Fannie's obituary and moved on.

"Go into 1897," Sadie suggested. "He was probably observing mourning for about a year, but he married again in 1898, so I want to see if there's any mention of him squiring around a new lady love."

Oddly, there wasn't. Carlton was mentioned several times as attending events, and there was even a photograph of him at a ribbon-cutting ceremony for a new building, but not a hint that there might be someone else entering his life.

Roz moved on to 1898, while Sadie read all the details of the articles she had gathered thus far. They both were touched to see that Carlton Maxfield had given large sums of money to several charitable endeavors in the name of his late wife and child.

"Oh, Sadie," Roz said, after they found the third such article, "he must have been so devastated to lose them."

Sadie nodded. "It seems so."

Finally, Roz gasped. "Whoa. I almost missed it. Sadie, here's a mention of Carlton's second wedding to Bridget Murphy, but seriously, it's barely a mention. And...oh my, it says she was an 'Irish domestic.'"

17

SADIE FELT AS IF A PUZZLE PIECE HAD DROPPED INTO PLACE WHEN she heard what Roz had just said. Carlton Maxfield, a well-to-do Silver Peak citizen, had married an Irish domestic. "That was still the Victorian era, and even though they weren't living in a bastion of high society like an East Coast or Deep South city, he was one of the most prominent men in town. I bet that caused a scandal that rocked the town. Anti-Irish sentiment was terrible in the middle of the nineteenth century, but I am sure the upper-crust society in Silver Peak was slow to change their biases, so even in the late 1890s, a marriage like that would have caused quite a scandal."

"An Irish girl named Bridget who worked as a housekeeper or some such surely didn't bring with her the prestige that his first wife's connections did." Roz's words were a huge understatement. "It must have been a love match."

"Maybe so," Sadie said. "I wonder how they met. Maybe she was part of his household staff. They had a child together, a daughter like his first one. That was just a year into the marriage, I believe."

Roz searched through 1899—twice—before she found a tiny mention of Carlton Maxfield's second daughter's birth. "Big difference from the first one," she said. "I think we were right about the scandal."

"There's one last thing I'd like to see," Sadie said. "Look at 1904. Both Bridget and Carlton died that year, although the child did not."

"This poor family certainly had its share of tragedy." Roz traded out the film for another roll and went back to her search as Sadie continued to absorb the information about the Maxfields' lives.

A few moments passed, and Roz spoke again, her voice hushed. "Oh, Sadie, I found it. There was a smallpox outbreak in 1904. It affected people all across the country, and Silver Peak didn't escape. This one article says that thirty percent of the town's citizens died. *Thirty percent*."

Sadie was equally stunned. "That's awful. It's a wonder the little girl, Iris, survived."

"Maybe they sent her away," Roz said. "People often did that, you know."

"Maybe. Or maybe she was just very, very lucky."

"She probably didn't feel lucky," Roz reminded Sadie. "She would have been five years old, and both of her parents died. Here, I'll print out the article about smallpox. Anything else you want me to check?"

Sadie shook her head. "No, I don't have enough information to point you in the right direction...no idea when Iris might have married, assuming she even did."

"And you're assuming she stayed in Silver Peak after her parents died," Roz added. "She might have been sent to relatives elsewhere. Unfortunately, I can imagine well-to-do people of that era choosing not to acknowledge a female child from an undesirable marriage. And if Bridget was an immigrant with relatives in another part of the state or even the country, Iris could have been sent to them."

Roz's blunt assessment was disheartening, although she knew it was a distinct possibility given the attitudes of the times.

How ironic, Sadie thought, that the letter written by E.M. had led her to discover so much about the Maxfield family, and yet it was looking more and more as if she would never know who E.M. was. The only things Sadie knew for sure about her were that she had been married, that she had known and loved Fannie and Magdalena enough to treasure their memory, and that her husband appeared to be a man who was tormented by their loss. A cousin or childhood friend, perhaps?

If Carlton and Bridget hadn't died at the same time, she'd have thought that perhaps Carlton had married one of Fannie's friends from his earlier years who would have known her and her infant and would have treasured their memory.

She and Roz parted ways outside the library, and Sadie checked the time. The high school had let out a few minutes ago, so if she went straight over there, she might get a chance to talk to the history teacher to see if he had been in her shop.

But before she drove in that direction, she placed a quick call to Rhea Ressler.

"Hi, Rhea," she said when the other woman answered. "It's Sadie Speers. I just have one more question about the armoire."

Rhea laughed. "You're persistent, aren't you? Ask away."

"You would not be the first to gently suggest I'm like a dog with a bone." Sadie chuckled. "You said you bought the armoire in the seventies, around when your daughter was born. Can you tell me when she was born and if you recall whether it was before or after her birth?"

"Before," Rhea said instantly. "We did up a nursery a few months before she was born. Let's see, she was born on July twenty-seventh of 'seventy-six, so probably April or May. I remember when the room was finished, I'd go in there and sit in the rocker and wish time would pass faster until my due date."

Sadie smiled at the sweet memory. "I remember that impatience well. I could hardly wait to get my hands on my daughter, Alice."

She thanked Rhea for pinpointing the date more closely and hung up. That had been helpful. When she met Buck Lanniter, she would have a much more specific window of time in which to search for a sale bill.

Starting the Tahoe, she drove over to the high school. There were empty spaces in the faculty lot, so she parked there, filled with nostalgia. In some ways, it seemed like only yesterday she'd been entering this building each weekday.

Familiar faces greeted her as she walked down through the halls, but she'd been gone a decade now, and there were as many unfamiliar faces as there were those that she knew. She stopped at the door of her old classroom as a colleague with whom she had once taught spotted her and called out.

"Hey, Sadie. What brings you back here?" Donette Laurent had been a single teacher just starting her career during Sadie's final year of teaching. Now she was a busy wife and mother of young children, and she'd moved up from teaching the general civics and history courses to some of the more challenging courses like the advanced placement options.

Sadie smiled. "I had a yen to see my old stomping grounds. Who's in my room this year?"

"Trey Collins," Donette told her. "He's new this year. He's got three sections of World History and three of Civics." She made a face. "And he hasn't been shy about letting the department head know he's not pleased that he didn't get any upper-level courses." She snorted. "He should be glad he only has two preps. I had four my first year."

Preps, Sadie knew, were preparations that a teacher needed to make in order to teach each class each day. Having two preps meant that he had two separate courses to prepare for, in addition to the adjustments needed for each particular class of students. And how convenient it was that Trey Collins was in her old room. It gave her the perfect excuse to visit.

"I'm on my way to a parent conference," Donette said, indicating a file she held, "or I'd chat longer. Great to see you, Sadie."

"You too, Donette." As the other teacher hurried away, Sadie walked down the hall and knocked lightly at the door frame of her old classroom. The door was open. When no one answered, she stepped inside. "Hello?"

The room was empty. Intrigued, she looked around, noting that a number of things remained unchanged. Textbooks were stacked along the windows, the desks were still arranged in rows, and colorful maps and posters covered the walls.

A leather satchel hung over the back of the teacher's chair behind the desk caught her eye. Her heart began to race. Surely that had to be the same leather satchel that Sue Clapsaddle had seen "the tall man" carrying the day he'd been in her shop. She moved a step closer. The satchel was unzipped, and the corner of a light gray bag poked out of one side. *Is that my deposit bag?*

She froze. It was the exact same color, and it looked like it could be the exact same size—

"Hello. Can I help you?"

A masculine voice behind her gave her a jolt. Turning slowly, Sadie forced herself to smile and extend a hand. "Hi. I'm Sadie Speers. I used to teach history in this room."

The young man who had prowled in wrung her hand in a tight grip, squeezing hard enough to make her suppress a wince. He smiled, revealing even white teeth. His hair was dark and slightly disheveled, and as Sue Clapsaddle had noted, he had lavish dark eyelashes so long and thick that his piercing eyes were the first thing she noticed. "I'm Trey Collins. It's my room now."

"Oh, of course." She gestured around them. "It still looks much the same, although I imagine you use more high-tech things to help with the learning process these days."

"We do." He went over to the desk and pushed a button. "Like this." As a screen slowly dropped down from a fixture above the blackboard, Trey said, "I use PowerPoint for a lot of my lessons now. Sort of like the old-school overhead projectors, but a lot more sophisticated."

"I haven't used PowerPoint for much," Sadie said, "but I'm familiar with it. It must be a terrific teaching tool."

"Only if the students are interested," Trey said, making a face. "I don't have any really great classes. This is my first year, but I'm hoping to get an AP next year, which would be a lot more fun, I think." He picked up a hefty stack of papers. "You here for a meeting or something?"

Sadie shook her head. "No, I just had a weak moment and decided to reminisce." She grinned. "I guess that's hard to imagine."

Trey laughed. "A little." He spun his chair and sat down heavily, regarding the pile of papers. "Well, I've got four dozen World History quizzes to grade, so if you'll excuse me..."

"Certainly." Sadie headed for the door. "It was nice to meet you. I hope your first year goes well." Out in the hall, she breathed slowly and steadily as she walked back to her vehicle. Did Trey Collins have her deposit bag? It certainly looked likely. She knew first-year teachers didn't make enough to get rich, but they certainly weren't dirt-poor either. Why on earth would he have stolen money from her? She realized she had missed a golden opportunity because she'd been so rattled when he'd startled her. If she'd mentioned the Antique Mine, he would have had to tell her he'd been in the shop. Or, if he'd concealed it, she would have felt she had enough reasonable suspicion to mention his name to Mac Slattery.

As it was, she still wasn't sure. She had to get a look at that bag!

Deciding she had time for one more errand before meeting Buck Lanniter at the storage place, Sadie stopped at a handsome log chalet on a lake not far from Milo Henderson's ranch where she kept her horse. Genevieve Olney and her husband, George, had retired there a few years ago. Sadie didn't know them well, but they also attended Campfire Chapel, and she knew Genevieve was the other knitter in the Needlework Guild who might have made the baby afghans.

Genevieve answered the door in a flowing caftan in shades ranging from pale sky to the deepest turquoise. "Why, hello, Sadie," she said, smiling broadly. "What can I do for you?"

Sadie returned the smile. She'd always wanted to get to know Genevieve better, because her pleasant nature was so contagious that it infected everyone she met. "I have a knitting question, and I thought I'd ask an expert."

"Oh, *pshaw*," Genevieve said, waving a dismissive hand. "There are people a lot more skilled than I, but I'll see what I can do."

"It's pretty simple, really. I'm trying to find out who left a gift bag for Anna Harrington on my shop door on Saturday. It had two knitted baby blankets in it, but there was no card."

"Wasn't me," Genevieve said promptly. "I stopped making afghans years ago. Too boring and time-consuming. I mostly make sweaters, vests, that sort of thing. Want to see a few?"

"I'd love to." Sadie followed Genevieve inside to what was obviously a craft room devoted mostly to sewing and needlework.

"Here are a couple of sweaters I've made recently," Genevieve said. "I'm trying to finish two more so I'll have Christmas gifts for all the grandchildren."

"Oh my goodness." Sadie held up a light gray sweater with a handsome navy-and-white pattern that Genevieve handed her. "This is stunning."

"It's a variation on a Fair Isle snowflake pattern. My eldest grandson is an avid skier," Genevieve told her. "And this is a short-sleeved hooded sweater for one of my teen granddaughters. She picked out the pattern because it had to be ever so fashionable, you know." She chuckled.

Sadie was truly amazed at the intricate work in both items. "Wow," she said. "You are really talented. Your family must be thrilled to receive these."

"Sometimes the younger ones roll their eyes when Grandma gives them another sweater," Genevieve said, "but I tell them if they don't like them they can give them away, and I've never given them one that isn't eventually worn to pieces, so I think they like them. I wanted to make sweaters for the new Harrington babies, but I'm not sure I'll have time before Christmas."

"Do you know a lot of other knitters?" Sadie asked. "No one at church has come forward to say they gave Anna those blankets."

"I'm in a knitting club that meets monthly at What's Needling You," Genevieve said. "I can ask them if anyone knows Anna and gave her those afghans."

"I'd appreciate it," Sadie said. "I'm running out of people to ask."

She was about to head for the door when a quilted wall hanging caught her eye. It was a view of Campfire Chapel atop its little crest with mountains in the background, stunning in its detail. "That's really lovely," she said. "Did you do that?"

"Goodness, no," Genevieve said. "That was done by Dottie Fraser. Do you know her?"

Sadie shook her head. "Is she local?"

"She's Anna Harrington's mother. She works at the drycleaner's, if you ever go in there. Her appliquéd quilts and wall hangings have won awards all over the state," Genevieve added. "She donated this one to the Heart Association benefit auction. I bid a ridiculous amount to win it." She grinned and winked. "But it was for charity, right? I just had to have it."

"I've never met Anna's mother," Sadie said. She was quite curious about the woman after hearing Anna's story of their falling-out.

"Very nice lady. I bet she's thrilled with those new babies of Anna's."

Genevieve apparently didn't know that the mother and daughter weren't on speaking terms.

"I've visited a couple of times," Sadie said. "They sure are precious."

"I think I'll wait until they're both home from the hospital. That way, I know I'll get to hold one." Her laugh was infectious, and Sadie had to grin.

Taking her leave of Genevieve, she headed out to the Placer Self-Storage facility along the highway to meet Buck Lanniter.

Parking outside the second row of units, Sadie walked into the climate-controlled hallway with a neat row of doors marching down each side. As Buck had said, number forty-one was on the left. He had beaten her there and was waiting outside the unit's door for her.

Buck Lanniter was tall and spare. He wore a faded Western denim shirt with patch pockets neatly tucked into darker blue denims. Fancy stitching defined the boots on his feet, and a huge rodeo buckle of "jeweler's gold," which was really red brass, with Old West floral designs in nickel silver and a Professional Rodeo Cowboy Association logo adorned his belt.

"Hi, Buck. I'm Sadie."

"Pleased ta meetcha, ma'am," he drawled.

"Were you a rodeo cowboy?" she asked, indicating his belt. It seemed a superfluous question, but she was always surprised at how many imposters would purchase prize buckles from down-at-the-heels cowboys and then claim them as their own wins.

Buck nodded. "Back in the day I won a bunch of bareback bronc titles. Then I tried my hand at bull riding, and after I got one too many bones broke, I decided to hang it up and do something else. My daddy was an antiques dealer, and I was loud and mouthy, so auctioneering seemed like a good fit."

Sadie had to laugh. "I guess so. Sounds like you've led an interesting life."

"And how about you?" He tipped back the black cowboy hat he wore. "How long's your shop been open? A decade, more or less, I'd say."

"Sounds as if you haven't completely gotten out of the business," Sadie teased. "That's about right. I was a teacher. After I retired, I opened the shop. And last week, someone brought me a gorgeous old armoire to restore. When I looked at it closely, I found a false bottom, beneath which were some family heirlooms, a photo and a christening gown. I'm trying to track down the original owners to see if they would like to have the items."

"That's a nice thing to do," the auctioneer pronounced. He fished out a key and opened the door to his locker. Then he flipped the light switch just inside the door, and an overhead light dispelled the dark shadows.

Inside the room, Buck had placed a number of metal storage shelves that contained boxes, all neatly labeled, along one wall. Various odds and ends filled the other side: a vintage rocking horse, an old oak chest on pedestal feet, several paintings, and more.

"You got any idea of the year?" Buck asked, looking down at her.

Sadie nodded. "Nineteen seventy-six. Spring of 'seventy-six. Probably April or May."

"And you know the purchaser?"

"Rhea Ressler."

Buck's eyes lit up. "Well, now, that's helpful. I thought you were going to try to get me to look through a whole decade's worth of paper." He stepped past her, removed a box from a shelf, and set it on top of the oak chest. Carefully wiggling the tight-fitting lid up and off, he thumbed through files and pulled out two. "I think this is the easiest way to do this. First we need to locate the sale, since you have that information. Then we'll go back and find out where I got the piece." He handed her a file. "This here's April, and I've got May. If we don't find what we're looking for, then we'll try March and June. Now, can you give me an exact description of this thing?"

"I can do better than that." As she recited the measurements and description of the armoire, Sadie tapped her phone and found several photos of the piece. She passed her phone to Buck so he could see them.

"Pretty thing," he said. "I almost think I remember it, but I'm not sure. It didn't come in with a whole house full of goods. I believe it was a single item."

Sadie glanced around, looking for a place to lay her folder so she could more easily page through it. Lanniter reached behind the shelving and pulled out a folder chair, which he opened and set to one side for her. "Be easier if you have a seat," he told her, pulling out a second one for himself.

"Thank you." Sadie sat and laid the file in her lap. Opening it, she found several sheets of paper stapled together, each with several columns on it. They included a short description of the item, an item number, the winning bid, and the name and address of the purchaser, along with the method of payment.

She scanned each sheet carefully, making sure she didn't overlook anything. On the third page, she found what she was looking for. "I believe I have it," she announced. "Here's the armoire. It was sold to Rhea and James Ressler on April twenty-fifth."

Buck slapped shut his file. "Good work. Now let me get my logbook, and we'll see where it came from."

Sadie's heartbeat quickened as Buck went to another box. He lifted out several large logbooks and opened them, then pulled one free. "Nineteen seventy-six," he said.

He returned to his seat and opened the large book on his lap. "You got a number for me? Usually nice pieces, especially unique ones like that, sold within a few weeks, so I think we'll find it in 'seventy-six. But it's possible it's back in 'seventy-five."

Sadie read off the number. "One-two-nine-eight-four-five-five. Is there any special meaning to that?"

Buck shook his head. "When I started up my business, the first item was number one. So we're hunting one in the second million items I handled."

"Wow." Sadie's eyes widened. "That's a lot of merchandise."

"Sure was." Buck chuckled as he paged through the book. "Here we go. Got a full description of the armoire, what I paid for it, et cetera. I bought it from a guy named Thomas Nally. Guess you want his address and phone number."

"You bet." Sadie grinned at Buck, realizing he was teasing her.

Buck read off the address. "Lived here in Silver Peak. Wonder if he's still around."

"I'll let you know." Sadie helped him replace the logbooks and files, and then preceded him from the storage room. She waited while he turned off the light and locked it, then offered him her hand. "Thank you, Buck. I really appreciate this. And I promise I'll let you know how this turns out."

"Nally," he said, as they headed toward the exterior door. "Wasn't there some lady writer named Nally, used to have pieces in the paper?"

"Lena Nally," Sadie said promptly. "She wrote a weekly column about life in the Rockies for years until she retired. I wonder if this Thomas is related to her."

18

Sadie got back in the Tahoe and headed straight home on Tuesday evening. As she pulled up her long driveway, she saw the mother bobcat on the porch again. The animal took off running when Sadie's vehicle came into sight, but Sadie felt sure she wouldn't go too far.

"Stick around, Mama," she muttered as she pulled in to the garage. "You're about to get your dearest wish."

The phone was ringing as she entered the house. "Hi, Sadie." The caller was Anna Harrington. "I was just writing a few thank-you notes, and I wondered if you'd had any luck figuring out who sent these little blankets."

"I didn't," Sadie said, "but would it be all right with you if I stopped by tomorrow?"

"Sure thing." Anna sounded delighted.

As quickly as she could, she took Hank out for a short walk. Then, shutting the dog in the kitchen one more time, she went to the front door and out on to the porch, where the baby bobcat waited. The little one was huddled in the back corner of the kennel, his customary spot when a human intruder entered his space.

Sadie smiled. "I'll see you around, little one," she said. "But hopefully not too close. You stay away from those traps now."

Opening the door, she propped it wide open and left it that way before going back inside. Then she took up a position at one side of the window so that she could see out without disturbing the curtain or making any noise.

She waited twenty minutes. Unfortunately, she didn't have a lot more time before she was going to have to feed Hank, grab a bite for herself, and head back into town.

And then the baby moved. He came to the front of the cage and sniffed, then stepped out on to the porch, and she heard him make a very plaintive, mewling cry. He moved to the edge of the porch and uttered the same sound again, and Sadie could see that he limped a little, still favoring the injured foot. She hoped Ben was right, and that the little one would continue to heal out in the wild.

Suddenly, she was there.

Sadie hadn't seen the mother bobcat approach. She hadn't heard a thing. With little fanfare, the mother leaped onto the porch and nuzzled her baby, sniffing him all over as he rubbed against her and made happy little noises Sadie could hear even through the glass.

Then the mother moved. She placed her mouth over the back of the baby's neck and lifted him in the air, dangling by the loose skin at the back of his neck. She leaped off the porch and ran across the driveway, bounding up the hill to the edge of the forest from which she had been keeping watch for several days.

At the very edge of the forest, Sadie saw her hesitate. She turned around and surveyed the house, and Sadie fancied that in her own feline way, the mother bobcat was expressing her gratitude for the care they'd given her little one.

She was smiling as she went to feed Hank. He'd be more than delighted that their guest was gone.

When dinner was over, she called Alice. "You'll never believe what I saw today," Sadie said the moment her daughter said hello.

Alice laughed. "Coming from you, I would believe anything, Mom. An-y-*thing*. So what did you find?"

"I went to the high school and met Trey Collins."

"Oh? Did he say anything about the money?"

Sadie laughed. "No. But then, I didn't ask him if he happened to steal my deposit."

"Oh, I guess not." Alice sounded a bit sheepish.

"Besides, I was afraid if he is 'the tall man' and he realized I owned the shop, he might get suspicious about why I'd suddenly showed up right after he was in there. But I did see what might be my deposit bag in his satchel," Sadie added.

"*What?*"

Sadie held the phone away from her ear, amused by her daughter's uncharacteristic squeal. "At least," she amended, "I saw a light gray leatherette-looking bag that resembled my deposit bag sticking out of his satchel."

"Oh my goodness," Alice said. "Are you going to tell the sheriff?"

"Not yet." Sadie shook her head, although her daughter couldn't see her. "I'm not sure if it's my deposit bag, and I wouldn't feel right about reporting him if he's innocent. Plus, it seems odd to me that he would still be carrying it around. Seems like something he'd want to deal with quickly and privately. In fact," she said, inspired, "any chance you're going over to the high school soon?"

"Actually, I have a meeting there tomorrow after school. Why?"

"I wish I had thought of this while I was in the room with him, but I'm just thinking of it now...I was thinking perhaps you could get a picture of his satchel and the bag in it. Maybe you could get someone to distract him, get him out of his room long enough for you to get a quick picture or two?"

"Mother..." Alice sounded as if she was reaching for patience. "Are you joking? I couldn't do that."

"All right." Sadie knew her daughter wasn't the risk-taking type. But she was somewhat disappointed. "Fair enough."

"It's just that I don't do things like that, Mom." Alice paused for a moment. "On the other hand, there's no reason I couldn't at least try to help. Does Donette Laurent still work in that department?"

"She does. I just saw her when I was there today. She could probably be talked into getting Trey out of his classroom. She'd think that was a great joke."

"All right." Alice sounded excited and determined now. "I'll do my best."

"Thanks, honey. If you can't, it's no problem. I appreciate your giving it a try. Luz also had an idea. I laughed at the time, but now I think it might be worth a shot."

"What's that?"

"Since Hector saw the tall man, I was wondering if we could find someone to try to do a sketch of his face."

"You mean, like a criminal profiler?"

"Yes, except obviously I can't ask the sheriff. And besides, I think that those kinds of artists are attached to federal agencies like the FBI, anyway. It would have to be someone local."

"I suppose I could ask the art teacher at my school if he'd consider trying it. It's a pretty specialized skill, but maybe he'd be interested enough to give it a shot." Alice sounded wholeheartedly enthusiastic now about the investigation. "I can let you know tomorrow."

"Thanks, honey. I appreciate it."

Sadie set down the phone, but an impulse had her picking it up again and dialing Anna Harrington's number. A few minutes later, she hopped in the Tahoe and headed to Anna's house for a short visit. Although she truly did want to support the young widow, she also wanted to find out how Anna would feel if her mother made contact. And she had to do it on the sly without raising Anna's hopes, because she didn't know when or if she would find it appropriate to speak to Dottie Fraser. Family misunderstandings were so tricky. While Sadie knew Anna clearly felt herself to be the wronged party, perhaps the mother thought Anna owed her an apology. Who knew?

Anna greeted her at the door. "Hi, Sadie. Any news on my mystery gift yet? I didn't hear anything from the church, so I assume either the sender isn't from Campfire Chapel, or they simply weren't at church on Sunday and didn't hear the announcement."

Sadie shook her head. "Not yet," she said. "I was really hoping that announcement would give us the answer." A thin cry from another room interrupted her, and she halted. "Oh, did one of the twins come home?"

Anna smiled. "Aaron was released this morning." She sounded surprisingly confident. "He's nursing really well. The lactation consultant stopped by this afternoon and said she could have saved herself the trip."

Sadie laughed with Anna, pleased and relieved. "And Alex?"

"If all goes well, he comes home tomorrow. His respiratory issues resolved much faster than the doctor expected." Anna said. "And then things should get interesting. Jeanne Sweeting has meals lined up for me for two months already, if you can believe that. More people are signing up to help, and I've had several folks stop by with casseroles I can freeze and eat as needed. I told Jeanne I didn't think I'd need anyone until there were two to take care of."

"Wonderful," Sadie said. "Anna, I know this is a touchy subject, but I wondered if you had heard from your mother yet."

Anna paused, and Sadie could almost feel her balloon of optimism leaking. "No. She was invited to the shower the church gave me, but she didn't come. I don't think I'll ever hear from her again."

"Do you want to? It sounds as if she hurt your feelings pretty badly."

"She did," Anna agreed. "But the thought of my boys growing up without ever knowing their maternal grandmother breaks my heart. I wish she hadn't been so rigid. She knew Grandma intended for me to have that ring, and I still don't understand why it became such a big deal."

"Who knows?" Sadie said. "It seems to me people who are grieving do an awful lot of irrational things. Years later, they look back and are sorry."

Another infant squawk made Sadie chuckle.

Anna turned away. "Please come in. I need to change Aaron's diaper and feed him, if you don't mind."

"Not at all," Sadie assured her. "Could I clean up your kitchen or throw in a load of laundry? Please put me to work."

Anna smiled. "The kitchen does need a little work, if you're sure you don't mind. It's amazing how one little person can take up so much time."

Anna's kitchen was by no means a disaster. It took Sadie only a few minutes to wash up the few dishes, empty the dishwasher, wipe down the counters, and set out clean dishtowels.

Back in the living room, she folded a few burp cloths and receiving blankets and set them within reach for Anna, who was settled on the couch nursing Aaron. On the coffee table was the scrapbook of her pregnancy that Anna had shown Sadie at the hospital.

"I'd like to look through this again." Sadie said. "It's such a lovely idea."

"Be my guest." Anna pointed at a small table by the window that appeared to be covered with scissors, paper, and other craft supplies. "I need to get working on the boys' baby album."

Sadie just shook her head. "You are amazingly industrious." She pulled the scrapbook toward her, taking more time than she had in the hospital to read each caption and examine it more closely. Anna really had a gift for design. Genevieve's words about Anna's mother came back to Sadie, and she realized that like her mother, Anna had a wide streak of creative ability.

Sadie drew a deep breath. "You must get your eye for design from your mother. I understand she's an award-winning quilter."

Anna was silent. She repeatedly smoothed over Aaron's tiny head where he lay nestled against her. Finally, she said, "Yes, she's very good at appliqué."

"Did she teach you to quilt?" She wasn't sure if she should try to keep Anna talking of her mother, but some part of her felt that the young mother needed to be reminded of good times that she had shared with her own mother.

"I was never very interested in quilting," Anna said. "But she encouraged me to work in whatever medium I wanted to try, like scrapbooking."

Sadie turned another page in the scrapbook. About to make some reply, her attention suddenly was riveted on a photo. It was of Anna and her mother. Sadie had noticed it before. Neither woman was smiling, though her mother's arm was about Anna's shoulders. Opposite it was the obituary notice she'd read before about Anna's grandmother.

But what really drew her attention was a table just behind them in the photo, on which lay a set of something that looked exactly like knitting needles.

Anna rose. "I'm going to change Aaron," she said. "I'm pretty sure he just left me a mess in this diaper too. I'll be back in a minute."

"All right," Sadie said absently.

The moment Anna left the room, Sadie zipped over to her capacious handbag lying on a table near the door. She dug deep and withdrew a magnifying glass that she kept there in case she was presented with antiques that had tiny writing or detail.

Quickly, she moved to the photo book she'd left lying open on the coffee table. Leaning close, she trained it on the photo of Anna and her mother. Now there was no question in her mind that there were knitting needles lying on that table.

The afghans she'd received from the mystery gift-giver lay on the coffee table. As Anna reentered the room with the baby, Sadie said, "Do you mind if I take a picture of these?"

Anna waved a hand. "Go right ahead. But why?"

Sadie shrugged, trying to seem nonchalant. "I thought if anyone wanted more information about them, I could show them a picture. Maybe that would jog someone's memory or something." Which wasn't quite the truth, but it certainly wasn't a lie, and she was afraid to get Anna's hopes up by mentioning her new theory.

She spread the little blankets out, one partially over the other, and took several photos with her phone. As she did so, she noted that they were fairly simple, both with the same stitch repeated over and over, and what looked like an equally simple edge stitch. It certainly didn't appear to be the work of someone as talented with knitting needles as Genevieve. It looked far more like the work of someone who wasn't highly skilled in the art of knitting yet...someone who was just learning to knit. And she knew just where to go tomorrow to find out whether her theory was correct.

As she headed up her driveway, it felt odd not to see the bobcat loping across the driveway and up the hill. She doubted she'd ever see either the mama or the baby again, although she might well *hear* them occasionally. And that was fine with her, she decided with a grin.

She took Hank for a brief walk, but it was beginning to get dark earlier, and they couldn't go far. Returning to the house, she hauled out her local telephone book. The name *Thomas Nally* had been lurking in the back of her mind ever since she and Buck had found that bill of sale earlier. Oh, how she hoped the man still lived in the area.

Running her finger down the column through the *Ns*, Sadie let out a whoop when she saw that there was a listing for Thomas Nally. Little butterflies dodged back and forth in her stomach as she punched in the number and held the phone up to her ear.

"Hello?" It was a woman's voice.

"May I speak to Thomas Nally, please?" Sadie crossed her fingers.

"He's not available right now, but this is his wife. Can I help you?"

"Mrs. Nally, my name is Sadie Speers. I own the Antique Mine in Silver Peak, and recently someone brought me an armoire to repair. I believe your husband may have sold it through Lanniter Auctions in 1952, and I have some questions about it."

"Oh! The armoire!" Mrs. Nally sounded unbelievably excited. "I've regretted selling that ever since we did it. We didn't have room for it at the time, but it was handed down through my family, and boy, have I ever felt guilty about letting it go. Is there any chance we could buy it back?"

Rather stunned by the outpouring of information, Sadie said, "I don't know. I'll be happy to approach the owner and ask. Mrs. Nally, I'd like to talk to you about that piece. Would it be possible for me to stop by tomorrow, perhaps right after I close my shop at five?"

"Of course. We'd love to find out where the armoire has been living since we sold it," Mrs. Nally said.

Sadie quickly confirmed the Nallys' address and set a time for as soon after five o'clock tomorrow as she could get there.

19

Sadie closed the Antique Mine for lunch on Wednesday and walked down the street to What's Needling You. Entering the little fabric and yarn shop, she found Gemma Meijor just finishing up a bargello quilting class, where the four people involved were making sets of handsome placemats.

"Hey, Sadie," Gemma said as soon as she broke free. "What's up? Do you have more tatting questions for me?"

Sadie chuckled. "Not this time." She fished her phone from her pocket. "Gemma, do you know Dottie Fraser?"

"Oh sure. She occasionally teaches an advanced appliqué class in my quilting series. Why?"

"Is quilting the only needle art she knows?"

Gemma shook her head. "I don't know what all she might be able to do, but I can tell you for sure that she has learned to knit, because she was in my Beginning and Intermediate Knitting courses last spring and summer."

Sadie swiped her phone several times and brought up the picture of Anna's blankets. "Do you know if she might have made these?"

"She sure did." Gemma beamed. "Her daughter is having twins—might have had them by now, come to think of it.

Anyway, Dottie was determined to have these blankets finished in time to give them to the babies." Her easy smile faded into a look of concern. "Why are you asking? Did something happen to Dottie?"

"Not that I know of," Sadie assured her. "Dottie and her daughter had a falling-out a few months ago, and Anna, the daughter, received these blankets anonymously."

"Oh, that's so sad." Gemma's face fell. "She was so excited about those babies. I hope they can patch it up."

"I hope so too," Sadie said. "Knowing her mother made these blankets may help. Thanks, Gemma."

As she left the shop to return to her own store, the cell phone rang.

Pulling it out, she recognized Alice's number. "Hi, honey."

"Hi, Mom. I don't have much time. I'm on my planning break, but I wanted to let you know the art teacher said he'd work with Hector and see if they could come up with a sketch of the man Hector saw in your shop. I already called Hector and he's coming in today after school to meet us and give it a try."

"That's wonderful!" Sadie beamed as she walked briskly back to the shop.

"He just wanted to make sure you understand he's never done this before, and that anything he produces could never be used for any legal proceedings."

"Oh, you can assure him it won't be. I just need to know if Trey Collins is the guy Hector saw."

"Well, if that's all you need, after the art session, I will show Hector a photo of all the new teachers that we received on the first day, and ask if he can identify anyone on there."

"Oh, brilliant. But go ahead and see what comes out of the art session first. That will be interesting."

"All right. Why don't you come for dinner? Then I can give you the update on all of our Sherlock Holmes–type sneakery."

"'Sneakery'?"

"Well, since there are no bodies involved, I didn't think 'skullduggery' sounded quite right. This is mere 'sneakery.'"

Sadie laughed out loud, causing several passersby to cast her odd looks. "See you later, Watson."

Later that afternoon, Hector came through the connecting door, which Sadie had left ajar to encourage browsers to enter the Antique Mine after they finished partaking of Luz's goodies.

"Sadie, I just came from the school. Guess what? I found the guy."

"You did?" Sadie clasped her hands together. "The art teacher did a terrific job with the sketch from your description and Alice was able to identify him?"

Hector grimaced. "Not so much. It turns out it's a lot harder to describe what I saw in a way that the guy was able to draw. The sketch ended up looking a lot like Mac Slattery, if you want the truth."

Sadie had to laugh. "So Alice showed you his picture then?"

"Alice showed me a bunch of pictures," he corrected, "and asked me if anyone in them looked familiar. I recognized one lady who comes in for coffee every Saturday and Sunday morning. And the other one I recognized was the tall guy who was in your shop."

"That's terrific, Hector. Thank you so much."

So what, she wondered, *is the next step?* Should she talk to the sheriff? No, better to wait until Alice got proof. If she could get a picture of Sadie's bank bag sticking out of his satchel, then Mac would have to question Trey Collins.

———

She couldn't wait for suppertime, so she could see if Alice had managed to get a photo of the bag. As she prepared to leave the shop at five, she thought about Anna Harrington and her mother again. She decided it was time to plant a seed.

She had not been able to gauge how receptive Anna might be to reconciling with her mother; the young woman shut down her emotions like a computer powering off any time the topic was introduced. But now that Sadie knew Dottie Fraser had made an overture, albeit an anonymous one, she thought Anna should be aware of that.

She called Anna and asked if it was all right to stop by, and when the young widow agreed, she decided to stop on her way to Alice's.

Anna must have been keeping a lookout, because she opened the door before Sadie could even knock.

"Do you have news about the blankets?" she asked.

"You're perceptive," Sadie said, smiling. "I do."

"Great. I don't know why I'm so hung up on figuring out who sent them. New mother hormones or something."

Sadie laughed. "It's natural to want to know where such a beautiful gift came from. After all, they were handmade."

"So…?" Anna rubbed her hands together in anticipation. "Come. Sit. Speak."

They chuckled together as Sadie followed her into the living room, where Aaron lay sleeping in a little bassinette. Sadie took a seat on the couch, pulling the pregnancy scrapbook toward her as she did so. "When I looked through this yesterday, something caught my eye," she told Anna, leafing through the book to the page with the photo of Anna and her mother. She laid the book in Anna's lap and tapped the photo with her index finger. "Look at the table," she said. "What do you see?"

Anna's face immediately pokered up. "I don't think this photo is relevant to..."

"Just tell me what you see on the table," Sadie said gently.

There was a silence. "Knitting needles," Anna said finally. "My mother told me she was going to take a Beginning Knitting class at What's Needling You. I forgot."

"Yesterday," Sadie said, "after I left you, I went down to What's Needling You and asked Gemma, the owner, if she knew your mother. She does. I guess your mother sometimes teaches an appliqué quilting class there. She also took both the Beginner and the Intermediate Knitting courses earlier this year. I showed her the photo I took of your blankets, and she confirmed that they were made by your mother during her classes."

Anna reached for a tissue on the end table. Sadie saw that her eyes were filled with tears. "Oh, Sadie, do you really think my mother made those?"

"I'm certain she did," Sadie said gently. She let the silence hang. Any further move had to be Anna's decision.

Finally, Anna said, "Do you think she wants me to get in touch with her?"

"I can't speak for her," Sadie said, "I've never been in a situation like this. But I think it's a positive sign that she gave these to the boys, don't you?"

"Even without letting me know they came from her?" Anna's question sounded heartbroken. Then, quietly, she said, "I miss her."

"And I suspect she misses you and would love to be involved in these babies' lives. Why else would she have sent you the blankets?"

Alice sighed. "You think I should contact her."

Sadie shook her head. "Not unless you feel ready. But I think it would be lovely if the two of you could reconcile."

Sadie didn't get a chance to discuss the "sneakery" with Alice until after supper. During the meal, Sara reported that she and her friend Eve Avery were nearly finished with their English project. "She'd read almost all those books in less than a week," she said with awe.

"If she's anything like her brother," Theo put in, "she's a brain. Tobias is really smart."

"His mother said he's gotten some scholarships and is putting himself through college," Sadie said. "It's hard to imagine that selling ice cream is very profitable."

Alice nodded. "Especially since he also has to maintain that truck and put gas in it, as well as pay for his inventory."

"But he's going to the community college, so he doesn't have room and board and all those expenses," Theo told them, unaware that Sadie already knew that. "And at the awards assembly last year, I heard he got all kinds of scholarship money."

"And if the family qualifies for FAFSA assistance, as well, he may be doing all right," Alice pointed out.

After they cleared the table and the kids headed to their respective rooms to work on their homework, Sadie couldn't stand it any longer. "So," she asked, "were you able to get photos of the bag today?"

"I was." Alice snatched up her phone and proudly found the desired pictures. "I told Donette I needed a few minutes in his room to help you with something. She didn't even ask why, just told him she needed him to help her hang some posters, and he went right into her room."

"Way to go." Sadie beamed. "So was the satchel open?"

Alice nodded. "It was in almost the same exact position you described to me yesterday, and it doesn't close all the way because the gray bag sticks out of the top. I got three pictures—and then I was afraid I'd get caught, so I skedaddled out of there. As I went by Donette's doorway, she gave me a thumbs-up." Alice grinned.

Sadie scanned the pictures as Alice pulled each of them up. The gray leatherette bag was clearly visible in each photo, which Alice had taken from different angles. "May I?" she asked her daughter, who handed her the phone.

"Sure. What are you looking at?"

Sadie zoomed in on the first photo. Her bank's logo should be easy to see, or at least part of it should be.

But instead, what she saw was an unmistakable logo that was *not* that of her bank, but the one used by the American Red Cross.

"What?" she murmured. Quickly, she looked at the next picture, and then at the third and final one. In each picture, from every angle, the Red Cross, bright red with the four points of the "cross" all the same length, was plainly in view. In two of the three, colored pencils in several hues could be seen peeking from the bag.

Alice, leaning over her shoulder, murmured, "Oh dear."

"Oh dear, indeed." Sadie hadn't realized until that moment how much she had been presuming that Trey Collins was the thief who had stolen her deposit. "Tell me what you see," she demanded. She was still having trouble accepting the fact that she still had no information on who had stolen her money.

"I see a frequent blood donor who uses his free gift to store art pencils," Alice said in a wry tone. "My first attempt at evidence-gathering appears to have been a miserable failure."

Mother and daughter looked at each other and burst out laughing.

"It was worth a try," Sadie finally managed.

"But you got no information," Alice said. "I'm so sorry."

"*Au contraire*," Sadie said. "I have learned that Trey Collins is not carrying around my missing deposit bag in his satchel. That's information, even if it's not the type I was expecting."

"What will you do now?" Alice asked.

Sadie shrugged. "I guess I'm back to square one. The only thing I can think of to do is to call those people I met at the Heritage Festival who were in my shop that day, and ask again if there is anything else they can think of that they might have noticed."

"Do it right now," Alice urged. "I'm invested in this now. I want to hear what they have to say."

Sadie chuckled. "All right." Pulling her own phone from her handbag, she found the number she had saved in her phone and dialed. Moments later, a woman's voice said, "Hello?"

After identifying herself, Sadie said, "I'm sorry to bother you again, but I am still trying to track down that missing deposit I told you about."

"We're happy to help," Sue Clapsaddle said, "but I am not sure what else we are going to be able to tell you."

"You mentioned the tall man who was in the shop," Sadie said. "I'm pretty sure that he isn't the thief."

"My husband said he didn't see how he could be," Sue said, "since he left when we did."

"He what?" Sadie was stunned. How had she missed getting that information before? She could have saved herself and Alice both a lot of time and... and *sneakery*. "The tall fellow left when you did?"

"He did," Sue confirmed. "He actually preceded us out the door."

Which might explain why Sadie hadn't noticed him. "Was there anyone else, anyone at all, who was still there when you left?"

"Well, there was that boy," Sue said.

"What boy? I didn't see a boy in the shop." Sadie was beginning to wonder if she'd been temporarily blind that day, given the people she appeared to have missed seeing.

"The boy who came in behind us," Sue clarified. "He was still in the shop when we left. Young teen, maybe, with a cap on?"

Sadie gasped. "I thought that was your eldest child."

"Oh no. We only have two children," Sue said. "You saw them at the festival last Saturday."

Sadie's mind was a whirling mass of confusion, as she thanked Sue for her time and concluded the call. Was this the answer? She remembered a young teen boy coming in with the family, slouching along behind them as if he didn't want anyone to know he was with them... because he wasn't?

It made perfect sense. Her thief had entered with that family, but he didn't leave with them.

20

———

"WHAT DID SHE SAY?" ALICE STOOD, HANDS ON HER HIPS, expectantly.

Sadie shook her head, feeling dazed. "When that family came into the shop right before closing on Thursday, I thought there were five of them. The oldest child was a young teen boy. But Sue just told me they have no son of that age. Their children are the younger two who were with them at the festival on Saturday. According to Sue, the tall man—Trey Collins—left the store right before them, but the other young person was still inside when they left."

"Which means he may be your thief," Alice said. "The fifth person, whom you think is a young teen—or at least looked like one—may have hidden in the shop."

"Exactly."

"Where?"

"Where did he hide? I don't know. Maybe in the back room." The thought gave her the shivers. She recalled the sound, which she had thought was simply the spool of thread rolling off the worktable. Had she walked into the back at the wrong time, she could have found herself in a struggle with a thief. And while it was true that he had looked like a young boy, the reality could be far different.

"I wonder if he was a tourist," Alice said.

"But how would he have known my end-of-day routine?" Sadie asked.

"Maybe he didn't. It could have been a crime of opportunity," Alice theorized. "It's reasonable to expect that most shopkeepers would be handling money at the end of the day. Maybe he just hid and waited for a chance to snatch and run."

"I like that better than thinking it could have been someone who watched me for days, learning my routine," Sadie confessed.

Sara came into the kitchen then, carrying her laptop. "Hey, Grandma. Want to read my part of the final Laura Ingalls Wilder report?"

"Sure," Sadie said. She took a seat at the table and accepted the little laptop. Then she looked at Sara again. "I forgot to tell you I released the baby bobcat last night."

"Was the mom there?" Sara asked.

"Close by," Sadie said. "She came and picked him up by the scruff of his neck and carried him away."

Alice laughed. "Sometimes I get that urge."

"I'm too big to scruff," Sara said, grinning. Then her eyes lit up as familiar music was heard in the distance. "Hey, it's the ice-cream truck. Sometimes Eve helps Tobias. Maybe she's with him tonight." She bolted to her feet. "Come on, Grandma. Let's go get ice cream."

"Get me a Nutty Bar," Alice called as Sara rushed out the door. Sadie followed more slowly as Sara hurried to the ice-cream truck. Its eye-popping colors and blaring organ tune drew every kid in the neighborhood...and more than a few adults, she noted, smiling.

She watched as folks placed themselves in an orderly line. At the window, Tobias was smiling and chatting as he served his customers. It wasn't until he tossed a comment over his shoulder that Sadie realized there was a second person in the truck. Then she recalled that Eve might be helping Tobias, as she joined Sara in line.

When their turn came, Sara leaned to the side so that she could see into the truck. "Hi, Eve."

Sadie caught the flash of a shy smile as the girl stepped into view. "Hi, Sara. Have a craving tonight?"

Sara grinned. "When *don't* I have a craving for ice cream?" To Tobias, she said, "Two Nutty Bars and—what do you want, Grandma?"

"An ice-cream sandwich," Sadie said to Tobias. "Please."

A stifled sound from the back of the truck had her glancing back at Eve questioningly. Eve's eyes looked wide and startled. They were the same striking, misty green as that of the other members of her family. "Hello, Eve. I'm sorry we couldn't give you a ride the other night."

"That's all right. I needed the exercise." The girl ducked her head, her long blonde hair falling in wings on either side of her face, effectively hiding her expression. "I'd better get back to work," she mumbled to Sara, and she turned and headed for the darkest corner of the truck.

As they walked back to the house a moment later, unwrapping their treats and taking first bites, Sara said. "Well, that was weird, even for Eve. She's usually not quite *that* shy."

"I don't think she realized you had anyone with you at first," Sadie said thoughtfully.

Alice met them at the door, hand out.

"We forgot to get you anything," Sara told her.

Alice mimed cuffing her daughter along the side of her head. "You'd better not have."

Sara grinned, handing over the Nutty Bar. "As if I could ever forget you, Mom." She stretched up and kissed her mother's cheek.

"They certainly seem like nice kids," Sadie said to Sara. "Does your friend help her brother with the truck often?"

"Recently, she's been helping a lot," Sara told her. "Eve said Tobias almost didn't have enough money for his college tuition this fall, so she's been trying to help him as much as possible."

Sara dropped her empty ice-cream wrapper into the trash can, pulled a lip-gloss tube from her pocket, and applied it to her lips. "I need to get back to work," she said. Before she sat down at her laptop again, she came over and wrapped her arms around Sadie from behind, hugging her hard.

"What's this for?" Sadie asked.

"Just because I love you." Sara began to straighten.

"Hey." Sadie sniffed. "What's that smell?" She sniffed again, and she was certain the scent was the same one she'd noticed the day her deposit had been stolen. And the same one she'd caught a whiff of the night of the performance at the opera house. "Is it strawberry perfume?" she asked.

"Strawberry lip gloss," Sara said. "Do you like it? All my friends wear it. Everyone loves it."

"It's unforgettable," Sadie said, recalling the scent that had lingered in her shop last Thursday. Her youthful thief might have been wearing it, but— "Do boys wear it?"

Sara shook her head, giggling. "No, Grandma. It's definitely for girls."

Sadie headed home—again—after finishing her ice cream, thinking all the way about the young man with the green eyes, someone who might have left behind a strawberry scent, and a thief who hadn't left her shop when the Clapsaddles and Trey Collins had.

At the shop on Thursday morning, Sadie called Rhea Ressler. "Rhea," she said, "I may have a buyer for the armoire if you're serious about selling it."

"I guess I am," Rhea said.

"I recently learned who the original owners were, and they've expressed an interest in getting it back. Apparently it was a family heirloom they sold, and they've regretted it ever since."

"I'd be willing to sell it back to them," Rhea said. "I love the thing, but nobody in my family wants it, and I am determined to get rid of some of the accumulated clutter I've got from forty-plus years of marriage."

Sadie made appropriately regretful comments, but inside she was jumping for joy. What a treat it would be to tell the Nallys the armoire could be theirs again.

"What do you think I should charge?" Rhea asked.

Sadie reviewed the armoire's condition with Rhea, told her what comparable pieces in the shop had sold for, and suggested a range, and Rhea decided upon a figure. "You can quote that," she said, "if they're interested."

Recalling the excitement in Mrs. Nally's voice, Sadie suspected they would be very interested, but she merely agreed to call Rhea if she had an offer.

At lunch, Sadie closed the shop and walked several blocks over to the only dry cleaner in Silver Peak. The business had a bell over the door to alert the staff, as she did.

A woman with dark hair streaked liberally with silver came toward the counter from the depths of the store with a friendly smile. "Hi. Here for pickup?"

"No," Sadie said. "I'm looking for Dottie Fraser."

The woman's smile remained, but her eyebrows rose. "I'm Dottie. How can I help you?"

Sadie cleared her throat and extended her hand. "I'm Sadie Speers. I go to Campfire Chapel." She paused. "You're Anna's mother, right?"

The woman's smile collapsed, and her lips quivered. "Yes. I believe I may have seen you there when I was visiting."

Sadie looked at her steadily, compassionately. "I've seen your grandsons. I've held them."

Tears swam in Dottie's brown eyes, and in that moment, Sadie knew there was hope. "Are they well?" She bit her lip. "You probably know what a terrible person I am, or you wouldn't be here. Just tell me if the babies are okay."

"They are doing wonderfully," she said to Anna's mother. "Wouldn't you like to see them?"

"I wish I could." Dottie half-turned away and wrapped her arms around her own waist. "But I was awful to Anna. You don't understand. She would never want me in her life again."

"I think you're wrong." Sadie kept her voice soft, but she was determined. "The Anna I know is longing to have a relationship with you, for her sons to have a grandma." She paused. "You made the little blankets, didn't you?"

Dottie nodded through her tears.

"They were beautiful. Anna was really touched that you sent them."

"How did she know?"

"She remembered you had started knitting," Sadie said. "Gemma Meijor verified that you had made them." Deliberately, she downplayed her part in the search for the giver of the blankets.

"I want to see Anna and the babies," her mother said. "But what would I say to her? When my mother died, I went a little crazy. It was so sudden. She had coffee with me one morning and she said she didn't feel well, that she had really bad indigestion. As she was walking back to her car, she collapsed. It was a heart attack. She was gone by the time the EMTs arrived."

There was a counter between them, or Sadie would have put an arm around her. "That's often the way heart disease happens in women. We don't get many second chances," she said quietly. "I'm so sorry."

"I wasn't ready to lose her, you see." Dottie sobbed once and clapped a hand over her mouth. "I can't even explain to myself why I behaved so badly. I'm sure Anna will never forgive me."

"You raised a wonderful young woman," Sadie said. "She might surprise you."

Dottie was silent for a long moment, composing herself. "Maybe I should call and see if I can visit."

Sadie smiled. "What do you have to lose?"

There was another short silence. "Nothing." Dottie straightened her shoulders. "You're absolutely right. I have nothing at all to lose. Because without family, I have nothing."

"The second twin came home from the hospital today, I believe," Sadie said. She hauled out her phone, smiling. "Would you like to see a picture of them?"

Dottie's eyes widened, once again reminding Sadie of Anna. "Oh yes," she said, clasping her hands together.

As Sadie shared the photos she had taken, Dottie looked over at her. "I know this sounds silly, but would you go with me to Anna's house?"

"Of course," Sadie said.

Dottie took a slow, deep breath. "I'll call her right now. Be back in a minute." As she left the counter and headed for the back of the dry-cleaning shop, Sadie reflected that Dottie apparently hadn't deleted Anna's phone number in the time they'd been estranged. That was a good sign.

She examined a flier for wedding gown preservations done by the company and looked at a photo album with several examples of preserved dresses. Before she could grow bored or even restless, Dottie came rushing back to the front counter. "She said yes," she said. "She'd be happy to have me visit. Is tonight okay?"

"Sure." Sadie had planned a quiet evening at home, but really, quiet was overrated. "I'll be happy to go with you. What time?"

"How's seven?"

"I'll meet you there."

Not long after lunch, Sheriff Slattery came into the shop.

"Hi, Mac," Sadie said.

"Sadie." He tipped his hat. "Sorry to tell you I don't have anything new to report about your missing money. I called that couple you talked to, but they didn't recall anything very helpful. And I re-canvassed the other shops like I said I would, but no one recalls seeing a tall fellow."

"I have something to share with you though," she said. She told him about last night's call to Sue Clapsaddle without sharing her earlier suspicions about Trey Collins. Since he clearly was innocent, there was no point in mentioning him to the sheriff.

"What do you remember about the boy?" Mac asked, getting straight to the point. "If he was still in the shop after closing, he's probably the one who took your money."

Sadie shook her head. "Not much. He had on a black watch cap, even though it's warm for that."

"A lot of kids today wear those," Mac said.

"Anyway, he had a little blond hair sticking out from under it, and big green eyes. Light eyes, very striking. Jeans and an oversized dark T-shirt, I believe. Maybe sneakers?" She shrugged. "I wasn't really examining him so I could describe him to the police later, you know?"

Mac allowed a small smile to crack his impassive expression. "That's a pretty good description for someone who wasn't paying attention. How tall?"

Sadie hesitated. "Maybe a hair shorter than I am? Not very tall at all, I guess, for a man. But as I said, I had the feeling he was young. Maybe still in his early teens even."

"Weight?"

"Not much," Sadie said. "But I couldn't put a number to it. Certainly no more than one-forty, and probably not even that much. He seemed scrawny under that big shirt."

"Any jewelry or unusual features on the clothing that caught your eye?"

Sadie shook her head. "No jewelry—wait. He might have had an earring. Maybe a stud? But I'm not sure about that. And the clothing wasn't memorable at all, except that it seemed huge and baggy. Mostly, the clothing was just dark except for—oh yes, I *do* remember. White sneakers. Like tennis shoe sneakers."

"Tennis shoes? Not many young men wear tennis shoes anymore."

"Maybe they were clunkier. Sports sneakers. I really can't tell you for sure, Mac. I'm sorry."

"No problem. You're doing fine. Anything else? Anything at all. Tattoos?"

"Not that I can think of. His eyes were his most unusual feature. And I didn't see him smile or really even change expression. I just assumed he was being a typical teen and trying to pretend he wasn't really associated with his family. But as it turns out, they weren't his family at all."

"Any idea where he could've hidden?"

Sadie looked around the shop. "He wasn't very big, and I wasn't looking for someone. He could simply have been standing behind some of the bigger items of furniture, I guess. Some of them have cupboards large enough to conceal a small person, but I think I'd have heard that. Most of them have some squeaks and clunks, you know?"

She gestured for Mac to follow her to the place she'd been the day the deposit bag had been taken. "I was standing here talking to Luz. We both had our backs to the shop. And although Hector glanced in at one point, he easily could have missed a small person hiding."

Mac turned and surveyed the shop. "And if he just reached up and slipped the bag off the counter, he probably could have even crawled into the back room without giving himself away."

"And then let himself out the back door. Hard to believe no one saw him."

"You'd be surprised," Mac said, "at how often people completely overlook the obvious."

Left alone in the shop, Sadie, deep in thought, pulled out the silver polish, polishing cloths, and an old toothbrush and started working on erasing the tarnish from an elaborately wrought set of William IV silver candlesticks on square pedestal bases. Surely someone must have noticed someone running out the back. He certainly hadn't flown away or made himself invisible.

———

The rest of the afternoon dragged. Sadie couldn't wait for her visit to the Nallys. At long last, she gathered her things and locked the shop, taking with her the christening gown, the *memento mori*, and the handwritten prayer. She told herself not to get excited. The Nallys would probably know very little of the armoire's early history, and it was highly doubtful that they would be able to shed any light on who E.M. was. But a gal could hope.

She drove to the Nally home on a quiet street not far from where Alice lived. The Nallys lived in a wood-sided rancher surrounded by thick, well-trimmed shrubbery. A camper was parked on an extended lot next to the driveway.

Sadie got out and approached the front door. As she rang the bell, the inner door opened and a short, smiling woman in jeans and a soft pink sport shirt waved at her. She proceeded to hold open the storm door. "Hello. Come in. I'm Lena Nally, and this is my husband, Tom." She indicated a silver-haired man only a few inches taller than she.

He stepped forward and shook Sadie's hand. "Hey there. Nice to meet you. My wife's been over the moon since you called and mentioned the armoire."

Sadie laughed, as the couple ushered her into a comfortable living room. "I'm delighted to have found you. I'm sure you have questions, and I also have some for you. But first, I must tell you, Mrs. Nally, that I read your column for many years and enjoyed each and every one. It was a sad day for the *Sentinel* when you retired."

"Thank you." Lena flushed with pleasure. "It was a difficult decision, but after Tom retired, we wanted to be able to travel and visit our children and grandchildren, and it was time for me not to be tied to a weekly production schedule."

Sadie knew from recalling the column that Lena had retired close to two decades ago, but the couple still radiated a youthful, vibrant energy.

"Please sit." Lena indicated a chair and perched on a love seat close to her. "You talk first. Where did you find the armoire? You said someone who owns it brought it to you to repair?"

Sadie grinned. She explained how Rhea had brought the piece to her to repair. "But before I go further, may I ask you a few questions?"

"Certainly." Both of the Nallys nodded as Lena answered.

Sadie glanced around the room—and froze.

"Where did you get that?" she blurted, indicating a framed piece of needlework on the wall.

Lena looked a little confused, but she rose and went to the piece, and Sadie went with her. A chill ran up her spine as she recognized the same tatted design, the pretty lacy heart that was sewn on to the front of the christening gown.

"I can see why you would notice this, as someone who treasures antiques. This is a family heirloom," Lena told her. "It's a type of needlework called tatting, and it's over a hundred years old. It was done by my grandfather's first wife, who died very young. My mother was the daughter of his second wife, so she wasn't really related to me, but my family has treasured this for many years."

Sadie was so happy she had to swallow and take a deep breath. She was convinced now that she had found the family to whom the items in the armoire belonged.

"It's utterly stunning," Sadie said. "And especially precious in light of what I have to share with you. Are you related to the Maxfields who used to be so prominent in Silver Peak, Lena?"

Lena looked surprised. "Why, yes. How did you know? There are no Maxfields around here anymore, and I thought the name had been largely forgotten."

"It's important to this story," Sadie told her. "How, exactly, are you related?"

"My mother was a Maxfield before her marriage," Lena said. "Her name was Iris. She was the only daughter of Carlton Maxfield and his second wife, Ellen Mary Murphy Maxfield. His first wife, Fannie Hayes Maxfield, was the woman who did that lovely tatting."

"Ellen Mary Murphy!" Sadie couldn't hide her surprise. "I thought her name was Bridget." *E.M.,* was all she could think. Finally she had found E.M.

21

LENA LAUGHED. "A LOT OF PEOPLE BACK THEN CALLED ELLEN Mary 'Bridget,' because she was Irish and she had been the nanny to the first Mrs. Maxfield's baby daughter, Magdalena. Bridget, I have gathered, was sort of a derogatory term for working-class Irish nannies, and a lot of the snobby upper class probably never even knew her real name. As I said, she was Magdalena's nanny, but Magdalena died as an infant, and then Fannie, her mother, died just a few months later. My grandmother, Ellen Mary, married Carlton two years later, and my mother was born in 1899. She was their only child. And believe me, that marriage was, according to my relatives, a *huge* scandal at the time. It was quite unfashionable for a well-heeled gentleman to marry an Irish immigrant. It put them beyond the pale, and he was never invited to the social events of the most exclusive set again. Isn't that the silliest thing you've ever heard?"

Lena waved a hand as if to bat away the small talk. "But we can talk about this more later." She drew Sadie back to her seat. "I am dying to hear the story of the armoire. Tell me, have you asked the owners if they'd consider selling it?"

"I have," Sadie said. "And they are." She had to restrain herself from babbling all the information she had yet to share, but she wanted to tell the story properly.

"Oh, wonderful!" Lena clapped her hands to her mouth, and her eyes filled with tears. "My mother treasured that armoire, and I never should have sold it. We'll pay anything to get it back."

"Well, not anything," Tom said, laughing, "but we're willing to make a generous offer."

"I imagine we can come to an agreement," Sadie assured the couple. "But first, let me tell you what I found when I examined the piece."

"Oh no. Is it damaged?" Lena demanded.

Tom put a hand on his wife's knee. "Let the lady talk," he commanded.

"It's not damaged at all," Sadie told the couple. "A few minor things that would have occurred with any use through the years. But as I took a look at it, I realized there was a false floor in it."

"A false floor? Was it there when we owned it? I never saw anything like that, did you?" Lena turned to Tom.

"Nope." Tom shook his head. "I imagine that was put in after we sold it."

"Actually, it's been there since at least the turn of the last century," Sadie told him.

Tom looked astonished. "How can you tell that?"

Sadie grinned. "Because I found some very special things hidden beneath that false bottom that have been in there since 1899, or pretty close to that date."

"You're kidding. What did you find?" Lena leaned forward.

Sadie picked up the large handbag she had brought along and pulled out a large manila envelope, into which she had placed the heirlooms. "Brace yourself." Carefully, she withdrew the photograph of Fannie and Magdalena Maxfield. "This is called a *memento mori*," she said. "I believe this is Carlton Maxfield's first wife, Fannie, with their baby girl, Magdalena." She went on to explain that the child in the photo was already deceased, and how she had visited the photographer's studio to uncover who the pair were.

Lena studied the photo. "Dear little soul," she said. "I wouldn't be surprised if her mother died of a broken heart." Then Sadie drew the christening gown from the envelope. She had folded it carefully in a clear bag to keep it safe, and she gently laid it across the coffee table before them. "This, I believe, was Magdalena's christening gown, the one she is wearing in that photograph. Look at the tatted design sewn on to the breast."

Lena gasped and clutched her husband's hand. "Tom! It's the same as the tatting we have." Together, the elderly couple studied the tiny garment, awe in their faces.

"This is amazing. Just amazing," Tom kept murmuring, while his wife simply wept.

"There's one more thing." Sadie withdrew the letter. "This was written, I believe, by your grandmother, Ellen Mary. If you look, the author signs with the initials *E.M.* When I researched the Maxfields in newspaper articles, she was always called Bridget, so I didn't connect it until just now. But this makes perfect sense. If Ellen Mary was Magdalena's nanny, she would have known—and from this letter, we know she loved—both Fannie and Magdalena."

Silently, Lena and Tom read the lovely little prayer with its short preface. Both of them had tears on their cheeks when they looked up. Silently, Lena got up and retrieved a box of tissues from a corner desk. She blotted her tears daintily while Tom blew his nose and mopped at his eyes with a handkerchief he had pulled from a pocket.

"I can tell you a little more about this," she told Sadie. "My mother told me once that my grandmother treasured the armoire, but my grandfather couldn't bear the sight of it. She kept it locked away in a little-used attic room. I imagine, if it was something Fannie loved and used for her child, that it would have been hard for him to see."

"It sounds as if Ellen Mary might have shown him the christening gown," Sadie said. "Maybe hoping to use it for their child?"

"But he couldn't bear it," Lena concluded. "And when he wanted her to get rid of the things that reminded him of those losses, my grandmother hid them away. That fits with what I know of her from my mother's family. She was someone who cherished tradition and would never have wanted to let something so precious go." She made a wry face. "Which makes me feel even worse for ever letting that armoire be sold."

Tom patted her shoulder. "But we're going to get it back, and that's the important thing. We can give it to our Magdalena now."

"Your Magdalena?" Sadie blinked. "What do you mean?"

Lena chuckled. "Oh, I guess I neglected to tell you that detail. My mother, Iris, named me Magdalena, Lena for short, to remember her little half sister who didn't get a chance to live very long. I gave the name to my own daughter as a middle name. Her daughter is also a Magdalena, but we call her Maggie. And she's expecting her first child any day now. If it's a girl like the ultrasound showed, she will be called Magdalena."

Sadie was moved beyond words at the coincidence that had led her to find this family…only she knew better. This was no coincidence. There had been a divine hand leading her. No wonder she had felt so compelled to find E.M.

"I wanted to find out who E.M. was and restore the things I found to Fannie and Magdalena's family, if there was still anyone living," Sadie said, "but I confess this is much, much more than even I had hoped for—and I'm generally known as a starry-eyed optimist."

They all chuckled.

"It all makes sense to me," Lena said. "My mother said my grandmother Ellen had been very close to her employer's wife, and of course, she would have loved that baby, being her nanny. Even though she went on marry Carlton and start a family of their own, she never forgot Fannie and the first Magdalena."

"I read in a census report that both your grandmother and grandfather passed away in a smallpox epidemic."

"Yes. My mother was only five. She was raised by Carlton's family. They had opposed the marriage vehemently, but after Carlton and Ellen died, they were deeply sorry they had wasted those years not speaking. From everything my grandmother said, she had a wonderful childhood despite being orphaned young."

Sadie made a mental note to tell Roz that they'd been mistaken about the elder Maxfields' treatment of their orphaned grandchild. "Thank you," she said, reaching out to clasp Lena's hands in hers. "Thank you so very much for sharing your family's story with me."

"No, thank *you*." Lena clung to her hands, gripping tightly. "There is no way to tell you how deeply grateful we are that you persevered in trying to find the family to whom these treasures belonged. I know a lot of antique dealers would have just kept them and sold them."

Thomas and Lena stood, as Sadie did. "Let me send along a quart of our homemade ice cream. We just made it this afternoon and put it in the deep freeze, so it should be hard enough now for a short trip."

"Oh yes." Lena bubbled over with happiness. "It's a family recipe. Who knows? It could even have been handed down from Ellen Mary Murphy Maxfield!"

Sadie drove home for dinner feeling euphoric with pleasure. She could hardly believe she had finally found E.M., and that Fannie and Magdalena's sad story had come to such a sweet close. They had been loved, and in the end, Sadie felt she could be happy with that.

As she placed the homemade ice cream in the freezer to share with her family later, something teased at the edges of her brain. Ice cream... the ice-cream truck... *yes.*

She drove back into town after supper and a short hike with Hank, feeling that her day had disintegrated into a dash from one activity to the next. *It's your own fault,* she reminded herself. But really, she couldn't have said no to Anna's mother, could she have? The poor woman needed support. Sadie sensed she was deeply regretful for causing the rift with her daughter, but more than that, Sadie feared that Dottie felt she should be punished for it. And Sadie wanted to help her past that feeling. Everyone made mistakes, and she knew Anna had a big enough heart to forgive Dottie... if Dottie could forgive herself.

When Dottie joined her on the sidewalk in front of Anna's house, the woman was visibly shaking. Before she could get any more nervous, Sadie turned and headed up the sidewalk to the house, so that Dottie had to follow or be left behind.

Before they could even ring the bell, Anna opened the door. Her face crumpled, and she put a hand over her mouth. "Come in," she managed.

As they walked inside, Dottie said, "Anna, can you ever forgive me? I'm so ashamed of the way I acted..."

"Of course." Anna hastily handed Aaron to Sadie, and then the two women fell into each other's arms.

Sadie beamed. It was exactly the reunion for which she had hoped.

Eventually, Anna stood back.

"Mom, would you like to hold Aaron? I'll go get Alex."

Dottie gently took the baby Anna settled in her arms, looking down at him with such a tender expression Sadie felt her throat form a lump. "He's beautiful," Dottie whispered.

"Why don't we sit down?" she said to Dottie, leading the way toward the sofa in the front room, as Anna vanished back down the hallway.

They sat. Dottie regarded the tiny boy in her arms. "He looks so much like Anna did as an infant."

Sadie watched as the grandmother gently rocked the infant while he stretched and yawned. "God certainly knew what He was doing when He made babies so precious and helpless, didn't He? I've signed up to spend some nights here helping Anna. I can't wait."

"Spend nights?" Dottie echoed. "Oh, that's thoughtful. She does need a good bit of help now."

"I do." Anna had returned to the room. She stood in the doorway, patting the other baby, whom she held against her shoulder. "My church family has taken me under their wing and is providing assistance until I can manage two infants on my own."

Dottie looked at her daughter, and there were tears in her eyes, although her voice was strong and steady. "I hope there will be room for a grandmother on that schedule. Anna, I owe you an apology. I owe you more apologies than there are hours in the day to say them to you."

Anna looked at her sadly. "Why did you do it, Mom? Grandma had told me she wanted me to have that ring since I was old enough to remember."

Dottie began to cry. "I don't know, honey. I was so shocked and upset when Grandma died so suddenly, I just sort of snapped. All I could think was that I didn't want to lose even one little thing that belonged to her. It wasn't rational. I wouldn't have had the courage to come here if Sadie hadn't come to see me. I am hoping you have a big enough heart to forgive me."

"Only if you'll forgive me too," Anna said tenderly. "I said some pretty harsh things, and I know I made you feel that I would never be willing to forget what happened." She held the second twin out so that Dottie could see him. "They have a doctor's appointment tomorrow morning. Would you like to go with us?"

"I'd love to." Dottie beamed.

Sadie rose as silence fell over the room. "I'm going to let you two visit now. Dottie, I'm sure I'll see you again when I visit."

"I hope so." Dottie looked at Anna.

"I know so," Anna said. "Thank you, Sadie, for everything. If not for you, I might never have known where those blankets came from."

"Yes, Sadie, we owe you so much for bringing us back together," Dottie added. "Thank you."

"You're welcome," Sadie said to the mother and daughter. "I'll be in touch." She left with a light heart, sensing that each woman truly wanted to resolve the distance between them.

She returned to the Tahoe, on the verge of driving home again, but a sudden memory assailed her. Anna had mentioned a doctor's appointment...and so had someone else. May Belle Avery had said she had a doctor's appointment on the afternoon Sadie's deposit had been stolen.

Sadie had assumed Tobias took her, since he was the only other driver in the family. But Tobias had been working the ice-cream truck that day, so he couldn't have. May Belle must have gotten to the doctor some other way. Lucy had gone with her...but what about Eve?

Eve, who sometimes helped her brother in the ice-cream truck.

Sadie fished her cell phone from her handbag and called Sara. When her granddaughter answered, Sadie said, "Hi, honey. Quick question: Does your friend Eve also wear strawberry lip gloss?"

"Sure," Sara said. "She's the one who got me started wearing it. Why?"

Sadie snapped her fingers. *Gotcha.* "Yes!" she said out loud.

"Yes, what?" Sara asked.

"Nothing," Sadie said hastily. "Just talking to myself. Thanks," she said to Sara. "I'll explain later. 'Bye."

Eve Avery wore strawberry lip gloss, and she'd helped backstage at the Heritage Festival, where Sadie had noticed the odor for the second time. Eve had green eyes. Eve was about the height of the "boy" who'd entered her shop, and she had blonde hair the same color as the wisps that had poked out from beneath the black watch cap.

And finally, the noise Sadie had heard had probably not been the spool of yarn but was someone slipping out the back door. And there was no one anywhere in sight except for the ice-cream truck when she'd checked.

So why, she asked herself, hadn't Tobias turned her in? Because she was family? "Or maybe," she said out loud to herself, "he doesn't even know she stole anything. If she was slick enough to get in and out of my shop undetected, her brother might not have seen anything."

Tobias was trying desperately to make enough money to stay in school. The mother wasn't able to work, so finances in the household were extremely tight. Sadie suspected Eve was hoping to help her family in one way or another.

Still, stealing wasn't the way to go about it. Sadie started the Tahoe and instead of driving home, turned the SUV in the direction of the Averys' modest home.

22

SADIE DROVE ACROSS TOWN TO THE SMALL WHITE HOUSE WITH the burgundy trim where the Avery family lived.

She parked and sat there, studying the house for a moment. The ice-cream truck was parked in the small driveway. Lights blazed in the living room, which fronted the street. The dining area, behind it, could be seen through the windows because the curtains were drawn, and more light spilled from the rectangle of the doorway into the kitchen. Of the three windows across the upstairs, two were lit. Yes, there was someone—probably most of the someones—at home in the Averys' residence.

She debated about the course of action she'd chosen. Was she right or wrong? Should she simply call Mac tomorrow morning and let him handle it? Part of her thought that would certainly be the easiest thing to do...but it would also lack any heart whatsoever. If Eve was indeed her thief—and Sadie felt certain she was—Sadie wanted to know why she'd resorted to stealing money before involving her in a criminal matter that had the potential to follow her for the rest of her life.

She recalled the haunted look she'd glimpsed in the girl's green eyes last night when she had realized who was standing beside Sara at the ice-cream truck. No, arrest was not the way to go here. At least, not until she had given the girl a chance to speak.

Climbing out of the car, she mounted the porch steps and knocked on the door.

As before, the youngest child, Lucy, yanked open the door. Unlike the last time, she recognized Sadie immediately. Her little face lit up. "Hi! Mrs. Speers, right? This is a weird time of night for you to visit."

"Lucy." The deep male voice from inside the house must belong to Tobias, since he was the only man living there. A moment later, he loomed in the doorway behind Lucy. "Hello, Mrs. Speers. Please come in." He picked up Lucy under one arm and clapped the other over her mouth, grinning. "Please excuse that less-than-gracious welcome."

Lucy wriggled and made exaggerated noises behind his hand until Tobias set her down.

Sadie enjoyed their silliness. It spoke to a warm family relationship between the two. As she entered the living room, she eyed Tobias's height out of the corner of her eye. He definitely couldn't have been her thief. He was way too tall, even taller than Theo.

"My mom's lying down," Tobias told her. "I'll tell her you're here."

"Oh, don't bother her," Sadie said quickly. "I'd actually like to speak to your sister Eve."

Puzzlement creased Tobias's brow.

"She's not here," Lucy volunteered. "She walked to the library to return some books. She should be home pretty soon though."

No sooner had the words left Lucy's mouth than the front door opened. Eve stepped into the room, dropped her backpack—and froze as she spotted Sadie. Her expression instantly grew stricken, and in that second Sadie knew her hunch had been right—she was looking into the face of her thief.

Sadie glanced at her brother, judging from his expression that he had no idea what Eve had done. He was looking from Sadie to Eve with growing suspicion. "What's going on?" he asked gruffly.

Eve didn't answer. She seemed frozen, staring at Sadie as if she were a snake and Eve a hapless mouse.

Sadie cleared her throat. "Would it be possible for me to speak privately with Eve?"

Tobias frowned. "Did something happen to Sara?"

Sadie realized that as far as Tobias knew, the link to Eve's friend was the only reason Sadie would be here now. "No," she said gently. "Sara is fine. I just need to speak with Eve."

"Tobe." Eve found her voice at last. "Would you take Lucy upstairs and give us a few moments please?"

"I don't want to go upstairs." Lucy appeared fascinated, her gaze following the conversation from one face to another.

"I guess," Tobias said grudgingly. He appeared to grasp that something was wrong, but he looked quite bewildered. "But you're only getting five minutes, and then I'm coming back. And I'm bringing Mom."

Tobias put his hand on Lucy's shoulder and urged her toward the stairs. "C'mon, Luce." He looked over his shoulder. "Five minutes," he repeated.

"Aw. I miss all the good stuff," Lucy was complaining as her brother shepherded her up the steps.

Sadie took a seat on the couch and patted the space beside her. Gently, she said, "Sit down, Eve. I believe you have something to tell me."

Tears were swimming in those large, familiar green eyes as the girl collapsed on to the cushion. She didn't even try to pretend innocence. "How did you find out? Did someone see me?"

Sadie shook her head. "I ran into the couple you came in with and realized they only had two children, and they told me you had stayed in the shop after they left. You have those distinctive eyes," she said. "And last night, I saw you working with your brother," Sadie went on. "And then Sara came home smelling of strawberry lip gloss and mentioned she'd gotten it from you. I smelled it in the store last Thursday night. After my deposit bag went missing."

"It didn't go missing, Mrs. Speers," Eve burst out. "I stole it. I came into your shop, saw the bag on the counter, grabbed it, and left."

"Why?"

Eve's tears were streaming down her face now. She gulped and said, "What do you care? Aren't you going to have me arrested?"

"I'd like to know why you took the money," Sadie said. Her heart ached for the child. She couldn't help but imagine Sara if her life was as difficult as Eve's seemed to be. She hoped her granddaughter would never resort to theft, but who knew what desperation could drive a person to attempt?

Eve gestured bitterly. "Look around you. My mom can't work. My brother's trying to stay in college. I was going to help Tobias so he doesn't have to drop out of college."

"'Was going to'? You didn't?"

Eve shook her head miserably.

"So tell me the rest." Sadie suspected Eve needed to make a full confession if she was ever to forgive herself. "You watched my shop for...how long? Before you decided to steal from me, I mean?"

Eve looked shocked. "I didn't watch you at all. It was just one of those things. I was riding in the ice-cream truck with Tobe, and he told me he probably isn't going to go back to school next semester. I was so upset I was crying, so I put on his hat so no one would see my face and then I jumped out and walked down Main Street. I looked in your window and saw you counting money. I followed that family in, thinking maybe I could steal it—and then you set down the bag and walked away from it. It felt like my answer was right in front of me."

"And then you hid until the family left, then snatched the bag when I wasn't looking, ran out the back door, and jumped back in the truck."

"Yeah." Eve met her eyes. "You notice an awful lot, don't you?"

"I do." Sadie fought not to smile. She might still feel conflicted about Eve's decision to steal, but she could understand the impulsiveness of a teenager.

"Another question. I smelled your lip gloss the night of the Heritage show. Were you backstage?"

"I was working as a stagehand," Eve said.

Sadie nodded. "That's right. Lucy told me that and I forgot."

"I was terrified you were going to recognize me that night. It was wrong to steal from you, no matter how badly we needed the money," Eve said, "but I couldn't figure out a way to put it back. And then you saw me at Sara's house, and I almost *died*."

"Wait." Sadie held up a hand, palm out. "You were going to return the money?" That simple statement gave Sadie even more to consider.

Eve nodded. "Yeah. I get that you still have to turn me in, but at least I can give you back your money. I haven't spent a dime." She stood and went to her backpack, pulling out a shapeless gray sweatshirt tied into a makeshift bundle. A moment later, she lifted the deposit bag and carried it over to Sadie. "Here. Everything's still there. I was thinking about taking it to the post office tomorrow and mailing it anonymously." She looked away. "I know this doesn't make up for the stealing. Do you think I'll go to jail?"

The child looked utterly terrified at the thought.

Sadie was stunned. She was holding her bulging deposit bag, and she believed Eve when the girl said there wasn't a penny missing. She was certain all the checks were there, untouched. Since she hadn't called anyone to cancel them and it had only been a week, she'd still be able to deposit them.

She thought for a long moment, mulling over possible ways to address such a unique situation. Finally, she said, "Eve, it means a lot to me that you realized your mistake and planned to rectify it. You didn't spend any of the money, and you were planning to return it. I think, if you agree, we can come up with a solution that satisfies us both."

The girl stared at Sadie, hope dawning. "You're not going to press charges?"

"I'm not going to press charges. But I would like you to volunteer to do something to pay me back for the week of worry that I've experienced."

"Sure. Anything. You want me to come clean your shop? I . . ."

"No, you don't need to do anything for me. Do you enjoy spending time with children?"

Eve's eyes lit up. "I'm in the pediatric care club at school. Once a month we visit the hospital and supervise the playroom, do little craft activities with any children in the hospital, that kind of thing. I especially love it when there are babies and toddlers to visit."

"Perfect," she said, "there's a young mom at my church who just had twins, and we have people signing up to help her for various shifts. Would that be something you're interested in?"

"That would be *awesome*," Eve said reverently. "Twins? Cool." She sobered again. "You'd let me do that? How come you're being so nice?"

"I think maybe you deserve a break," Sadie said.

Their quiet words were interrupted by firm footsteps on the steps. "What's going on?" Tobias asked.

"Um, nothing," Eve said.

Sadie almost chuckled out loud. It was so clearly *something* that she couldn't blame the boy for being suspicious.

"Would you ask Mom to come down here?" Eve said to her brother. Sadie realized the young girl intended to tell her mother everything, and her respect for the girl's courage grew.

Tobias looked at them both. Finally, he said, "All right. And I suppose you want Lucy and me out of the way."

"Lucy for sure," Eve said. "You can be here if you want though."

He shook his head. "She'll never stay in her room if she thinks she's missing something important. I'll play a game with her. You can fill me in later."

He vanished again.

"So we have a deal?" Sadie asked. "You returned everything you took, and I agree not to press charges if you make the additional volunteer commitment to help my friend with her twins for... what do you think? Two months, one four-hour visit per week?"

"I can easily do that," Eve said. "I might even be able to help more. I love babies." Her head was up, and her eyes had lost their haunted look. She met Sadie gaze directly. "Mrs. Speers, I am deeply sorry I stole from you. I felt desperate, but once I'd taken your money, I felt so much worse that I have learned dishonesty isn't the answer. Thank you for giving me a second chance."

———

One week later, Sadie and Edwin were having dinner at Los Pollitos, a cozy Mexican restaurant not far from Sadie's shop on Main Street. It was a little too cool to eat out on the dining patio as they enjoyed doing in warmer months, so they were seated inside in a booth with a large, decorative sombrero on the wall.

"Tomorrow I'm headed for an auction," Sadie said after their orders were taken and the waitress had brought them coffee. "It's a private estate that's been in the family for over a century, and there are some lovely pieces advertised. Now that I've gotten the money from my missing deposit bag back, I'll be able to afford to indulge myself a little."

Edwin grinned. "You never did tell me what Mac said when you told him you found your deposit bag."

"He gave me that gimlet-eyed stare," Sadie said, chuckling, "and asked me exactly where I found it. And when I prevaricated, he said, '*Exactly*, Sadie.' He's no fool."

"What did you tell him?"

Sadie shrugged. "I said someone took it and had an attack of conscience, so the person returned it. 'Exactly where' was never mentioned. He pointed out it was still a crime, and I told him I was satisfied with the resolution, and that I preferred not to press charges."

She already had told Edwin the whole story of Eve's confession and what Sadie had asked the girl to do.

"That took a lot of courage to confess," Edwin said, "but what impresses me just as much is that she already was planning to return the money. All of it."

"Every last penny," Sadie said. "I almost felt bad taking it back when she was going to use it to help her brother pay his tuition."

"About that," Edwin said, "I've been thinking...I would like to establish a scholarship for a local student to attend the UC Silver Peak branch campus. I'd like to offer it to students who are experiencing financial hardship. I thought Tobias Avery might be a good first recipient. He's clearly dedicated to his education. How many college-age boys do you know who would drive an ice-cream truck to pay their way through school?"

"Not more than a few, probably," Sadie admitted. "I think that's a lovely idea, Edwin, and Tobias would be so very grateful. Thank you for thinking of it."

"Well, well." Edwin was distracted by some new patrons coming in the door. "Look who's here."

Sadie had been sitting with her back to the door. She turned around to see Anna Harrington and her mother, Dottie, being seated at a table not far away. "My goodness. I can't believe she's managed to get out of the house," Sadie said. "What a break for her."

Just then, Anna spotted them and lifted a hand. She said something to Dottie, who smiled and waved. Then Anna got to her feet and came toward their table.

"Sadie, Edwin. It's great to see you," she said. "How are you?"

"We're fine," Edwin told her. "And how are you getting along with your busy schedule?"

"Surprisingly well," Anna said. "My mother comes every day to help before or after work, and Mrs. Sweeting has a list of church members who are coming to spend the night. They get up and change the boys, bring them to me to feed, and then rock or walk them back to sleep, so I am getting more sleep than I expected." She laughed. "I even get a shower every day. It will be wonderful when they are big enough to sleep through the night, but I was expecting to stagger through this stage in a fog, so I'm very grateful for all the help."

"And here you are," Sadie said. "Getting out of the house, even for a few minutes, can be so invigorating when you're cooped up with babies all day."

"Yes, Jeanne Sweeting called the other day. She had a mother and daughter, the Averys, who had offered to come in and stay for a while if we wanted to do something. The mother has rheumatoid arthritis and doesn't get around well, but she can cuddle babies. The daughter is fourteen and loves them, so she can do the legwork with her mom's supervision. It was so nice of them to offer. I fed the boys and then Mom and I decided to get out for dinner before the next feeding. We're going to try to do it once a week. Isn't that wonderful?"

"It sure is." Sadie glanced at Edwin, who unobtrusively lifted his coffee cup to her in a silent salute. "I believe my first overnight with you is Friday. I can't wait to see the boys again. I bet they've grown in just a week."

"They're already getting very distinct little personalities," Anna said. "Aaron is very calm and laid-back. He reminds me of his daddy. Alex is much more impatient and quicker to squawk the minute he gets wet or hungry."

After another moment's chatter, Anna returned to her table.

"Well done, Sadie," Edwin said, laying his hand over hers and squeezing her fingers. "Very well done."

Sadie thought back to the hectic week she'd had last week, caring for the baby bobcat, trying to support Anna, looking for the descendants of the Maxfield family, and searching for the missing money. "Thank you," she said. "I had faith that everything would work out eventually, and in the end, it exceeded anything I could have dreamed of. There's a line in that poem written by Ellen Mary Murphy Maxfield that has stuck in my mind: *'Accept my most humble intercession.'*"

She paused, thinking of the valiant young immigrant who had married far above her station, been shunned by society, and still had a big enough heart to pray for her husband's first wife and save Fannie's creation for future generations. "That's all I tried to do. And I'm very grateful that God found a path for me to help in any way I could."

Once again, Edwin lifted his coffee cup. "He may have shown you the path, but you took the initiative to walk it. Would that we were all so open to His guidance. Sadie, you are an inspiration."

She grinned, lifting her own coffee cup and clinking it lightly against his. "I think that would be a wonderful legacy for anyone's life. I'm happy to be considered an inspiration."

About the Author

CAROLE JEFFERSON IS THE PEN NAME FOR A TEAM OF WRITERS who have come together to create the series Mysteries of Silver Peak. *Things Unseen* was written by Anne Marie Rodgers. Anne Marie is the author of nearly fifty novels, including sixteen for Guideposts. A best-selling, award-winning writer, she also is deeply committed to animal rescue and welfare. In addition to working at an emergency veterinary clinic near her home in State College, Pennsylvania, she volunteers with wildlife rescue and local animal shelters, where she specializes in orphaned infant mammal care.

Dangerous Beauty

"Now what in the world is this?" Cecile Daly said, holding up a large metal pot with beautiful blue-and-white stripes painted on it.

Sadie looked into Cecile's blue eyes, which were bright under her blonde pixie cut, and smiled. Then both Sadie and Cecile looked at Alfred, Cecile's husband, who was standing beside Cecile under the cool, bright sunshine that lit the Silver Peak afternoon.

All three of them, along with what seemed like close to half the population of Silver Peak itself, were standing on the sidewalk outside the Antique Mine, where all kinds of antiques were spread out under the Colorado sunshine on a large maze of tables and display cases.

Alfred's eyes crinkled with pleasure at Cecile's question.

"Well, professor?" Sadie asked. Alfred taught American History at Colorado Mountain College, and was an expert on

Rocky Mountain history, and one of the first calls Sadie tended to make when she was stumped in her own research on a particular item.

But the twinkle in his eyes now let her know that he might be up to something more than just relaying his formidable knowledge.

"This?" he asked, adopting his most professorial tone. He took the large pot, which was about the size a modern woman might use for boiling a big pan of pasta, from his wife, and knocked his wire-rimmed glasses down his nose, making a big show of getting a closer look at it. After a long moment, he gave a decisive nod, pushed his glasses back to the bridge of his nose, and looked triumphantly from Sadie to his wife.

"Well?" Cecile demanded, her own face crinkling into a smile.

"I think it's perfectly obvious what this is," Alfred said, in a teasing tone of voice.

"Maybe if you're a professor of history, it's obvious," Sadie joked back.

"Oh, you don't need to be a professor of history to recognize this," Alfred shot back. "I'd say just about any child in Colorado ought to be able to do it."

"Any child?" Cecile said, putting her hands on her hips. "Are you saying any child would know more than me about this?"

Alfred put his arm around her shoulder and gave her a loving squeeze. "Of course not, my dear," he said. "It's just that, as we get older, sometimes we forget the things we knew as children."

"Well," Sadie said, "before we have to admit how long it's been since we were children, why don't you clue us in? I have to say I was curious about the origins of this thing as well. What do you think it is?"

Alfred held up the striped pot with a flourish. "As I was saying," he said with a grin, "I think it's obvious. This is clearly Paul Bunyan's coffee mug."

Cecile gave him a gentle thwack.

"No need to resort to hand-to-hand combat!" Alfred said, trying to fend her off with the mug.

"You're impossible," Cecile said.

Alfred adopted a look of long-suffering. "It can be very hard for a visionary professor to get the public to accept his ideas," he said. "But I have no doubt that the truth will win out in the end."

"Uh-huh," Cecile said, with more than a hint of sarcasm. Then she turned to Sadie. "And where in the world did you find this treasure?" she asked.

"The same places I found most of this," Sadie said. "Estate sales. Antique wholesale events. And this year, I've been to several sales at storage units."

"Storage units," Alfred said with a nod. "Where people are helpfully archiving their own lives for the historians."

"Well, yes," Sadie said. "At least as long as someone is paying for the storage. But if they stop, quite a bit of those things wind up going to the highest bidder."

"That's so sad," Cecile said.

"Yes," Sadie said. "But it can also be hopeful. After all, I'm going to find all these things a good home. Get them to someone who can use them."

"Well, I always love coming to your outdoor sales," Cecile said. "It seems like you must have over half the store dragged out here into the street."

"Actually," Sadie said, "The store is just as stuffed as it always is. If you go in there, you won't find one thing out of place. What you see here on the street are things I've been collecting in my own storage."

"Well," Cecile said, handing over the striped pot, "I believe we'll take this."

"Don't forget to stop for some food," Sadie said as she rang them up. She nodded across the sidewalk to a busy stand that was set up in front of Arbuckle's Coffee Shop.

"That's where we were just headed," Alfred said. "It smells delicious. Is Arbuckle's catering?"

"I wish," Sadie said. "I tried to get Luz to cook up something, but she passed me off to a friend of hers. It's street foods—empanadas and tacos. I'm not sure it could ever compare to Los Pollitos, but still it sounds absolutely delicious."

As they went off, Sadie surveyed the scene with pleasure. All around her, people pored over the antiques that were spread on the surrounding tables and cases—and the "not-so-antique"—items that Sadie wouldn't normally display on the Antique Mine's carefully curated shelves, but were still of some value or interest.

The whole "staff" of the Antique Mine were on duty today, as well. She saw Theo dutifully carrying a large art-deco mirror to the car of a young couple who had just snapped it up. Alice was leaning over a beautiful milk-glass pitcher, talking quietly with a middle-aged gentleman who had been dithering over whether or not to buy it for the past several minutes. Sara was manning one of the other check-out stations, diligently adding up tabs and making change. And Josh and Julie floated through the crowd as well, answering questions and directing foot traffic.

But the appearance of another customer quickly brought Sadie back to her own station. This time it was Rita Dodd, who had gone to high school in Silver Peak with Sadie, and Roz. Now she worked as a receptionist for Dr. Tom Conroy. And Sadie wasn't at all surprised to see a pair of interesting cat's-eye glasses in her hand. Rita was well-known around town for her fondness for eye-catching eyewear. It seemed like she wore a different pair of frames every week.

"Rita," Sadie said, nodding at the frames. "I thought those just might have your name on them."

"Well," Rita said, laying them down on the long folding table that was serving for the day as Sadie's checkout counter. "You've got my number, I guess. Can you tell me anything about these?"

"I can give you a couple of guesses," Sadie said, looking down at the frames, which were a delicate silver filigree, with vines entwining to make the stems that folded out from the frames and sat behind the ears. "As you can see, they're quite old."

Rita nodded. "Older than us!" she joked.

"Well, of course," Sadie said. "But then again, you and I are only sixteen, right?"

Rita grinned. "If you won't tell, I won't," she said with a wink.

"I'm guessing these are turn of the century," Sadie said. "Commercially made, but at a time before plastics were in wide use. That would place them right about that time. But I'm no expert on the history of eyeglasses."

"Where did you come across them?" Rita asked. "Do you know anything about their specific history at all? Like who might have once owned them?"

Sadie shook her head. "I'm sorry," she said. "These came from a storage sale. So I don't know much. The guy who bought the unit was only interested in paper documents, photographs, and the like. But after he opened the unit, he only found one box of documents. So he auctioned off everything else he could to the rest of us who were still here. So he made back some money. But that doesn't leave me with much to tell you."

Rita looked at the glasses, clearly still curious about anything she might be able to learn about them.

"I did get this from the same collection, though," Sadie said.

"What?" Rita asked.

Sadie pointed to a beautiful locket that hung from a jewelry stand beside her register. "This may be the item I'm most excited about in this whole place," she said.

"May I?" Rita asked, reaching for it.

"Of course," Sadie said.

Rita cradled the locket in her hands, and popped it open.

"There's nothing in here," she said.

Sadie nodded. "No," she said. "But it's still a very remarkable piece. I've never seen anything like it."

Rita shut the locket and gazed down at the beautiful scrollwork that covered the thick oval. "It's a pretty pattern," she said.

"And it's very unusual," Sadie said, warming to the topic with the same excitement she'd felt when she first discovered it, wrapped up in a small piece of plaid calico in a cigar box that she'd been just about to toss out. Something had made her look inside the box—and when she had, she'd discovered her favorite find of the entire antique hunting expedition that day—even though she hadn't actually meant to buy it. The cigar box had simply been thrown into the same box as a beautiful quilt she'd been bidding on—which was now hung proudly in the shop, part of the wares that would still be available at the Antique Mine as part of their regular stock, after the sale had finally wrapped up that evening.

"It is?" Rita asked, fingering the pattern wonderingly.

Sadie nodded. "In fact," she said, "I'm curious to see if it's a one-of-a-kind piece. It looks like hand engraving to me. And if you'll notice, the pattern isn't exactly symmetrical. You see here?"

She pointed from one side of the locket to the other, where there was a small but clear variation in the size of two matching whorls that would otherwise have been mirror images of each other.

"You're right," Rita said, her finger tracing where Sadie pointed. "They are a little bit different. So who do you think made it?"

"That's the other thing that's so interesting about it," Sadie said. "I don't wear much jewelry myself, but there's a lot of call for it here in the shop. They just don't make jewelry these days the way they used to."

"You know," Rita said, "I think you're right about that. I buy myself a new piece of jewelry now and then, but I always find myself reaching for the things I inherited from my mother. And even my grandmother. There's just—something—about them."

Sadie nodded. "Yep," she said. "You're not the only one who feels that way. So I've learned a little something about maker's marks, especially in the Rocky Mountain region. They're one of the simplest ways to establish the provenance of a piece."

"I thought provenance was a town in France," Rita said with a wink.

She turned the locket over in her hands, opened it, and closed it again. "I don't see anything that looks like a maker's mark on this, though."

"I couldn't find it either," Sadie said. "That's what makes it so unusual. Usually jewelry makers love to mark their work. Even if they weren't active for very long, they always invented a mark, and slapped it on everything they put out."

"That's like my sister," Rita says. "She likes to paint. By which I mean she paints about one painting a year. But her signature always takes up the bottom quarter of the canvas."

"I've seen canvases like that too," Sadie said, with a grin.

"This doesn't have it," Rita said, turning it over in her hand. "But it's so much prettier than so many of the things I've seen," Rita said. "You think they'd be proud to put their name on it."

"If I ever made anything that pretty," Sadie joked, "I think I might have to take out a full-page ad in the Silver Peak Register."

Rita hung the beautiful locket back on the stand beside the register. "Well, that's a regular mystery," she said.

"It is," Sadie said. "But there's no mystery about how beautiful it is. I have to say, it's my favorite item on display here today. I can't wait to see who takes it home."

"I might be tempted to," Rita said. "But it's a bit out of my price range. You think someone will?" Rita asked.

"You can never tell," Sadie said. "And to tell the truth, I wouldn't mind keeping this one around. If I spend some more time with it, I may be able to find out a bit more about it."

"So if I want it, I ought to buy it now," Rita said. "Before you discover how valuable it really is, and the price shoots up."

"I like the way you think," Sadie said. "Now if you can just spread that rumor around the crowd, I'll think about making you a salesperson at the shop."

"That'd be lovely," Rita said. "But I'm afraid it would probably be a wash for me financially. I know if I were here every day, I'd be spending my whole paycheck on antiques."

"That's why I opened this shop!" Sadie said. "It lets me buy antiques for a living."

"You always were a smart one," Rita said, settling the eyeglasses she'd just bought into her purse.

As Rita threaded away through the crowd, Kimama Temoke, the librarian at the Silver Peak Library, came up to Sadie. The look on her face was quizzical, but also eager, a smile playing just out of reach beyond her expression of curiosity.

"You've got such a great collection here today," Kimama said. "It feels to me more like a museum display than a commercial endeavor."

"Coming from you, that's a real compliment," Sadie said. "Nobody puts on anything like the exhibits you've been creating at the library."

As they were talking, Harry Polmiller came up. At ninety-four, he was one of the oldest residents of Silver Peak, but he was still on his feet, still active around town—and still smiling. His face was wrinkled, but his grin was as fresh as a teenager's.

"Good afternoon, ladies," he said. "I hope I'm not interrupting anything."

"Well, I was just helping Kimama," Sadie began.

Kimama took a graceful sidestep out of the line for the register. "Actually, I had a question for you about one of these pieces," she said. "But please, take care of Harry."

"Thank you kindly," Harry said, stepping up to the table with a pair of comic books in hand. He put them down beside the locket and tapped them both with his fingers.

"Now, these may look like just a pair of old comic books to you," he said. "But I tell you, they make me feel just like a boy again."

"That'll be three dollars," Sadie said. The comic books were old, but Theo had checked their value before the sale began. They were quite well-used—and quite common—so Sadie had assigned a tag-sale price to them.

"Three dollars," Harry said, and gave a low whistle. "But the cover says they're only pennies each!"

He pointed to the original prices, prominently drawn in the corners of each booklet.

"I'm afraid there's been a bit of inflation since they first came out," Sadie said.

Harry handed over the few dollars with a grin. "I'm not worried," he said. "There aren't many things that make me feel like a boy again, these days. To me, that's worth every penny."

As Sadie carefully settled the delicate old comic books into a flat paper bag, Harry bent down to inspect the locket hanging by the checkout counter.

He popped it open, turned it over in his hands, then swung it shut and replaced it. "Well, that's real pretty, right there," he said. "It'd be a real nice present for some young lady."

"That's one of my favorite pieces here today," Sadie told him.

"You just need to find me a young lady to give it to," Harry said. "If you can do that for me, you'll have made yourself a sale."

"I'll keep my eyes open," Sadie said, with a wink.

Harry winked back. "You can tell my dream woman to look for this young whipper-snapper at the town square, reading comics under the pine trees."

"Will do," Sadie said, as Harry ambled off.

Then she turned to Kimama. "Well," Sadie said. "What's this question of yours? Usually I'm the one coming to you for answers."

"Do you have a minute to come look at something with me?" Kimama asked.

Sadie glanced quickly around the crowd.

"For you, always," Sadie said, stepping out from behind the table to follow Kimama. "Lead on."

To Sadie's surprise, Kimama headed toward the only spot on the sidewalk by the shop that *wasn't* occupied by an antique, under the shadow of the awning, near the shop door.

Then Sadie's eyes adjusted to the shadow of the building, and her face broke into a smile.

"You're interested in Matilda!" she said.

Kimama, who had come to a stop before a large painting, which stood on a makeshift easel that Josh had rigged up for it that morning, looked back at Sadie in surprise. "Matilda?" she repeated.

Sadie came to a stop beside her, shoulder to shoulder before the art. "Well, that's what I've been calling her anyway," Sadie said. "Isn't she fascinating?"

The painting was a portrait, about three feet high by two feet wide. It was of a woman, perhaps in her late twenties or early thirties, with chestnut hair piled on her head and escaping in curls over her brow, and green eyes. She was good-looking, but there was something even more arresting in her face. Sadie hadn't been able to explain what it was yet to herself, but whatever it was, it had spurred her to place a bid on the portrait at the storage unit. And to engage in quite a healthy bidding war with another prospective buyer, in which Sadie eventually triumphed.

"She is," Kimama agreed, staring deeply into the woman's eyes.

"There's just something about her eyes," Sadie said. "I don't know if they're wise, or determined, or thoughtful, or…"

"All of the above?" Kimama suggested.

Sadie laughed. "Maybe that's it," she said. "But I just couldn't leave her behind."

"So you don't know anything about her?" Kimama said.

"Not yet," Sadie said gamely. "Other than what we can see here at first glance. You've probably noticed that her clothing looks to be from around the turn of the century. The high collar, and the hairstyle."

The woman's hair was done in a simple but elegant updo, and white lace fringed the collar of her sky blue jacket.

"Yes," Kimama said. "But that's interesting, because the frame…"

"Exactly!" Sadie exclaimed. "What in the world is a picture from this period doing in such a modern frame?"

"Well," Kimama said, reaching out to touch the simple silver frame, which was devoid of any of the faux-baroque decoration that might have been expected in frames from the turn of the century, "relatively modern, anyway. This looks like it's seen some years itself."

"Well, it's considerably better made than a lot of things you'd find these days at a cut-rate frame shop," Sadie agreed. "I could believe this dates back to the nineteen sixties."

"I'll have to take your word on that," Kimama said.

"And before we get much further, I should probably tell you," Sadie said, breaking the gaze of the woman in the portrait to turn to Kimama. "It's not for sale."

In response, Kimama grinned. "I see she's really made an impression on you," she said. She spoke almost as if the two of them were already acquainted, Sadie noticed. But also, Kimama was right.

"She definitely has," Sadie said. "For the time being, I'm keeping her for myself. At least until we get to know each other a little better. And after that, who knows?"

Kimama nodded. "I understand," she said.

Now Sadie glanced at Kimama, curious. "But you said you had a question about her," she said. "I don't know that I can answer it, but if you tell me what it is, maybe I can be on the lookout in the course of my own research."

"Actually," Kimama said, "I think you probably know the answer to this question. At least, I hope you still do."

"Well, go ahead," Sadie said, crossing her arms. "Shoot."

"Where did you get it?"

"Get it?" Sadie repeated.

Kimama nodded. "You said you couldn't leave her there," she said. "Where did you find her?"

"Yes," a man said behind them. "I'd be very interested to know the answer to that question, myself."

Surprised, both Kimama and Sadie wheeled around.

Just behind them stood a red-headed man with pale freckled skin, dressed in a green plaid shirt. As far as Sadie could tell, she'd never seen him before.

She offered him a big grin in greeting, as she had to just about everyone who had walked into the sale that day.

But the stranger was having none of it. Instead, he gazed back at her with a steely glare, and handed her a small figurine to ring up.

Sadie glanced at Kimama, who gave her a quick look that told her that Kimama had no idea who the new arrival was, either.

Quickly, Sadie did the math for the tax on the figurine, and gave the man the number.

"I'll just need you to write your address and phone number," she said, handing it back to him.

The man scrawled an address in a nearby town and handed the slip back to her, still clearly displeased with something.

"Please," he said, nodding at the portrait. "Do tell us where you found this." He put a special emphasis on '*found*,' almost sarcastic, as if he didn't really believe something she'd said.

Out of patience with his confusing antics, Sadie decided simply to pick up where she and Kimama had left off before the man had interrupted them. Especially since he claimed that all he wanted to know was the answer to the same question that Kimama had just asked her.

"Oh," Sadie said. "You're right, that is easy. You know those storage units between here and Bent Pine?"

Kimama nodded.

The red-headed man continued to stare daggers at Sadie.

"They have quarterly sales," Sadie said, trying to keep her tone light despite the man's attitude. You could never tell what was going on with people, she always told herself. And no matter what was happening, it was always best to treat them with respect, and not get upset yourself.

"The last one was a few weeks ago," Sadie went on. "That's where a good bit of this stuff came from. I wound up with most of the contents of one of the units, just because I couldn't leave this one"— she glanced again at the portrait—"behind. I tried to negotiate just to get her portrait. But the auctioneer was under pressure to clear all the units assigned to him, and he was tired of haggling. He said take it all, or don't take any of it. Which is part of why we needed to have this big sale today," she said with another smile at the red-headed man.

His expression didn't seem to have changed since he had first interrupted them. It was every bit as belligerent as when he'd first barged into the conversation.

But Kimama's expression was quizzical now.

"What else did you find in that unit?" she asked. "Were there any papers? Any documents at all?"

"No," Sadie answered.

Kimama's face fell in obvious disappointment.

Why was Kimama so disappointed? Sadie wondered. "I know," Sadie said. "And that's actually very unusual. But there was one other really wonderful find from that same lot."

"Oh?" Kimama asked. "And what's that?"

"Well, that locket," Sadie said. "The one that Harry Polmiller was planning to give to his imaginary girlfriend."

Kimama's eyebrows jumped. "Very interesting," she said. "And you don't know anything else about it?"

"Really?" the red-headed man broke in, his voice still sarcastic, verging even on angry. "You're sure you don't know *anything*?"

"I'm sorry," Sadie said to him. "Do you have some personal interest in this portrait? It seems like it's important to you."

At this, the man looked taken aback. He glanced around the crowd, as if suddenly coming to his senses about where he was, or waking up from a dream. As he did, Sadie could see a different expression on his face: confusion, and perhaps sorrow. He seemed very different from the angry man who had pushed himself uninvited into her private conversation with Kimama. Her heart went out to him.

But still, he wouldn't answer her question. "This isn't about me," he said. "It's about you. And how you wound up with all of these things."

With that, he turned on his heel and stalked off.

Kimama and Sadie's eyes met in a questioning glance.

"That was ... interesting," Kimama said.

"There's never a dull moment here at the Antique Mine," Sadie said. She was trying to joke, as she usually did, but something in her still felt the heaviness of the man's bad attitude and suspicion. She looked back at the painting, as if she might read something that could give her a clue in the woman's eyes. But although they were just as intriguing as ever, they didn't give away anything more than they ever had.

She turned back to Kimama.

"I guess I could ask you the same question, actually," she said with a smile.

"What question is that?" Kimama asked, her gaze still slightly troubled, as Sadie had been, by their interaction with the red-headed stranger.

"Well," Sadie said. "I can't help noticing that you seem to have a particular interest in this piece too. It's almost as if the two of you have met before."

She glanced from Kimama to the portrait and back again with a smile.

Unlike the man who had just left them, Kimama answered with a smile. But her lips still pressed together, holding something back. "It's hard to keep anything from you, Sadie Speers," she said. "And you're right. I do have a particular interest in this portrait."

"Then do you know something about it that I don't?" Sadie said, eagerly. She was surprised by how excited she was about the prospect of learning anything more, anything at all, about the mysterious woman with the intriguing gaze.

"I suspect I do," Kimama said. She took a step back as she said it, as if she were a runner getting set for a race, and eager for the shot to sound so she could take off running. "But before I get your hopes up, I just want to double-check a few things, first."

She pulled her phone from her purse and put it on the camera setting. Then she held it up to the portrait. "Do you mind if I ...?" she asked Sadie.

Sadie spread her hands wide. "Please," she said. "If you think it'll help me to learn anything about her, be my guest."

Kimama took a rapid fire set of pictures, then replaced the phone in her bag.

"I promise I'll let you know as soon as I'm sure about anything," she said.

"You can't even give me a hint?" Sadie asked with a grin.

Kimama shook her head. "You'll just have to wait to find out."

A Note from the Editors

WE HOPE YOU ENJOYED MYSTERIES OF SILVER PEAK, PUBLISHED by the Books and Inspirational Media Division of Guideposts, a nonprofit organization that touches millions of lives every day through products and services that inspire, encourage, help you grow in your faith, and celebrate God's love.

Thank you for making a difference with your purchase of this book, which helps fund our many outreach programs to military personnel, prisons, hospitals, nursing homes, and educational institutions.

We also create many useful and uplifting online resources. Visit Guideposts.org to read true stories of hope and inspiration, access OurPrayer network, sign up for free newsletters, download free e-books, join our Facebook community, and follow our stimulating blogs.

To learn about other Guideposts publications, including the best-selling devotional *Daily Guideposts*, go to Guideposts.org/Shop, call (800) 932-2145, or write to Guideposts, PO Box 5815, Harlan, Iowa 51593.